SHE'D NEVER MISSED
ANYONE BEFORE

"Don't punish me by staying away," Mariah said.

"Is that what you think I'm doing?"

"That's what it feels like," she answered honestly.

"No, no," he said, brushing his thumb across her bottom lip. "I don't mean to punish you. It's just that you make me crazy when I'm with you. Then again, I'm crazy when I'm not with you."

Typically, Mariah giggled. The giggles turned to laughter that made Ford think of wind rippling across fertile fields of flowers. The sound of wind blowing away years and years of his loneliness.

Ford asked the one question he was afraid to ask. "Are you leaving tomorrow?"

"Tell me not to."

"Don't go."

Mariah let his words, the fire in his eyes, warm her. She'd spent a lifetime being reckless and daring, but what she'd just asked of Ford was the most reckless thing she'd ever done. For it set her on a journey she'd never traveled. A journey of self-exposure. A journey of dependence. A journey there might not be a return from. Slowly, damning caution, she raised her lips to speak. Once more she worshiped at the feet of danger.

"No," she whispered, "I won't leave."

Calloway Corners

A VERY SPECIAL CORNER OF

Louisiana!

It's not often that we get to enjoy the uniqueness of life imitating art, but the Calloway Corners series affords us that special pleasure. This tiny crossroads in northern Louisiana was a creation of four authors' imaginations—but their vision was spurred by a lovely house sitting vacant on the road between Minden and Sibley.

It is vacant no more. Since these stories were born, the house has undergone a rebirth—as a charming bed and breakfast whose gracious owner is conscious of her home's singular place in the hearts of Superromance readers. Calloway Corners really has come to life, for the house now bears that name—and the spirits of the four Calloway sisters imbue the structure with the warmth of their familial bond.

Mariah

SANDRA CANFIELD

Harlequin Books

TORONTO • NEW YORK • LONDON
AMSTERDAM • PARIS • SYDNEY • HAMBURG
STOCKHOLM • ATHENS • TOKYO • MILAN
MADRID • WARSAW • BUDAPEST • AUCKLAND

First printing November 1988
Published January 1989
This edition published September 1993

ISBN 0-373-83278-8

MARIAH

For my Calloway sisters, Terri, Kathey and Penny.
Thanks for the memories.
and
For M—for always and forever.
A special thanks to Jeanne Cole Woods.

CHAPTER ONE

"MARIAH'S DONE IT AGAIN!"

Jo Calloway, her olive-green eyes flashing, her tone of voice as fiery as the blaze of red hair tumbling about her shoulders, bellowed the announcement as she swung wide the kitchen door of the Calloway home. The two women inside glanced up, Tess Calloway from where she'd been staring out the window into the cold December afternoon, Eden Calloway from where she was mechanically preparing finger sandwiches.

"Leave it to Mariah to miss Dad's funeral," Jo railed. The memory of the awkward hour and a half delay before the decision to go on with the ceremony, minus a daughter, was still fresh in the three women's minds. "Obviously planes fly into Monte Carlo, but not out."

"The Riviera," Tess corrected. "Mariah was at the Riviera."

"Monte Carlo, the Riviera, St. Moritz, who cares? They're all the same," Jo said, not bothering to hide her sarcasm. "Besides, that was two days ago. Since then she's probably been a half dozen other places doing a dozen dumb things." Jo frowned. "She did have the money for a ticket, didn't she?"

"I volunteered the money," Eden said, meticulously trimming the crust from white bread, "but she said she didn't need it." The oldest Calloway sister halted in mid-slice, her face, which she'd always thought remarkably plain, suddenly etched with worry. "You don't think something's happened to her, do you?"

"You've got to be kidding," Jo said, smirking. "Something happen to Mariah? Did anything happen to her when she skydived out of that plane? What about when she rock climbed up the face of El Capitan? Or kayaked down the Snake River? Was she hurt scuba diving, driving fast motorcycles, or racing in the Grand Prix? No, thank you very much, she was not. Nor was she hurt running with the bulls in Pamplona, although I understand a couple of bulls almost got trampled by her. Why do you use white bread, Eden?" she tacked on, as if it was somehow pertinent to her previous points. "The additives'll kill you. Of course, that cholesterol-filled ham will probably get you first. Watercress, bean sprouts, avocados—they make wonderful, nutritional sandwiches."

"I know she hasn't been hurt in the past, but there's always a first time," Eden answered, adding, "and not everyone wants to be a vegetarian or join a 'ban the additives' cause."

"She'll be here," Tess said in a typically quiet tone. "If Mariah said she'll be home, then she will be."

Home was Calloway Corners, a spot in northeast Louisiana some two and a half miles from the outskirts of the small town of Haughton. Appearing on no map, it was only a crossroads that could be missed in a blink of the eye—in a fast blink of the eye. The Calloway house, a simple white frame structure located off a winding dirt road, sat on one quadrant, while on another sat the Calloway lumber mill. In yet another was a general store, which sold everything from bread and milk to nuts and bolts. Dan Morgan, who leased the land from the Calloways and owned the store as his daddy had before him, gave his advice away free. The fourth quadrant housed nothing except dead grass in winter and pastel field flowers in the spring and summer.

A few of the residents, mostly old-timers who religiously congregated at the Morgan General Store, remembered when Ben Calloway had bought the land, some two hundred acres, nearly fifty years before. He'd been a young man of twenty-five, a man with big dreams and little money. From the seeds of nothing, nourished by the sweat of his brow, he'd built a lumber mill, which had grown and prospered until Calloway had become a name to be reckoned with. With the fruits of his labor, on the privacy of his tree-rich land, he'd built a modest house and lived there alone until the age of forty. It was then that bachelor Ben Calloway had met the young and vivacious Grace Whitaker, who'd traveled that spring from St. Louis to visit her cousin in Haughton. In two weeks he had married her. It would have been sooner, but she'd insisted, with her gay laugh that had endlessly delighted him, that someone had to counterbalance his impetuousness. Ben had settled his bride in his simple house, and there they'd lived and loved for the next ten years until Grace had died giving birth to their fourth daughter. Many of the old-timers said that Ben Calloway had died that day, too, but that nobody had bothered to bury him.

The daughters left behind by Grace Calloway and Ben Calloway, who had died twenty-five years later, were as different as night from day, and yet, just as night and day are necessary to complete time, so all four daughters were necessary to complete the Calloway clan. There was Eden, who at thirty-three, was the oldest. A nurturer both by nature and circumstance, she had assumed a maternal role and was the only one who had remained in Calloway Corners. She still resided in the old family home, where she baby-sat for a living, occasionally lending a helping hand

in the running of the mill. At thirty, firebrand Jo lived in
Baton Rouge. There she worked as a lobbyist, professionally and personally embracing one cause after another.
Twenty-nine-year-old Tess, on the other hand, was as in-
troverted as Jo was extroverted. A soft-spoken, sensitive
woman, she taught school in Dallas and waited for her divorce from Vance Langford to become final. And then
there was Mariah, the youngest at twenty-five—Mariah,
the risk-taking world traveler. Mariah, the prodigal
daughter. Mariah, the wayward child who'd missed her
father's funeral.

"It's going to seem odd not seeing Dad at the arbor this
spring," Tess said, the words falling softly into the stillness.

As she spoke, her gaze once more drifted to the tree-
dotted backyard. To the left stood a white, lattice-work
arbor, its hexagonal sides plant-bare with winter. The
bench inside, where Ben Calloway had often sat, looked
noticeably vacant. The sloping lawn beyond, brown and
barren, seemed equally bleak. Even the nearby creek, a red
wooden footbridge spanning its silver water, trickled with
a reverent quietness.

"Yeah," Jo said, the snap gone from her voice. "He
loved sitting out there when the wisteria was blooming."

"I remember him and Mamma sitting out there every
evening when the weather was pretty," Eden said, then
laughed. "I think he only built it so they could have some
time to themselves, away from us kids."

A poignant silence followed.

"I'm gonna miss him," Tess said, her eyes suddenly
glazing. The death of her father had been particularly
painful, coupled as it was with the recent failure of her
marriage.

"Yeah, me, too," tough Jo said, a definite huskiness to the admission.

"The house is gonna seem so empty without him," Eden said, not bothering to fight back the tears. Sniffing, she again threw herself into whittling the crust from the bread. Tess just continued to stare out the window, while Jo, typically, grabbed pen and paper and began to compose a list of things to be done in the wake of Ben Calloway's unexpected demise.

Suddenly the kitchen door was pushed open, admitting the sound of several hushed voices and one voice in particular. "Everything all right in here?" Reverend Ford Dunning asked.

That the psychologist-turned-minister was an unconventional instrument of God had long been acknowledged, even partially accepted, by his small nondenominational congregation. The rest of the world, however, often had trouble reconciling the image of a man who'd perform a burial ceremony in tight jeans and a sports coat with that of a cleric. Or, to be more precise, how could he be a messenger of God when he had hair as dark as sin, eyes the color of whiskey, and a body even Satan would have coveted?

"Yes," the three women answered amid sniffs and swipes.

"Would you get Eden out of here?" Jo added. "She's making a sandwich for every man, woman and child in America."

Ford Dunning laid his large, hair-dusted hand on Eden's arm. "The people gathered in your living room came to express their sympathy, not to eat."

"But—"

"No buts," Ford insisted, ushering Eden toward the door.

She managed, however, to snatch the tray of sand-wiches. "Don't you try your sweet-talking wiles on me, Ford Dunning," she said.

The minister laughed, sending a pleasant sound skip-ping around the room. "Trust me, Eden, not even the Devil would be that foolish." As the three women passed through the opened doorway, Ford asked, "Have you heard anything from Mariah?"

"No," came a trio of replies.

"She'll be here," Tess stated optimistically.

Then Eden murmured, "I hope nothing's happened to her."

"Nothing's happened to her. Mariah's happenproof."

This last comment was said with Jo's usual rugged as-surance, though deep below the surface was a note of concern. So indiscernible was it, however, that not even Jo herself heard it.

THE TAXI CRAWLED with obvious uncertainty through the rustic pathways of the quaint cemetery. The driver, a man of enough years to have sworn that he'd seen everything, had ceased to be shocked by his passenger. He'd equally ceased to question her about her destination. Instead, he just let the meter tick away in what was well on its way to becoming one of the biggest fares he'd earned.

The strange odyssey had begun at the Shreveport Re-gional Airport, then continued through Shreveport itself and on to Shreveport's sister city, Bossier City, which lay just beyond the rust waters of the Red River. From there, Haughton had been the object of their journey. Once in-side the sparse city limits, the woman had insisted he cruise the streets of the small town, as though there were mem-ories there that she was trying to physically gather to her-self. She'd also ordered him to stop at a florist, which had been in the process of closing. Its proprietor had opened up its doors again to sell her a single red rose. Somehow, the driver hadn't been surprised at her persuasive powers. No more than he was surprised at the endless meandering they'd done afterward through the Hill Crest Memorial Cemetery. What she was looking for he wasn't certain. He was certain, however, that she'd tell him when she found it.

And she did. Minutes later.

"Here," the woman said suddenly, softly, and for just a second the driver wasn't certain he'd heard anything more than the whispering of the wind. "Stop here."

The driver eased the cab to a halt. The woman, dressed in black leather pants, a red turtleneck sweater and black, high-heeled boots, over which hung a full-length sable-colored coat, picked up the scented rose, opened the door, and stepped from the car. Her emerald-green eyes, concealed behind sunglasses, conspicuous in the gray gloaming that was fast falling, went immediately, mesmerically, to the mound of brown, freshly tilled earth in the distance. At the same time a cold wind purled across the monument-studded landscape, tumbling her platinum-blond hair, which was shoulder-length and rippling in wild waves with the newest fashion. A froth of fire-engine-red lace, the same shade as the color on her full lips, tied back her hair. It, too, fluttered in the wind, as did her earrings—at least the jangly pair, which fit alongside two studs, diamond and gold, making a total of three earrings per crowded ear. The woman shivered. Whether from the cold or the sight of the new grave wasn't clear.

"Wait for me," she called over her shoulder as she started off across the winter-dead grass that mournfully crunched beneath her feet.

"Yeah, sure, miss. It's your money." The cab driver shook his head in disbelief when he realized his passenger, with a childlike trust, had left her purse on the back seat.

Trust, however, was the farthest thing from the woman's mind, for with each step she took, her breath shortened, her hands trembled. The rose threatened to fall from her unsteady fingers. She tightened her hold, ignoring the pain of a thorn.

Confronting death was always like this, Mariah Calloway thought. It was always like living out your most frightening nightmare, like staring into the jaws of the blackest beast, like standing in the coldest of cold winds. An idle thought occurred to her. Had she deliberately missed her flight connections in Atlanta so she wouldn't have to attend the funeral?

Funerals... Lord, they were such pagan rituals! So deceptively sweet smelling. So filled with both thanksgiving and grief. Grief over the loss of the loved one, but a personal sense of thanksgiving that the one stone-cold and breathless wasn't you.

Fear.

Mariah could never remember not fearing death. Just the way she could never remember not having the unshakable belief that she, herself, like her mother before her, would die young. She cast the thought aside, letting it disappear with the sun sinking into the lavender and pink sky.

All too soon, she stood at the graveside. A spray of flowers, in every bright color of spring, sprawled atop the swollen earth. Mariah stooped and read the card. It said: The Family. The family... Eden, Jo, Tess and Mariah. That was the family. All of the family. All of the family had been there to see Ben Calloway begin his journey into eternity. All except her... who roamed the earth like the wind... who deliberately missed her flight connections...who didn't have the courage to face a funeral. Not even her father's.

Suddenly a sense of grief overwhelmed her, and Mariah wanted desperately to cry. No. She would not cry, she thought, fighting against the salty sting. She'd spent a lifetime crying secret and silent tears over her father, and she would not add others to the impotent number already shed. What would be the use? Likewise, what would be the use of remembering that he'd always hugged her less than he'd hugged her sisters? And why recall that she'd sometimes found him staring at her, as if he were looking at her, but seeing someone else?

Someone else. Some special someone else.

Mariah shifted her gaze to the settled grave of her mother and the wisteria bush, bare-boned for winter, that grew nearby. Grief instantly changed to guilt. It was a familiar emotion. If it hadn't been for her, her mother wouldn't have died. It was a fact of life, a fact of death, a fact Ben Calloway had known only too well. Mariah smiled wryly. And one he hadn't been worth a damn at hiding.

Were her parents together now? She hoped so, though the truth was that her father really had never been separated from his wife. At least not in spirit.

"Hi, Mamma," Mariah whispered to the woman she'd never known, a woman whose name she bore. Choosing to call his last daughter Mariah Grace was, Mariah believed, her father's grief-stricken attempt to save as much of the woman he loved as he could.

But she hadn't been his beloved Grace. No matter how hard she'd tried to take her place, Mariah hadn't been able to. Just as no matter how hard Ben Calloway had tried, at least from Mariah's perspective, he hadn't been able to love his youngest daughter.

"Goodbye, Daddy," Mariah whispered, gently laying the rose across the raw, heaped earth. "I'm sorry I couldn't have been her."

The pungent smell of freshly shoveled dirt assailed her nostrils, while the ground's coldness permeated the air around her. Both drawn and repulsed, Mariah reached out for a handful of the clotted soil. It felt moist, chilled, and as heavy as her heartbeat. It felt like her enemy, her friend. It felt like death. Without warning, she was face to face with the blackest of beasts, the coldest of cold winds. Despite the frigid weather, perspiration formed on her forehead. Suddenly she felt like running, racing, fleeing with the wind. Throwing down the dirt, she started for the cab. By the time she reached it, she was almost sprinting. Sliding on to the seat, she slammed the door behind her. The sound was loud in the silent twilight.

"Let's get out of here," she said, adding, "and I'll give you an extra ten bucks if you make it fast."

"Sure thing." The driver shifted the gears, sending the car once more into motion. "Where to?"

"The Midnight Hour," Mariah said, simultaneously whipping the sunglasses from her eyes and digging in her enormous black handbag.

"I don't kn—"

"It's a bar. Down on the highway. At least it used to be down on the highway."

Popping open a compact nearly as big as a saucer, Mariah viewed her image, then rummaged through her handbag for a tube of lipstick. She found everything but. Finally, her fingers connected with a thin cylindrical object and, uncapping it, she applied a shiny layer of crimson to her lips. She smeared them together as she whisked the lipstick back into her purse.

"Tell you what I'm gonna do..." She halted the hand fluffing her hair. "What's your name?"

"Harvey."

"Tell you what I'm gonna do, Harve. I'm gonna buy you a drink for being such a good sport. That is, if Duke Boyd hasn't gone out of business." Mariah spritzed herself with a sweet, clingy scent. "You from here, Harve?"

"Nope. From Milwaukee originally."

"Yeah? I was in Milwaukee once. Actually, I was everywhere once, some places twice." She rearranged her hair again. "Hops," she said suddenly.

"Huh?"

"Hops. Barley. That's all you can smell in Milwaukee." She grinned. "You can get drunk there on a breath of air. Can do that in some of the French wine country, too. And there's this little village in Germany that'll knock your socks off. Course that may be the sauerkraut, I'm not sure." Without a pause, she asked, "Get back often?"

The cab driver had to think before realizing she was referring to Milwaukee. "No, not as much as I'd—"

"I just hate it when they change things while you're gone, don't you? I mean, the nerve of home towns. Don't they know it's their duty to stay just as you left them? It's been two years since I was home, and everything's different." A faraway look stole into her eyes, an ache into her heart. "Everything," she repeated quietly and again, for just a moment, Mariah felt like crying. In the same way she always did at such times, she laughed instead. "But, hey, life goes on, huh, Harve?"

"That's what they say."

"Well, doggone it, if *they* say it, it must be true. Ever wonder who *they* are, Harve? I have this theory. I think *they* are a select committee appointed by God—that can be interpreted as Buddha, Allah, the Force, the Orchestrator of the Harmonic Convergence, depending on your religious preference, of course. Anyway, the committee varies around the world, but in the good ole US of A the committee consists of Frank Sinatra, Mother Teresa, Jonas Salk, the current vice-president, Annette Funicello and Donald Duck. Donald Duck chairs the committee.''

The cab driver laughed. ''Whatever you say.''

''Uh-uh. It's not what *I* say. It's what *they* say that counts.'' She idly wondered what *they* would say about a young girl who sometimes deliberately misbehaved to get her father's attention. Or what would *they* say about a young woman who still felt very much like that little girl? Abruptly, and thankful for the interruption to her thoughts, she hugged the back of the front seat and pointed with one long red nail. ''There it is! Well, what do you know? Old Duke Boyd's still in business.''

The neon sign in front of the bar burned as invitingly as a naughty girl's smile. The car pulled alongside it, and Mariah hopped out.

''C'mon, I'll buy you a drink,'' she offered again, the wind rustling through her white-blond hair.

The driver shook his head. ''Can't. I'm working.''

''Ah, c'mon, Harve. Just one beer.''

He shook his head again.

She smiled . . . temptingly. ''An Old Milwaukee?''

The man laughed. ''Another time.''

''I'll hold you to it,'' Mariah said, rummaging through her handbag and, as always, unable to find what she wanted. Sifting through a plethora of junk, her hand closed around her wallet. ''How much do I owe you?''

She whistled at the horrendous sum named by the driver.

''Is that gonna be a problem?'' Harvey asked, the concern in his voice making him sound a lot like a friend and not a cab driver she'd just met.

"Naw," Mariah said, forking over the money, plus the extra ten dollars she'd promised, "it's just money. I've got..." She counted the bills and coins remaining in her wallet. "I've got a whole $22.18 left."

The small amount of money didn't even faze Mariah. Though an irritant, perhaps, it wasn't the thing that problems were made of. The truth was that she'd never held a job for more than a few months; she'd never stayed in one place long enough. Money was simply a means to get you from one exciting, daring place to another. In the beginning, when the money ran out, she'd worked at whatever was available, but she soon learned that she needed a skill. A high school diploma touting general studies and a typing course in which she'd received no grade—only the instructor's comment: "Can't grade. Student can't find her typewriter, nor her place in the manual"—opened few doors. She ultimately settled on two skills—tending bar and working as a croupier. Universally, it seemed, everyone wanted a drink and/or to try out his luck.

"Be good to yourself, Harve, and don't let life sneak up on your backside," Mariah said, slinging the purse strap over her shoulder.

Harvey nodded, then watched as the woman weaved her way among the Friday-night, good-time convey of cars. When her hand closed around the door handle of the bar, he called out, "Hey, take care!"

Mariah turned and smiled. It was a smile more poignant than flippant. "Can't, Harve! There's no fun in that!"

And then she disappeared inside the Midnight Hour, leaving the cab driver to shake his head. A smile played at his lips. He'd had a lot of customers, and plenty of them had been memorable, but he'd never transported a passenger quite like the woman in red lace and black leather. Whoever she was, whatever joys embraced her, whatever sadness chased her, she was one of a kind. On that he'd bet the exorbitant fare he'd just earned.

Inside, dim lights caressed the darkness, while incessant chatter, raucous laughter, and the ping of a pinball machine created a cacophony of noise. From the bright-colored jukebox George Strait wailed that all his exes lived in Texas, which was why he hung his hat in Tennessee.

Mariah welcomed the gay warmth, allowing it to envelop her emotionally chilled body. Her eyes, adjusting to the curious blend of neon and shadow, took in the busy crowd before singling out the small Christmas tree reposing at the far end of the bar's countertop. The tree, tinseled and lighted, looked as if it had been haphazardly decorated by too many hands. The man behind the bar, big and husky and with a blond mustache that rode clean across his easy-going mouth, looked as though he'd be at home around haphazard. Mariah smiled and strutted forward. She didn't notice that half the women and all the men in the room watched her...as they'd been doing since the moment she'd first walked in.

"Hey, sailor," she breathed huskily, her hip at a sultry angle, "been kissing any fast ladies?"

Duke Boyd looked up from the foaming beer he was filling from the tap. His frown said he clearly didn't appreciate being accosted by a female even if women's lib were the fashion. Suddenly, however, the frown fell apart, replaced, instead, by a smile that split his face wide.

"Heaven help us, Mariah Calloway's back in town," he said as he wiped his hands down his stained apron and rounded the counter. He scooped Mariah up in a fierce hug. "Dammit, girl, where you been?"

"Everywhere. Nowhere," she answered, squeezing him so tightly her arms ached. It felt so good to be with someone she knew! And she did know Duke Boyd. In fact, she'd known him since second grade, when his family had moved from Springhill, Louisiana, down to Haughton. Because the town was as small as it was, everyone knew everyone else's business, or thought he did, so it was common knowledge that Duke Boyd had given Mariah Calloway her first kiss. Beside the playground seesaw. When both were eight years old. Duke Boyd now gave all his kisses to his wife, Patti, who had been Mariah's best friend in second grade.

After several seconds, he thrust her away to arm's length. "Let me look at you." He did, proclaiming at last, "You look great. Absolutely great."

"So do you."

"Liar. I need to lose twenty pounds. I'm drinking more beer than I'm pouring."

"You look great to me," Mariah said earnestly.

Duke sobered. "I was sorry about your daddy."

"Yeah," Mariah said, her voice thickening. "Listen," she said with an abrupt overbrightness, "could a girl get a drink here?"

"You betcha," he said, stepping once more behind the counter. Mariah shrugged off the fur coat and, plopping it on a stool, heaved herself onto the adjacent one. "What'll it be?"

"A Vodka Collins."

Duke looked up. "Since when did you start drinking?" If it was common knowledge that Duke and Mariah had kissed at eight, it was equally common knowledge that Mariah didn't drink anything stronger than herbal tea.

Since I lost a father who didn't even know I existed. Since I lost a father who would have preferred someone else existed in my place. "It, uh . . . it just feels right today. Okay?"

The owner of the Midnight Hour studied his friend's suddenly serious, obviously pained, expression before complying with her request. Shoving the glass forward, he cautioned, "Go easy, huh?"

"That's the trouble with life," she said, stirring the drink with the swizzle stick. "Conflicting advice. You say 'Go easy,' Thomas says 'Do not go gentle into that good night.'"

Duke Boyd frowned. "Thomas?"

"Dylan."

"Was he the one in our class?"

Mariah giggled. "Of course not, silly. That was Thomas Graves." She took a sip of the drink, fought back a grimace and asked, "Ever been to St. Thomas?"

"St. Thomas? I thought you just said Dyl—"

"It's an island. In the Caribbean. Looks like a crown of jewels in the night." She took another swallow of the drink. It tasted like silk, but had the potential to strike like a serpent. "The night is truly good there. It wouldn't be easy to go gently into it." Sipping again, she said, "Wouldn't it be strange if Dylan Thomas were from St. Thomas? He'd be Thomas of Thomas." Her brow puckered. "Graves. That's kind of ironic, isn't it? I mean, this discussion and Thomas Graves being in our class."

"Mariah, what the hell are you talking about?"

She looked genuinely perplexed as she started to rummage through her handbag. "Death, of course. What did you think we were talking about?"

Before he could answer, she'd slid from the stool and, drink in one hand, a quarter in the other, she approached the jukebox.

Duke Boyd just shook his head. Mariah was back.

Mariah was also in rare form. Excitingly erratic in her behavior, she captured everyone's attention, especially the men's. She was vague, she was fey, she was an irresistible siren in lace and leather.

"C'mon, let's dance," she'd say to one, then laughingly abandon him to play pinball with another. Then in the midst of a tumbling pinball, she'd stop, letting the ball die in order to sing off-key along with the lyrics of a song. She charmingly answered questions with questions— "Where're you from?" "Why must I be from anywhere?"—and never seemed to know where anything was, from her purse to her coat to her latest dance partner. Her smile beguiled; her eyes, shining like a bolt of emerald lightning, enchanted.

Increasingly, however, those green eyes began to haze from one too many drinks, drinks everyone insisted on buying for her. To reciprocate, she insisted on buying drinks for everyone.

"C'mon, cowboy," she said to the guy in the Western hat, "have another beer. Another Duke, beer." She giggled. "Another beer, Duke. For this cowboy, who's been rounding up them dogies all day."

"Mariah..." Duke began.

"Where's my drink? I've lost my drink. Has anyone seen—"

Duke shoved the Vodka Collins someone had just bought for Mariah forward. "Hey, babe, don't you think you ought to go easy?"

"'Go easy into that good night,'" Mariah misquoted, a slurred smile at her lips as she patted her friend on the cheek. "Everything's fine, Duke. Really. Honest. I'm going easy...easy...easy..." She flowed off the stool; her legs had to think twice about supporting her weight, but finally agreed to.

Duke listened to her launch into an inharmonic duet with Reba McIntire, then reached for the phone beneath the counter. He hesitated, as if thinking better of what he was about to do. When, with a giggle, Mariah stumbled over thin air and barely caught herself before falling, he dialed the number of the Calloway residence.

EDEN, THINKING, HOPING, it might be Mariah, answered the hall phone on the beginning of the second ring. People still roamed about her living room, talking in soft and sympathetic tones. She turned her back to them in an attempt to create the illusion of privacy.

"Hello?" At the sound of a male voice, her hopes were immediately dashed. "Oh, hello, Duke." The caller spoke again. With each word, Eden grew paler. "Mariah? Drunk? But Mariah doesn't drink." She listened, then threaded her fingers through her strawberry-blond hair. "I see. Yes. Yes, of course, I'll be right down. Oh, and thank you, Duke. Yeah. Yeah. Thanks."

Eden cradled the ancient black phone that her father had refused to replace with something more modern, looking for all the world as if she'd just been told that her youngest sister had sprouted two heads.

"Is anything wrong?" inquired a deep masculine voice at her side.

Eden looked up and into the eyes of Ford Dunning.

"That was...that was Duke Boyd. Mariah's over at the Midnight Hour. Drunk." The word staggered about the hallway before Eden groaned. "Lord, Jo's gonna eat her alive. Why, why did Mariah pick now to do this?"

Ford thought the answer rather obvious.

"I've, uh... I've got to go get her," Eden said, suddenly, frantically searching for her purse which held the car keys.

"Let me go after her," Ford said, quieting Eden by grasping her shoulders.

She glanced up. "Would you?"

"Sure."

"It might be better if...if she needs carrying or anything."

"You stay here with your guests," he said, already digging in the front pocket of his jeans for his keys, "and I'll be right back with her."

"Okay. I'll stay here. With the guests. Oh, Ford?"

He turned from where he already stood by the front door.

"She has blond hair and green eyes—"

"I'll find her," he interrupted, not bothering to explain that in the two years he'd known the Calloway family, enough had been said about the youngest daughter to enable him in all probability to pick her out of a crowd.

Eden smiled, not joyfully. "Yeah. She'll be the one drunk."

"Hey, Eden?"

Eden, who'd already started back to her guests with thoughts of making more finger sandwiches, turned.

"Drinking too much isn't a crime, you know?"

"*I* know that, but tell it to Jo."

THE WORLD GLOWED, its appearance somewhere between slapstick comedy and gauzy tragedy, when Mariah, sitting once more on a stool, saw the man enter the Midnight Hour. She saw him through a beaded glass of whiskey—she'd changed from Vodka Collinses to Old Fashioneds—which she rolled across her forehead in an attempt to ease the room's heat and her head's swirl. She wasn't quite certain why he'd caught her attention. Maybe it was the way he fit the room, or, more to the point, the way he silently demanded the room fit him. Or maybe it was the surprise on the bar patrons' faces, for, even in her

inebriated state, she could sense the astonishment, the
awkwardness, maybe even the downright embarrassment,
crawling through the room as he spoke to first one person, then another. He seemed to be searching for someone. Even as Mariah made this assessment, the man's gaze
swung to her. With this full face-to-face view, she was
forced to conclude that perhaps what had ensnared her
attention was simply his good looks. His dynamite good
looks. And those more-than-dynamite whiskey-colored
eyes.

Whiskey-colored eyes?

It had to be an illusion, she told herself, an illusion created by the amber liquid she was staring through. Nobody's eyes could be that straw-in-the-sunshine shade.
Could they? She lowered the glass. His eyes remained the
same golden color, a color that contrasted beautifully,
boldly, with his tanned skin and his dark-brown, almost
black, hair.

On some level she registered that he was heading straight
for her, on another that his broad shoulders filled out the
beige, cable-knit sweater, which he wore beneath a brown
tweed sports coat, to perfection. Stone-washed jeans encased his long legs in a way that could only be called
memorable. For an older man—she guessed he was in his
late thirties—he wasn't bad. In fact, he wasn't bad at all.
Her woman's heart fluttered at the modulated swagger of
his hips. *Ah, come on, Calloway, call a spade a spade. The
man's scorchingly sexy.*

The scorchingly sexy man was now standing right before her. Mariah's eyes openly climbed the length of him.
Up, up and up, over waist and chest and sun-brown throat,
until her hazy gaze met his. He didn't flinch, nor did he
seem the slightest uncomfortable meeting another person

eye to eye. In fact, he seemed content to hold the mute stare forever.

It was Mariah who broke the silence. And she did so in her typically blunt fashion, a bluntness perhaps urged on by the spirits swimming in her bloodstream. When she spoke, her voice tinkled like the sweet, ebullient notes of wind chimes.

"You're sexy."

CHAPTER TWO

A SLOW GRIN SPREAD across Ford's mouth, a grin that confirmed, to every woman present, that he was, indeed, what he'd just been accused of being. "And you're just a little tipsy."

Mariah smiled, too, and swayed forward as though to tell him a secret. "You're wrong," she whispered when her lips were tingly-near his ear. "I'm a lot tipsy." Her condition and the too-severe angle caused her to lose her balance. Ford extended his hand, but she righted herself before he could touch her. "I'm okay. I'm fine. I'm taking everything easy."

"You do that."

"I'll do that. I *am* doing that. I'm..." She frowned. Then hiccuped. "There's something wrong here. Something's-seriously-wrong." The last slurred together until it was delivered as one word. "I'm a lot tipsy and you're no tipsy at all." She frowned again. "No tipsy...not tipsy." She shrugged, her shoulders pleasantly stretching the red cashmere sweater. "Whichever...whatever...Duke, this sexy man needs a drink."

"No, thank you," Ford said, aware that every eye in the place was suddenly turned on him. How the controversial minister handled the smashed lady would make rounds faster than the hands on a clock.

"Nonsense, I'm buying," Mariah said, reaching for her purse. Her fingers met thin air. "Where's my purse? Has anyone—"

"Thanks, but I don't want a drink."

"Duke, this man needs a drink, and I can't find my purse," she said, ignoring Ford's refusal.

"Hi, Ford," Duke said.

"Hi, how're you doing?"

"I'm doing."

"You two know each other?" Mariah asked, answering herself with, "Oh, yeah, I forgot I'm back home. Everyone knows everyone. And everything about everyone. Did you know that Duke gave me my first kiss? A thousand years ago when we were eight. Isn't that right, Duke?"

The hulky bartender grinned indulgently. "Yeah, that's right, Mariah."

"Ford?" she asked abruptly. "Your mother like cars or Julie Andrews movies?"

Ford looked appropriately confused.

"*Sound of Music.* 'Climb every mountain, ford every stream, follow every rainbow...'" Her off-key rendition of the song died to a close. A pensive close. "Gotta chase those rainbows, right? Wherever they are, right? Right," she again answered herself. "Gotta chase, gotta race, gotta run. Gotta...I gotta have another drink," she announced suddenly.

"Please don't."

At Ford's low words, Mariah glanced at him. For just a heartbeat, she'd actually believed he cared. But why would this stranger care about her when no other man ever had? Not even her own father. Some honest something deep inside her admitted that maybe she never let any man get close enough to care; maybe she was too afraid he, like her father, wouldn't. The subject was altogether too awesome to tackle in her fuzzy state, and even more awesome to tackle outside it, so she did as always. She fought seriousness with gaiety.

"If we're not going to drink, then let's dance. Did you see *Dirty Dancing*?" she asked, referring to a movie that had started a trend. "C'mon, let's dirty dance," she said, gliding from the stool.

This time, her legs flatly refused their assigned task. Her knees buckling, she crumpled forward. Ford's arm shot out and snaked around her waist. He hauled her against him—not intimately, but close enough for each to feel the lines and curves of a body which nature had deliberately structured to be the opposite of the other. Ford felt softness, the flat planes of her stomach, the swell of her breasts. Mariah felt hardness, the rugged contour of his chest, the firmness of his muscular thighs. She also felt strength and gentleness. How was it possible to feel both strength and gentleness? And yet, she did. In the arm encircling her waist. In the body pressed against hers. In the honey-colored eyes peering down into her own.

"Are you all right?" he asked, his gaze fixing on the fire-engine-red lace in her hair, then on the fire-engine-red at her lips. Both were the same shade. Exactly. He wondered why he would notice something that incredibly incidental.

In the background the jukebox crooned that love was nothing but a misunderstanding between two fools. The rest of the room had grown unnaturally silent and still.

"Yes," she said, taking in his angular cheeks beginning to shadow with a day's growth of beard, the square of his chin that had a hint of a dimple, the dark lashes, indecently long, that fanned his eyes. "I'm fine. Easy. I'm taking it easy."

She pulled away from him; he let her go. Both were relieved when her legs accepted their responsibility.

"Let me take you home," he said, quickly clarifying. "Eden sent me."

At the name, Mariah's face brightened, yet softened. "Eden? You know Eden?"

Ford smiled. "Yeah. Remember, this is a small town."

"How is she?"

"She's worried about you."

"Ah, she shouldn't do that. Eden worries too much . . . like a mother hen . . . always worries too much . . . I've gotta go, Duke," she said, grabbing her coat. "Eden's worried. Eden's . . . where's my purse?"

Ford produced the black leather bag from somewhere.

"Thanks. What-da-I owe you, Duke?" The bartender figured her tab and quoted a price. Mariah whistled. "Gee, I'm generous, aren't I?"

"Look, forget—" Duke began.

Mariah shook her head, started to dig in her purse and slurred, "I'm a woman of honnor. A woman of honnor always pays her bills." She produced keys, makeup, a dozen bags of airline peanuts, a portable hair dryer, a book of poetry by Rod McKuen, a tin of Darjeeling tea, a toothbrush and toothpaste—everything but a wallet. "Now, where is my wal— Would you hold this?" she asked, handing a filmy bit of red silk to Ford.

The filmy bit of red silk proved to be a nightgown, or rather the suggestion of one. Ford took it—he'd had no choice.

Several onlookers snickered, then quelled themselves with the reality of who they were snickering at. Prudently one didn't have fun at one's preacher's expense. Ford seemed oblivious to everything, including the red silk crushed in his hand. That the suggestive softness was sliding across his fingertips like an erotic midnight dream was in no way visible on his face. Controlling his emotions was something he'd learned a long time ago—during a six-month tour of duty in Vietnam.

"Here it is!" Mariah called triumphantly, starting to riffle through the bills in her wallet—the scarce bills in her wallet. At the $22.18 she found, she frowned. "Oh, yeah," she said, the memory of the cab bill penetrating her drink-dulled brain. "This is all I have, Duke." She shoved the money forward. A nickel rolled off the counter and pinged to the floor.

Duke picked it up. "Forget it, Mariah."

"No," she insisted, reaching for a cocktail napkin and a pen lying at the far end of the counter. "I'm a woman of..." She seemed to forget what she was a woman of.

Duke reminded her. "Honor."

"Yeah. Honnor."

As she leaned toward the napkin and pen, the leather pants, as tight fitting as a pair of new gloves, stretched across her trim bottom. Someone gave a catcall. At this, Ford did glance out into the sea of ultra-interested faces. That he'd had to drag his eyes from Mariah's derrière to do so softened his look of censure.

"I'll write you an IOU," she said, straightening and beginning to scribble. "I...owe...Duke Boyd...how much do I owe you...take away $22.18?"

"Look, babe, just forget—"

"Here," Ford said, stuffing the red nightgown into the leather bag and reaching for his back pocket. He held the liquor bill so that only he could figure the balance. Shucking through his wallet, he tossed two twenties down on the bar. Mariah looked up at him. She was genuinely surprised that his eyes were still that crazy shade of amber. How could eyes be that color? And why was he paying her bill?

"You don't have to," Mariah said. "Duke'll take my IOU."

Ford shoved the money forward. Duke hesitated; Ford silently insisted. The owner of the bar then rang up the bill and gave Ford his change, which he pocketed.

Mariah scratched through the name on the napkin. "I owe...Ford..." She glanced up. "What's your last name?"

"Dunning. D-u-n-n-i-n-g."

"Ford D-u-n-n-i-n-g." Finished, she asked, "What-da-I owe you?"

"$38.92."

"Three eight point nine two dollars." This she followed with an illegible penning of her name, folded the napkin twice and handed it to Ford. "I always pay my bills, Ford Dunning. I'm a woman of honnor."

"I'm glad to hear that, Mariah Calloway," he answered as he tucked the napkin into the small front pocket of his jeans.

The action, which would have splayed the fabric if there'd been a millimeter of room to spare, drew Mariah's attention. "Can you breathe in those?" she asked without the slightest apology for the intimacy of the question.

A crooked smile claimed Ford's lips. "Barely, but I hear they make me look sexy."

Mariah laughed. When she did, everyone in the room was in some way affected. Even Haughton's controversial preacher.

Children, fools and drunks, Ford had always heard, were led by God's guiding hand. He believed it. There was no other explanation for how Mariah reached his car under her own power. She weaved and bobbed, even once lost her footing in the fine pea-gravel, but miraculously she made it.

At the sight of the low-slung, sporty vehicle in the color of dove white, she hiked a brow. "A 300ZX. I'm impressed."

"Don't be," he said, assisting her into the plush seat. "It's secondhand and not paid for." He closed the door behind her and, fishing the keys from his pocket, crossed to his side. When he opened the door and slid in, he said, as though the conversation had never been interrupted, "One of the guys in my encounter group needed to sell it."

She squinted her eye in a measuring way. "Encounter group? You crazy?"

Ford grinned, shifted gears and pulled from the crowded parking lot. "Maybe. Maybe not. Either way, I'm heading the group."

"You a shrink?"

"A psychologist," he answered, gearing down again. The car purred under his caress. "Among other things."

"What other th—? Ohh," she groaned suddenly. The motion, combined with the admixture of spirits, was causing a wave of nausea to wash over her.

"Are you gonna be sick?" he asked, looking at her.

She spread her hand across her stomach and considered. The sick feeling, like an outgoing tide, began to recede. "No. At least I don't think so." She grinned, lopsidedly. "Don't worry, Ford D-u-n-n-i-n-g. I wouldn't dare barf in your car."

"That wasn't what I was worried about."

The hand at her stomach wandered to her temple, and her grin faded entirely. "Is my head supposed to feel the size of a watermelon?"

"Yeah. A big one. Why don't you lie back and close your eyes?"

"Good idea...great idea...wonderful id—" Mariah yawned, lazily, fully, making no attempt to stifle it. At the end, she sighed and added, "The airline lost my luggage. They always lose my luggage. I think they stamp that on my ticket—Lose Her Luggage. But I know how to fake 'em out. I keep all the important stuff in my purse." She giggle-yawned. "'Course I never know where my purse is, but..." She yawned again, seriously, the weariness of travel, the heaviness of drink, catching up with her. Her eyelashes, golden tipped, fluttered downward; she immediately raised them, as though fighting slumber.

Ford eased the car to a halt at a red light. He glanced over at her.

She lay with her head cushioned against the seat. Her eyes, only sleepy slits, were leveled on him. She twitched her lips in a pixyish grin. "You really are sexy."

He gave her a half smile which defied logic by being twice as potent as a whole smile. "You really are drunk."

Her smile started to widen, but died slowly. A haunted look, like the fog on an English moor, stole into her huge green eyes. With a visible effort, she swallowed back the clotted knot in her throat. "My father's dead," she announced in a small voice.

The words held a note of disbelief, as if she hadn't yet accepted Ben Calloway's death and was compelled from time to time to touch the reality of it, the way an unsighted person explores the shape of an unknown piece of sculpture.

Vulnerable. She was totally, wholly vulnerable. And though she was unquestionably a woman—the red sweater couldn't conceal that—there was also a bit of the child in her. Ford felt the warm ribbons of compassion unfurl within him.

"I know," he said, feeling some other emotion stir as well. A protective emotion. An emotion that was warmer, deeper, part of his masculine makeup.

The light changed, someone impatiently honked behind them and Ford reluctantly drew his eyes from her. When he looked back, Mariah's eyes were shut and her breathing was even. She was asleep. For the remainder of the drive, Ford divided his attention between road and woman.

So this was the free-spirited Calloway sister, he mused, who, like the wind, never stood still. Ben Calloway, though a man who grudgingly shared his feelings, had betrayed himself more than once with a wistful look, and a too casual word, that indicated he wished his daughter would come home more often. Was she feeling guilty now that she hadn't come home on a regular basis? Was she feeling guilty that she hadn't seen him one last time before he'd died? Or had it been Ben himself who lived with guilt? After seeing Mariah, after almost a decade of studying and observing human nature, he suspected, and strongly, that Ben Calloway had harbored ambivalent feelings about his youngest child. The reason was simple: she looked too much like her mother. The picture of a youthful Grace Calloway, which rested on the mantel of the Calloway house, was a dead ringer for the woman who slept beside him.

It was the hair which bound the two women so closely, hair so silvery blond it was white, white like the stars gleaming in the trusting December night. Ford's eyes now roamed over that hair which tumbled attractively about a perfectly oval face. He smiled. Actually, it did a good bit more than tumble. It fell in a wild, frizzy, gypsylike abandon that probably two women in all the world could wear with a naturalness. Mariah was one of the two. In truth,

the waywardness seemed specifically designed for her.
Waywardness. The wayward wind. Like the restless wind,
what demons drove her to aimlessly wander the globe?

Right this moment, with a thick fringe of golden lashes
fanning against her cheeks, she looked possessed of no
demons. To the contrary, she seemed kissed by angels.
Kissed. Ford's eyes dropped to her lips, lips full, pouty and
parted ever so slightly. Red lips. She liked the color
red . . . and earrings . . . and leather and lace.

And I'd like to get to know her better.

On the one hand the thought surprised him; on the other
it didn't surprise him at all. The truth was, since the first
Pamplona tale of Mariah, he'd been intrigued by her.
Professionally, of course, he hastened to clarify. And what
about privately? He had no private life, he reminded himself. He didn't have time for one. And even if he
did...well, no preacher in his right mind wanted to tangle
with a scarlet-lipped, sultry-hipped Sadie Thompson.

The moment he pulled into the crescent drive of the
Calloway house, Ford noted that the guest cars were gone.
Good, he thought, slowing the sports car to a crawl to accommodate the driveway's gravel, the last thing Mariah
needed was an audience. Stopping in front of the gate of
the white picket fence—the fence, as well as the house, in
the tradition of all old homes, always seemed in need of a
fresh coat of paint—he killed the motor. And looked over
at Mariah. She didn't stir, but rather remained just as she
was with her head lolled to the side, her arms limp in her
lap. Her legs, which Ford realized were as long as a country mile, sprawled out before her.

"Mariah?" he called softly.

She didn't respond.

"Mariah?" He tried again, this time touching her
shoulder.

She sighed, shifted and fell instantly back into something between sleep and stupor.

Ford threw open his door and, crunching through the gravel, crossed around to her side. He pulled open the door. Without the slightest hesitation, he slid one arm beneath her knees, the other around her shoulders.

"Mmm," she whispered as he lifted her into his arms. For a tall woman—he guessed her to be five-ten or, perhaps, five-eleven—she was light, with not a fatted ounce on her willowy frame.

"We're home," he said, trying to juggle her and her purse. What in Hades did she have in it? A nightgown. A red nightgown. A red, filmy nightgown.

"Home?"

"Um-huh."

"I can walk," she mumbled.

"Sure you can."

"I can," she assured him, curling her arms about his neck and nestling her head against his shoulder.

"Next time," he answered, negotiating the gate by feel alone and starting up the cracked sidewalk.

"Next time," she mumbled.

Stars glittered in the black heavens, while a frigid wind whipped across the land, chilling all in its path. The two magnolia trees in the front yard, as big as fifty years could grow them, quaked, their enormous evergreen leaves rattling. Ford, too, grimaced at the cold, which blasted his cheeks and tore at his hair. Even Mariah, snuggled in his arms, her hair now scattered in blond confusion, shivered.

With care, he took each step leading to the porch. Beneath his feet the weathered wood creaked, while the chains of the porch swing screaked in the heavy silence. Whether it was the noise that alerted Eden, or simply that she'd been watching for their arrival, she swung wide the screened door as Ford neared it. Her face registered her concern.

"How is she?"

"She's all right," he said, edging through the opened doorway. Immediately the door closed behind him, shutting out the winter night.

Mariah said nothing. She was dead to the world.

"I made some coffee—" Eden began.

"I'd just let her sleep it off," Ford interrupted, tactfully not pointing out that she was too drunk to get coffee down.

"Oh, my word!" exclaimed the sudden voice—the sudden and disgusted voice—of Jo.

Ford and Eden glanced up. Jo and Tess stood in the living room doorway.

"Do you believe this?" Jo added. "And Daddy not even cold in the grave. And would you look at the leather? My, God, now she's into whips and chains."

"She is not into whips and chains," Eden said, acting her usual role of placater. "She's just had too much to drink. And drinking isn't a crime, you know?"

"Which is good," Jo agreed, "because, if it were, she'd be facing life imprisonment. I just can't believe it," she added.

"Will you calm down?" Eden said.

Through the verbal interchange, Tess had said nothing. Now, she simply looked at Ford and, moving toward the first step of the stairs, said, "Let me show you our room."

Ford followed, the woman in his arms beginning to grow heavy despite her slender build. Downstairs, Eden repeated that drinking wasn't a crime.

At the head of the stairs, Tess indicated the first door to the right. It led to the room the two of them had shared as girls. That it remained exactly as they'd left it was obvious. A yellow- and green-flowered wallpaper, faded from the years, covered the walls, while a ruffled, white eyelet coverlet spread across the double bed. The room had been divided into territories, one very neat and traditional, the other cluttered and in the modish style of ten years before. Ford would have bet next Sunday's collection on which side of the room Mariah had lived in.

"Here, just put her on the bed," Tess said, yanking throw pillows out of the way.

As Ford lowered Mariah directly onto the coverlet, Tess opened the closet and lifted a quilt from the top shelf. When she turned back, Ford was dragging the fur coat from Mariah's shoulders. Mariah, for all the movement she made, might just as well have been anesthetized for major surgery. Ford tossed the coat across a chair, while Tess spread the quilt over Mariah, fussing to get it just right, seemingly because it was the only thing she could presently do for her sister, seemingly because it was her way of saying "Welcome home."

Finally, after one last adjustment, Tess looked up.

"She'll be all right," Ford said, grinning suddenly. "If you don't count a record-setting headache."

Tess smiled. It made it all the way to her hazel eyes, which was a trip not many smiles had completed in recent months. "Trust me, her headache won't be anything compared to the one she's given Jo."

Ford's grin broadened.

"You want some coffee?" Tess asked.

"Sounds good." He motioned for Tess to precede him from the room, which she did after switching off the lamp. Just as he started to close the door, Mariah's whimper reached him. He jerked his head toward the bed. She had fought the cover back and, one foot pushing at the other, was trying—ineffectively—to remove her boots.

"Be right there," Ford said to Tess.

She nodded and started on down the stairs.

"Here, let me," Ford said, crossing the room and tugging at a high-heeled boot. It wouldn't budge. He tried again. It still wouldn't budge.

"Mmm," Mariah moaned, obviously annoyed with his clumsy attempts. "Off...get it off."

"I'm trying, I'm trying. Would you be still?" he said when she rolled to her side.

"Off."

"Okay, okay, give me a minute," he said, molding his palm to the calf of her leather-clad leg. With the other hand, he yanked. The motion, sharp and quick, shucked the boot. It also jarred her awake. Her eyes, sleepy and round, bit by bit focused until she was staring directly at him. Recognition dawned slowly. She grinned...just as slowly.

"Hi, sexy."

"Hi, yourself," he said, using the same technique to remove the second boot. This time the shapeliness of her calf imprinted itself on his senses. The word she had just used—sexy—seemed appropriate. He ignored the observation, reaching, instead, for the quilt she'd discarded. He drew it back over her. She immediately tossed it off, wiggling her toes, which were confined beneath red and black Argyle socks.

"Go to sleep," Ford said, attempting once more to cover her with the quilt. Before it could settle, however, she flopped out of its way and managed to haul herself to the side of the bed. She turned on the lamp. Somehow, the quilt ended up at the foot of the bed, where it plunged onto the hardwood floor.

"Gown . . . I need my gown . . . where's my—"

"No way, lady," Ford said, remembering the froth of red silk masquerading as nightwear.

"But I need my—"

Ford took the purse she was rummaging in from her. "Go back to sleep."

Stepping to the foot of the bed, he picked up the quilt. When he glanced back, Mariah was on her feet and, balancing as though she were on a surfboard, she was fighting the zipper of her leather pants.

"What are you doing?" Sheer panic had replaced the cool authority that resonated from the pulpit.

"Can't sleep . . . in these."

Ford had never heard anything as loud as the rasp of the zipper. "No! Wait!"

Mariah wriggled her slim hips, skinning the tight leather from her thighs.

"Mariah!" His hands closed around hers, trying to forestall her. Which he did, momentarily. His intervention also caused her to lose her balance. She gasped. He grabbed her shoulders to steady her. She righted herself. He heaved a sigh of relief. And then she shoved down the leather pants . . . grabbed a fistful of the lapel of his sports coat . . . and stepped, hopped, stepped from the pants.

"Mari—!"

The word halted as Ford's breath was whittled in half at the sight of the red scrap of lace called panties. He might have considered the implications of his speedy masculine reaction to her near nakedness; he might have considered how compromising the situation looked and what kind of fast talking he'd have to do to explain it; he might have considered how panty manufacturers could grow rich from the production of nothing. He might have considered all this . . . but he didn't. He was too busy dealing with the fact

that Mariah had grabbed the hem of her sweater in prep-
aration of shedding it, too.

"No!" he cried, imprisoning her hands. "Do not take
off the sweater. Mariah, listen to me. Do not...take
off...the sweater. Do you understand what I'm telling
you?"

She looked at him with eyes as big as the state of Louisiana, as innocent as every babe living therein. "Do not
take off the sweater," she mimicked prettily.

"That's it. Perfect. Do not take off the sweater. Thank
you, God," he mumbled in an aside. "Now, I'm just going to get these pants—" he stooped and picked up the
leather pants, careful as he did so to keep his eyes on the
floor and not on lace panties "—and then you're going
back to bed and..."

As if from the heavens, a red sweater rained down and
covered his head like a cashmere curtain. He yanked it off.
"Darnit, Mariah, you promised! You—"

If the sight of her in red panties stole his breath, the sight
before him now stopped it completely. A red lacy bra,
more imagination than substance, cupped small, but firm
and shapely, breasts. Through the gossamer webbing
peeked two rose-tipped nipples, which at the moment
looked as sassy as soldiers who'd won an entire war without firing a single shot. Ford dropped his eyes, hoping to
escape the sensual view, hoping to restore his breathing.
Instead, he ran once more into crimson lace. It was provocatively molding the juncture of her long willowy legs.
The Argyle socks, which might have negated some of the
sensual impact, did no such thing. They were too busy
adding an irresistible, little-girl sweetness to the provocative scene.

"Damn!" Ford swore, adding, "Sorry, Lord, that
seemed the lesser of two evils at the moment."

Raking his hand through hair the sweater had already disheveled, he stood and threw the clothes into a chair.

Mariah was chanting what she'd heard him say, "Evil...evil...evil..."

"I'm gonna evil you, if you don't get yourself into bed," he said, his patience, his control, worn thin. "Now." When she balked, he took her arm and proceeded to give her no choice. "If you don't get your little red-laced fanny in bed right now," he said, forcing her down and grabbing the quilt, which he quickly pulled over her...up to her chin, "I'm gonna paddle it good."

Mariah grinned with unabashed sultriness. "Promises, promises."

"I mean it, Mariah Calloway..."

"You're cute..."

"If you take another thing off..."

"You're sexy..."

"I'm gonna paddle your butt but good."

"And you're sweet." Her grin faded. Her tone became deadly serious. "You're really terribly sweet, Ford D-u-n-n-i-n-g."

Her hand snaked from beneath the cover and connected with the side of his face. Her touch startled him. He told himself later that this startled state was responsible for his allowing what happened next. With a total lack of inhibition, Mariah raised herself on one elbow and placed her lips against his.

Gentle. Her kiss was as gentle as warm spring rain and, like rain, it nourished Ford's dry, barren lips. Lips whose needs were frequently subjugated to overwork and overbooked appointments. Ford allowed the delicious sweetness to permeate his senses, telling himself that he should stop her, that he *would* stop her just as soon as this mo-

ment of madness passed. Just as soon as he was past being startled, just as soon as the kiss was past being sweet.

He knew precisely the instant the kiss changed tempo,
the instant it changed from sweetness to sultriness to soul-
ful need. It was when she whimpered. He knew, too, what
had inspired the transformation: the coldness of death that
pleaded to be turned into the warmth of life. The need to
touch and be touched, the hunger to know, even temporarily, that she wasn't alone in the vast universe, trembled
through her—he could feel its fiery, frightening strength.
It was a strength which had once, long ago, blazed through
his own bereaved body. Then, just as Mariah now, he had
needed, had hungered, in primal, instinctive ways.

As if sensing that life and death and sex were but different sides of the same metaphysical object, she greedily
sealed her lips with his, begging with each restless movement, each reckless stroke, for him to consume her, to
prove to her that she wasn't alone. His lips, of their own
volition—he couldn't have stopped them had he wanted
to!—hardened as he eased to her side, driving her back
into the bed's plushness. He followed her down, his lips
never leaving hers. Her hand found the nape of his neck
and tugged, leaving the imprint of her nails in his skin. Her
other hand crawled up his sweater, absorbing his heartbeat, absorbing his nearness, absorbing the fact that she
wasn't alone. His mouth opened over hers. Parting. De-
vouring. Giving what she asked for. Until there was a silky
slickness. Until their breath was but a mated whisper.

In a natural reaction to get closer, closer, closer yet,
Mariah opened her mouth to him. She moaned.

The sound was sobering. Because it was precisely what
Ford himself wanted to do—moan deep in his throat. Or
maybe groan—raw and roughly. Either or—moaning or
groaning with a desire that had come out of nowhere with

a startling swiftness—it was the last thing he should be doing with this woman. Especially at a time when she was so consummately vulnerable.

Ford pulled his mouth away from hers. And stared down at her passion-softened features, her limpid eyes, her wet lips. Her incredibly wet lips.

"Go to sleep," he whispered, forcing his eyes from her ivory shoulders and the scarlet straps of her bra. He pushed himself from the bed when every male instinct told him to stay and hold her. As he shut off the light, he wondered just how much of tonight she'd remember in the morning.

"Ford..."

"Go to sleep."

Out in the hallway, he gave a deep sigh and waited for time and nature to adjust the front of his pants. Coffee. He needed a cup of coffee. Make that a whole pot! He was three-quarters of the way down the stairs when he realized he had fire-engine-red lipstick smeared across his mouth.

At the same moment Ford was swiping a handkerchief across his lips, Mariah rolled to her side. She was sleepy, but couldn't sleep. Drunk, but curiously sober. Passionless, yet fully aroused. She also felt tired, weary...alone. Her father had just died. And with his death was gone forever the chance to make him love her. Forever. Final. Death was so damned final. This she'd always known intellectually. It was just that she'd never *felt* the word *final* before. It felt so...so final. As in forever. As in never again. A great sadness swelled inside her, and she reached for a handful of flippant gaiety. She found none. Instead, one lone tear seeped from the corner of her eye.

Her daddy was dead.

And no one seemed to understand her sorrow. No one. Except a stranger named Ford Dunning.

CHAPTER THREE

SHE HAD A HEADACHE. Or, more to the point, the claws of a headache had her.

As though testing the waters of a cold lake, Mariah opened one eyelid, peeped out and groaned. Who told the sun it could shine that brightly! Whipping the quilt back over her head, she wallowed in the warm, womblike darkness. Finally she garnered the courage to try again. Squinting, she eased the cover from her face. The sun was still grinning its blinding warmth.

Threading her fingers through her hair, Mariah dragged herself to a sitting position against the headboard. She looked around. She had the vague remembrance of someone sleeping beside her during the night. Tess? Yeah, Tess. Who else but perfect Tess would get up and make the bed with someone still in it? Another memory came to mind, this one shadowy, this one of warm and sexy lips. Warm lips? Sexy lips? Yes, unbelievably warm and sexy lips. Did they belong to...? What was his name? Ford. That was it. Ford something-or-other. The red of her skimpy bra caught her attention, and she raised the quilt to see what she wore beneath it. Her toes, at the end of long bare legs, waved an Argyle good-morning.

Oh, my, she thought with a naughty grin, had she undressed before this Ford something-or-other? Dunning. That was his name. Ford Dunning. Ford D-u-n-n-i-n-g. The smile proved too much for her hungover condition and promptly turned to a grimace. Lord, she must have been pie-eyed but good for a simple smile to do that kind of damage!

Holding her head, she slid to the edge of the bed. A poster of funky Kiss greeted her. Along with a nine-by-eleven of Led Zeppelin. And an assortment of other teenage memorabilia—a bulletin board filled with ticket stubs, photos and a dried mum with faded red and white streamers that read Go, Bucks. She stood, eased into the leather pants and sweater and crossed over to the eyelet-draped vanity standing in the middle of the room. Unsightly black tape, measured to precision and curling with age, ran down the middle of the mirror and the vanity top and all along the floor and up two walls. One side of the room was organized perfection, the other absolute chaos. From the chaotic side of the vanity top, Mariah picked up a bottle of hardened scarlet nail polish. She remembered, as though it was only yesterday, when her desperate father had divided the room in two, for the benefit of squabbling siblings. She smiled . . . despite the pain. He hadn't changed a thing since she and Tess had abandoned the room, Tess to marriage, she to whatever, wherever, caught her fancy. The smile withered like the homecoming corsage on the bulletin board.

Her father. He was dead.

Because sadness once more threatened her, because there was the promise of aspirin downstairs, Mariah pulled Tess's brush through her hair and hastened from the room. Before she did, however, she snatched the wide-lensed sunglasses from her purse and, in defiance of the taunting sun, shoved them on.

She found Eden exactly where she'd expected to.

"You know," Mariah said, "I always try to picture you somewhere other than the kitchen, but I never can."

At the unexpected sound, Eden whirled toward the doorway. An apron skirted her waist, while suds bubbled on her hands. Unadulterated joy jumped into eyes as wide as Mariah's, but eyes a far darker shade of green.

Wordlessly, Mariah stepped forward and, suds be damned, the sisters embraced.

"I was worried about you," Eden said at last, swiping back sudden tears.

Beneath the sunglasses, Mariah's eyes were misty, though when she spoke her voice gave nothing away. "You're a compulsive worrier, sis. Don't you know nothing's gonna happen to me?" Mariah wondered whether if she said it often enough, even she might grow to believe it.

"That's what Jo says, that you're happenproof," Eden said, plunging her hands once more into the sink.

"Well, for once, listen to her. Where is our little zealot this morning? Out saving whales or collecting contributions for farm aid?"

"I left her asleep, and her new cause is vegetarianism."

"Down with meat, long live the lentil," Mariah exclaimed.

"For shame," Eden chastised, though with a hint of a grin. "Your sister's serious about bettering the world."

"I know," Mariah answered, her sudden earnestness noticeable, contrasted as it was against Eden's lighter mood. "And the world needs all the Jos it can get. They're a counterbalance to the Mariahs."

Mariah had long accepted the fact that, of all her sisters, she and Jo were most often at odds. Both seemed to thrive on, to enjoy, needling the other: Mariah because of Jo's causes, Jo because of what she considered Mariah's irresponsibility. Despite it all, Mariah respected her sister... greatly. She even longed to have some of her older sister's commitment. Perhaps to anything. Yet there was some unresolved something below the surface of their relationship, some barb, which often emotionally pricked each to the quick. Both women recognized the thorn, but fought against confronting it.

"Where's Tess?" Mariah asked before Eden could comment on her atypically heavy mood.

"Out walking."

"What's the status of her divorce?"

"Pending."

"What's the status of Tess?"

Eden wiped her hands and shrugged. "Who knows? You know how she keeps everything to herself." She checked the teakettle which sat atop a blazing burner.

"Yeah. Is that water for tea?" Mariah asked, sitting down at the round oak table that she could remember sitting down at a hundred times before. Often with the hope that her father would notice her. Really notice her.

"Yes. What would you like for breakfast?"

"Just an ice pack and two aspirins. Not necessarily in that order."

"Feel that bad, huh?"

"Is the Sistine Chapel in Italy?"

"Actually, you couldn't prove by me where it is."

"It's in Italy...and I feel that b— Oh, Eden!" she wailed at the teakettle's sudden whistle. Grabbing her head, she held it against the blaring pulsations, wracking flesh and nerve endings. Her oh, so touchy nerve endings.

At the same instant, Tess, dressed in a sweat suit, came through the back door. The frosty morn had reddened her nose and had caused her olive-skinned cheeks to glow like shined apples. Her coffee-brown hair, however, had escaped the wind's wrath with the help of a turquoise knit cap. As she entered the house, she pulled the cap from her head. Her hair bounded free.

"Well, well," Tess said, looking over at Mariah's prostrate figure, "I see we're collecting the wages of sin."

Mariah glanced up. Tess had always been an enigma to her. While intrinsically sensitive to people, she always tended to keep them at arm's length ... just the way she tended to keep all of life at arm's length. That Tess and their father had shared something special had long been accepted as fact. Mariah, more than a little covetous of their bond, had always thought it was because the two of them could sit for hours, saying nothing, doing nothing, both just sightlessly staring into their private worlds.

From her fifth birthday onward, Mariah had been acutely aware of loving Tess. It had been on that long-looked-forward-to day that her father, in what was to become an habitual pattern, had made a cursory appearance at her birthday party, then disappeared to his room to drink himself into a stupor. Heartbroken, Mariah had slipped off to her own room. Tess had followed. Both still in party hats, both faces still smudged with chocolate ice cream, Tess had eased beside her on the bed and had slipped her small hand into her sister's. There, they had sat in silence, a sound far too mature for their youthful years.

"*We're* not collecting the wages of anything. *I'm* paying for last night. And you don't have to look so darned pleased that I am."

"How else am I supposed to look? You kept me awake all night long tossing and turning. By the way, I assumed I wasn't to wake you for an early-morning walk."

Mariah groaned at the prospect. "Don't even say it."

Tess took the chair across from Mariah—it was the seating arrangement the years had programmed—and reached for her hand. A silent tightening of their fingers said more than a thousand words ever could have.

Minutes later, Eden set a steaming cup of coffee before Tess and an equally steaming cup of tea before Mariah. The latter was followed by an ice pack and two aspirins. Mariah downed the tablets with a murmured "Thanks." She also promised God that if He'd just stop the jack-hammer chipping away at the concrete of her mind, she wouldn't drink again. Ever. With one hand she brought the coolness to her forehead, with the other the cup of tea to her lips. The warm taste of spiced apple melted across her tongue. Warm. Warm like the morning sun. Warm like a kiss.

"Who's Ford—"

"What is this?" a voice suddenly erupted from the doorway.

Mariah grimaced as the throbbing pulsations once more crawled over her. She glanced up. Jo, carrying Mariah's fur coat, looked like a fire-breathing dragon who'd just cornered its victim. Mariah, on the other hand, with the ice pack held to her temple, with wide, dark sunshades shielding her eyes, looked as if she'd already been vanquished by powers greater than any fire-breathing dragon.

"Good to see you, too, Jo," Mariah said.

Instantly aware of the jagged edges of her opening remarks, Jo mellowed. "How do you feel?"

"Ghastly."

"Good."

"Your compassion is duly noted."

"What in the world were you thinking of, getting drunk? You never drink—"

"Obviously I do."

"And where in heck were you yesterday?"

"Purgatory. It also goes by the name of the Atlanta airport."

"I don't believe it. I just don't believe it. And then you drag in drunk, and looking like a member of a motorcycle gang."

"Leather's in."

"Leather's—"

"Look, Jo-Jo, spare me the lecture. At least until I'm conscious. We wouldn't want to waste your sage words."

"What is this?" Jo repeated, undauntedly returning the conversation to the coat, which she shook at Mariah. It looked like a big brown bear flexing after a season of hibernation.

Mariah groaned at her sister's tenacity. Dragging the glasses down the bridge of her nose, she considered. She tried to focus her bloodshot eyes. "I'd say offhand it was a coat. What would you say?"

"I'd say it was a *fur* coat."

It took Mariah a moment to get the point. "Ahh, I see, your latest cause is saving those adorable synthetic creatures."

"It's a fake?"

"Could I afford the real?"

At the realization that she'd been mistaken, Jo backtracked with a grand, "Well, I'm glad to see that something I've said has rubbed off on you."

Tess and Eden fought smiles. Even Mariah spared a twitch.

"How about some coffee?" Eden asked.

Jo accepted.

After a breakfast which Eden insisted on preparing, but which Mariah ate only scattered bites of, and Jo denounced because of the killer bacon, the women remained at the table, lingering over additional cups of coffee and tea.

"I'm, uh . . . I'm sorry about yesterday. About missing the funeral," Mariah said at last. What she was saying was the truth . . . as far as it went. She *was* sorry she hadn't shown up for the funeral; she just wasn't certain she hadn't orchestrated the outcome.

"We held the service up for an hour and a half," Eden said, though there was no censure in the statement.

"I'm sorry," Mariah repeated.

"It was a simple, graveside service," Tess said. "I think Daddy would have liked it."

"The heart attack was quick, huh?" Mariah asked, though she'd already been told it was. She didn't know why she was asking again, except that maybe if it hadn't been quick, maybe if he'd had time, he would have sent a message to his youngest daughter, saying he really had loved her all along.

"The doctor said he probably never knew what hit him," Jo said. "I guess that's the way to do it, huh?"

"Yeah," Tess mumbled.

"That's the way to do it," Eden said, fresh tears in her eyes.

Mariah said nothing.

The silence grew, swelling until the slightest sound ricocheted like bouncing bullets—Eden's sniff, Tess's sigh, the creaking of Jo's chair, the clinking of the ice cubes in Mariah's ice pack. Into this stillness rose a warmth, the thick, heated emotions of family, with each member reaching out to the other as, in turn, she was reached out to. For that moment nothing mattered but the Calloway clan. Tess reached out and took both Eden's and Mariah's hand, while Eden slipped her free hand into Jo's. Jo eased her hand into Mariah's.

"I'm glad you're home, Riah," Jo said.

"I'm glad to be home," Mariah returned and surprised herself by meaning it.

"Why don't you stay awhile?" Eden asked later in the day, after a lunch of grilled cheese sandwiches, after the airline had delivered Mariah's luggage, after the two sisters had been left alone in the house. At what she was certain was going to be a negative reply, she hastened to say, "It's been forever since you were here. And you never stay for more than ten minutes at a time. If you want work, you could go down to the mill. We need a part-time receptionist badly. We can't keep receptionists anymore. We've been through three in five months. I've been trying to answer the phone, but I've been busy going over the books and talking with the foreman—"

"I thought you were keeping kids."

"I had to put it on a back burner for now. I've got to make sure the mill goes on. Daddy took care of all the books. As soon as I can find a bookkeeper and as soon as I satisfy myself that the foreman can handle everything else, I'll go back to baby-sitting."

For as long as anyone could remember, Eden Calloway had baby-sat. The consensus was that she'd rocked more babies than ten mothers and diapered many of the bottoms residing in Calloway Corners.

Suddenly, Eden smiled. Sheepishly. "I guess the truth is I want you to stay because I don't want to be alone in the house, with Dad gone. Jo's going back to Baton Rouge and Tess to Dallas and... I guess I just don't want to be alone."

It was a sentiment Mariah could understand. Increasingly, the world was growing larger, she smaller... and alone.

"Please say you'll at least think about it," Eden said.

"I'll think about it," Mariah said, surprising herself for the second time that day.

"Good." Eden pushed back her chair and started to gather up the dishes. Mariah, whose head had gone from a throb to an ache, rounded up the glasses and bunched them on the cabinet. "Oh, by the way," Eden said, "the preacher's coming to supper."

On this Mariah didn't have to think. She groaned. The last thing she needed was an evening with a dull, boring, fire-and-brimstone preacher.

CHICKEN, COATED IN a delectable crunchy crust, potatoes whipped mountain high and oozing gravy, and peas swimming in butter—all stared back virtually untouched from Mariah's plate. And for a good reason. The phenomenon keeping words from coming up was equally keeping food from going down. The phenomenon had a name. It was called shock. And it had started the instant the preacher had stepped into the house.

The preacher.

Ford Dunning.

Ford D-u-n-n-i-n-g.

Everyone had seemed surprised at her surprise. Everyone, that is, except Ford Dunning, who had just grinned. Or, more to the point, he had worked hard not to grin, thereby calling far more attention to his restraint.

Well, how in the name of everything righteous, Mariah mused, smashing the pile of potatoes, as if it was single-handedly to blame for the deception, was she to know the man who'd driven her home was the family minister? He didn't look like any minister she'd ever seen. Hair as sinfully dark as rich chocolate did not look ministerial. Broad shoulders and lean hips—didn't he own anything but thigh-tight jeans?—did not look ministerial. Neither did liquor-colored eyes that somehow managed to make a woman dizzy-drunk if she stared too long at them.

"Mariah?"

Distantly, she heard someone calling her name. That someone was Eden, who was holding the platter of chicken. Mariah blinked, only then aware that she'd been looking into whiskey-shaded eyes...and that whiskey-shaded eyes had been looking into hers, the way they'd been at unexpected times throughout the evening. Their owner was once more trying not to grin.

"No. No, thank you," Mariah said, looking away and refusing a second helping of what she had yet to eat the first of.

"You're not eating," Eden chastised.

"Yes, I am," Mariah lied, taking a bite of the potatoes. They felt fluffy. And warm. Warm like a kiss?

Yes, warm like a kiss.

Mariah frowned. Was the kiss the basis of the discomfort she'd felt ever since the door had opened and Ford Dunning had walked, in soft brushed jeans, back into her life? Ordinarily, she would have found the discovery that he was a minister amusing—laughably amusing, even a real hoot—but, instead, it had gotten buried beneath an avalanche of emotions. Warm, kissy emotions? Yes, warm, kissy emotions. Feelings dealing not only with seduction, but with something far more powerful. Namely, need. Her need. And that she was uncomfortable admitting, let alone confronting, because it was easier, safer, to need nothing and no one.

Not a mother.

Not a father.

No one.

Yet, she had a vague, troubling remembrance of needing this man last night in order to fill some empty, scary void within her. The death void.

"Are you still counseling vets at the VA?" Tess asked. Because her husband, her soon-to-be ex-husband was a psychologist, Ford and Tess invariably got around to the subject of psychology.

"Yeah," Ford said, his eyes subtly shifting from Mariah to her sister. "Two nights a week. I'm also volunteering an afternoon a week over at the Family Services Center, mostly seeing troubled kids."

"Still teach at LSU-S?" Jo asked.

"Only one course this semester, but I'm teaching over at Haughton High, too."

"Good grief!" Eden proclaimed. "What do you do from midnight to dawn?"

Rescue damsels in distress, Mariah thought, her eyes again seeking Ford's. Why did he keep looking at her? Why did she keep looking at him?

"That's when I write my Sunday sermon," he said evenly, as if he'd been totally unmoved by Mariah's green eyes. "I promise you my sermons put me to sleep before they do the congregation."

Everyone laughed. Except Mariah.

Eden pushed back her chair. "If everyone's finished, I'll get dessert—"

"I'll get it," Mariah insisted, shoving her chair away from the table and standing.

"That's all right—"

"You cooked the meal," Mariah said. "Believe me, my culinary skills include slicing apple pie and dipping ice cream."

"And mine certainly extend to pouring coffee," Ford said, rising.

Mariah's eyes flew upward from the dirty dishes she was stacking. "You don't have—"

"Nonsense, I need to work off that wonderful meal." Something in his eyes challenged Mariah to defy him. She didn't. Instead, she headed from the little-used dining room and for the often-used kitchen.

The smell of freshly brewed coffee danced on the kitchen air, along with the fragrance of spices and cooked apples. Mariah walked to the sink. Behind her, she heard the door once more swinging open. The heavy, certain footfalls of a man marched into the room…only moments before the crisp smell of an after-shave that overrode the aroma of coffee, apples and spices.

Mariah whirled, her hands planted firmly, defiantly, on her hips. "Why didn't you tell me?"

Ford's eyes roamed from the black, pencil-thin leather miniskirt, jutted to the side by one cocky hip, up to the black and white tweed sweater riding low onto the hipline. A wide black belt cinched the waist, while long black stockings sheathed her legs. Black heels, so high they made Ford's head spin at the thought of balancing on then cupped her feet. The only breach in the black and white severity was gold jewelry, more than a gauche gypsy would have worn, a handful of red silk flowers strategically dotted throughout her wildly tumbled silver hair and a splash of fire-engine red at her lips. Lips Ford hadn't been able to get out of his mind. All night long. Even though he'd told himself that his reaction to them, his masculine reaction, had been nothing more than nature had intended.

"You didn't ask," he said with a maddening calmness.

"That's a crock!" she snapped, green lightning sparking in her stormy eyes. "You told me you were a psychologist."

"I believe I mentioned 'among other things.'"

"Well, you conveniently failed to mention what other things."

"That's because you got sick, then passed out."

Mariah muttered something that sounded like a sheepish "Oh."

Another few seconds of eye-to-eye contact passed before Ford, making himself more than at home, started hunting through the cabinets for cups. He began pouring the coffee. Mariah was left no choice but to slice the pie and top each wedge with vanilla ice cream. They worked in a deafening silence, Mariah taking out her frustration by hacking at the pie.

Abruptly she stopped, shoved back a strand of hair from her eyes and said, "Look, last night's a little fuzzy."

"I'll bet."

She glared.

"Sorry. I couldn't resist." The light in his amber eyes said he was enjoying this.

"Did I or did I not tell you you were sexy?"

Ford's lips shifted into a grin. "You did."

"Did I undress before you?"

The grin widened. "Right down to the shocking red lace."

"Did I...kiss you?"

"Yep."

She swallowed. "And did you—"

"I did."

Throwing the dish towel down on the counter, Mariah cried, "Well, if that doesn't rip it! I thought you guys took vows or something."

"You mean as in chastity?"

"Yeah. As in."

"Some men of God do. I didn't."

She was fast moving from being frustrated to be flustered. Again, it had everything to do with the kiss...and the feeling that he'd somehow seen her emotionally naked. That she found...frightening. "Well, what kind of minister would kiss a woman back?"

Ford said nothing for so long she thought he wasn't going to answer. Finally, with his voice lowered to a provocative drawl, he said, "A single, male and very human minister."

They stared at each other, his gaze so hot, Mariah would have sworn the ice cream on the pie began to melt. To say nothing of what her insides began to do. She turned back to the cabinet, busying herself with pie already cut and ready to serve.

Unsettling seconds passed before he asked softly, "Are you upset that I, the man, or I, the minister, kissed you?"

"I'm not upset," she lied, fiddling with a scoop of ice cream threatening to tumble from the hot pie.

"It sounds like it to me."

"Look," she said, her eyes meeting his, "there's not much I wouldn't, or haven't, done, but seducing a minister is a little radical for even me."

Ford studied her, remembering her life-style and that people who lived as rootlessly as Mariah did were more often than not loners. Remembering, too, the force of the kiss. And what he thought was behind it.

"Maybe that's what's bothering you," he said, deciding to take an educated shot in the dark. "Maybe the kiss went beyond seduction."

The shot landed dead center of the bull's-eye, a fact Ford noted. "I don't know what you mean."

"I remember what it feels like to lose someone." Ford's voice was low, gravelly, haunted with the undeniable traces of emotion. So obvious was his pain that Mariah momentarily wondered whom he'd lost. Someone he'd obviously cared deeply about. This thought fled, however, in her need to protect herself.

"Look, Reverend or Doctor of whatever-the-hell-you-are," she said, her words clipped, her eyes flashing, "save your analysis for someone who wants it."

He threw up his hands, as if in defeat, as if clearly backing off. "Hey, I'm sorry. No more analyzing, no more sermonizing. Okay?" When she said nothing, he repeated, "Okay?" A sudden grin played around the corners of his mouth. "C'mon, give a guy a break. Are we okay here, or aren't we?"

She grinned because it was impossible not to reciprocate. "Okay. But no more—"

"No analyzing. I swear it. No sermonizing. I swear it."

"All right. And I swear I'm good for that IOU."

"I'm not worried. You're a woman of honor. You told me so yourself."

Mariah's grin widened, ushering in a glimmer of her usual self. "Numerous times, I'm certain."

He shrugged. "Who was counting?"

The room grew quiet, the seconds slow. Mariah and Ford stared, she into too-perceptive eyes, he into eyes not worth a darn at hiding feelings. Particularly lonely feelings.

"Friends?" he asked quietly, extending his hand. It was suddenly important to him that she answer affirmatively.

She hesitated, then eased her hand into his. "Friends," she whispered.

Warm.

Why did she always think of warmth with him?

And why did his eyes seem so capable of emotionally undressing her?

"Hey, do you two need any help?" someone called from the dining room.

As though shot, Mariah removed both her eyes and her hand from Ford. "Coming," she answered, once more addressing the issue of dessert.

The epitome of cool, Ford reached for the tray of coffee cups and started for the door. Abruptly he turned, his eyes assessing her. "Oh, by the way, friend, you've got a fantastic pair of legs."

As she watched his own long, lean and quite fantastic legs carry him from the room, Mariah was forced to draw two conclusions: one, even though sober, she thought him as sexy as she had when she'd been drunk. Maybe even more so. And two, for all of her mute protests to the contrary, he'd penetrated her inner sanctum. He'd seen a part of her that no one else ever had. She couldn't allow that invasion of her soul ever again. By this man, or any other.

CHAPTER FOUR

A GUITAR, A DRUM and a piano, played à la Jerry Lee Lewis, combined with the melodic voices of the choir to produce a rocking rendition of an old spiritual. Fingers snapped, toes tapped, while stained-glass windows, the pride of the small white frame church, rattled under the mighty noise made unto the Lord. Even Ford's toes, peeking from beneath a black robe, were tip-tip-tapping. Bible in hand, sitting on the dais to the right of the pulpit, a purple ribbonlike stole to symbolize repentance during Advent over his robe, he scanned the congregation. Not a bad turnout for the blustery winter morning, he thought, singling out individual members of the faithful. Blond-haired, blue-eyed Seth Taylor, who at the age of thirty-two didn't seem able to shake his bad-boy image, despite the fact he was now a respectable businessman, sat near the back. Beside him sprawled his thirteen-year-old son, Jason, who lived with his mother, visiting Seth only on holidays and for alternate weekends. Unless he was very much mistaken, there was trouble brewing with Jason, because he sensed in him some of his own teenage rebelliousness. Ford made a mental note to personally invite Jason to join some of the youth activities.

Ford's eyes shifted to the sixteen-year-old boy sitting in the very back row. A girl, pert, pretty and red-haired, sat in the seat next to him. Actually the two were draped as close as decency would allow. And therein lay this couple's problem. Jeff Simmons's and Megan Blake's hormones were working their way toward maturity. Ford sighed. It was his job to convince them that restraint was also part of a mature person's personality. If he wasn't able to, they'd certainly be sexually active soon...if they weren't already.

The Simmons family. It was a cornerstone of the church's foundation. David Simmons, a long-time deacon, had died within a week of Ford's assuming the pastorate. In many respects, Ford knew he had become a substitute father to Jeff, helping him to work through the anger and grief of his father's death. He and Jeff's mother, Laurel Simmons, were not that close, however. Clearly, his unorthodox, liberal views on religion and on life in general, confused her. Laurel Simmons was one of those people who not only liked to play by the rules, but also *needed* to play by them. More than once he'd wondered what she would say if she knew her elderly, widowed mother, Ruth Doege, was closely shacking up with J. C. Hardcastle, the church's septuagenarian treasurer. Knowing the two cared for each other, and knowing also that their getting married would work a financial hardship because of entailed property both owned and didn't want the legal hassle of trying to merge, Ford turned a blind eye. He wasn't presumptuous enough to say what God's reaction was, but he wouldn't have been greatly surprised to learn He, too, was looking somewhere else.

Ford's eyes meandered closer to the front, up one pew, down another. His surveillance ended on the third row. There, huddled in reverence—well, three of the four were huddled in reverence—sat the Calloway sisters, Eden, Tess, Jo and...Mariah. She had pulled her platinum-blond hair back in a sleek chignon, dramatically emphasizing her perfectly oval face, making her appear as stunningly attractive as a model. Like a pointing arrow, the severe hair-style also drew attention to the three earrings glittering in each ear. Equally glittering were the lights in her emerald eyes.

Even as he watched, Mariah, certain of his attention, discreetly—he would give her that—raised a hand to her chest and wiggled her index finger in a wave. She gave a pixilated smile designed for only one thing: to break Ford's pious appearance. It did as designed.

Ford's lips twitched, and he lowered his gaze back to his worn Bible. But not before he noted that Jo, aghast, poked Mariah in the ribs.

"What are you doing?" Jo whispered.

"Saying 'morning to the Reverend," Mariah whispered back. "What did it look like?"

Jo just groaned. Discreetly, of course.

Ford tried to concentrate on the dying notes of the hymn, but, instead, found thoughts of Mariah constant intruders. The uptight Mariah of the evening before had reverted back to her impish self. It was his professional guess that she was out to prove that the kiss had been a meaningless gesture. One merely of seduction. The truth was she would convince him long before she convinced herself. And there was no way, Jose, given the length of eternity, that she was going to convince him. He smiled to himself, thinking that this Sunday's sermon must have been truly inspired.

The music died; the choir reseated itself to the sounds of muted shuffling; Ford moved from the chair to the pulpit.

For a reason Mariah couldn't explain, she felt her heart jump into an accelerated beat.

"Let me begin by making two announcements that will do more to drive home the meaning of this special holiday season than any sermon I could give," Ford said, his demeanor so relaxed it was obvious he was comfortable with public speaking.

His voice, curiously soothing, washed over Mariah.

"Ruth Doege . . . where are you, Ruth?" The congregation turned around in their seats. Ruth Doege, sitting beside J. C. Hardcastle and wearing the woolen tam she wore all winter because she fervently believed it kept her from taking a head cold, blushed at all the attention. "Ruth tells me that the cushions for the pews are finished and will be in place by next Sunday. I know you join me in thanking all who volunteered money and talent for this project. Nowhere in the Bible does it say that man must worship God on hard benches."

Titters of laughter skipped through the sanctuary. Mariah smiled.

"Also, Laurel Simmons has learned that our choir robes are on the way."

This drew a round of applause, which Mariah joined in as if it were her heart's fondest desire that the choir of twelve be dressed in robes.

"Our thanks to the anonymous donor for his overwhelming generosity. Dan Morgan, however, tells me that he's uncertain he can sing in such finery."

Everyone laughed again, and all eyes swung choirward to the tall, lanky owner of the Morgan General Store. And then, as though a silent cue had been given, everyone settled in for the awaited sermon.

Ford gave everyone a moment before beginning with, "I want to talk to you this morning about the subject of fraud." His eyes shifted to the third row. "Or put another way, how we as Christians, how we as human beings, go about deceiving ourselves."

Mariah frowned. She wasn't certain, but he seemed to be looking directly at her.

Thirty minutes later, as one of the deacons led the congregation in the benediction, Ford unobtrusively made his way to the door. While the amens were still echoing, people, bundling up in coats and scarfs, began to file out. Ford greeted each one with a handshake.

"Good to see you, Seth. And who's this young man with you?" Ford asked, taking Jason's hand as if he were an adult. "How's it going?"

Jason shrugged and muttered, "All right."

"You any good at basketball?"

"I don't know," he answered, studying his feet in true adolescent fashion.

"I hear the church team's looking for someone." Before Jason could cop out by saying he was only in Haughton on a limited basis, before he could give a definite no, Ford added, "They only play on weekends, and the play isn't real structured. If you had to miss, it'd be okay. Why don't you think about it?"

Jason shrugged again, which might have meant anything, except Ford thought he saw a flash of interest deep in troubled eyes.

To Jeff and Megan, who looked as though they were trying to sneak off, undoubtedly to neck, Ford shouted, "Don't forget the pizza party tonight after church."

They shouted something back.

"Excellent sermon," said a male voice.

Ford glanced up. "Thank you, J.C."

"How 'bout you coming to dinner this week?"

Ford took in both the man and the woman with him. "Is Ruth cooking?"

"You betcha," the man said, beaming at the woman.

"I'll be there, then." The elderly couple moved on down the steps, followed by several more church members. Finally Laurel Simmons, wearing a frown that negated her pretty features, reached the pastor. "Morning, Laurel, how are you?"

"Deaf from that music."

Ford smiled indulgently. "Now, Laurel, we wanted to get it loud enough for God to hear."

"Well, he certainly d—" Her eyes had roved to the young woman exiting the church. The young woman with three earrings in each ear, which made a total of six, which were four more than Laurel considered any civilized person would wear.

Ford turned around. His eyes met Mariah's. A twinkle still glinted in hers. Ford idly noted that Laurel was moving on down the steps. Silently moving on. Which was one of the few times he'd ever seen the woman at a loss for words.

"Hi ya, Rev," Mariah drawled.

A smile sauntered into one corner of his mouth. "Well, hello, Miss Calloway."

As he had with everyone else, he took her hand. Though definitely not a petite woman, Mariah felt her hand disappear in his. The way she had the evening before. She also felt that same warm gentle strength. Ford felt warmth, as well, a delicious warmth that singlehandedly combated the cold of the winter day. At the same time, both realized they had gone from a handshake to simply holding hands. Again, it was what had happened the evening before. Both pulled their hands away. Mariah rammed hers into the pocket of the fur coat.

"Eden, Tess, Jo," Ford said, taking each of their hands in turn. "Good to see you in church." He made this last comment at large, but his attention had returned to Mariah.

She grinned. "Don't get the wrong idea, Rev. These three hogtied me and made me come. I just hope God wasn't too shocked. I'd hate to be responsible for giving Him a coronary."

"If you hadn't already," Jo muttered, "it isn't likely you did this morning."

Ford's almost-but-not-quite grin was back. It was still devastating. "I imagine God's pretty shockproof."

"And how about you, Rev?" Mariah asked, aware that she was playing the flirting little games she always played with men.

Jo groaned, Eden blushed, while Tess just shook her head.

Ford laughed, visions of red lace tripping through his mind. "Let's just put it this way. I haven't had a coronary yet."

Because others were impatiently waiting to greet the minister, the Calloway sisters had to move on. Ford admonished Tess and Jo, both of whom were returning that afternoon to their respective homes, to drive carefully. He told Eden he'd see her later.

"And what about you, Mariah? You staying for a while?"

"I'm trying to talk her into it," Eden interjected.

Mariah shrugged. "I don't know. Depends on how the wind's blowing."

Minutes later, as the four women climbed into Jo's car, Jo said, "I vote we eat dinner out."

"But I've already cooked a roast," Eden protested.

"Save it," Tess said, adding, "I vote to eat out, too."

"Mariah?" Jo asked. "Hey, Mariah?"

"Hmm?" she asked, drawing her eyes away from one last look at the minister and easing into the back seat.

"How do you vote?"

"On what? Say, why don't we eat out?"

Jo groaned.

"Well, hey, it was just an idea," Mariah answered. "You don't have to get bent all out of shape."

As the car drove off, Ford watched. A brisk wind tumbled across the field adjacent to the church, whirled up the sanctuary steps and whipped the robe about his legs. The wind was cold; the wind was strong. He wondered if it would be the wind that would once more blow Mariah Calloway away from Calloway Corners.

"YOU REALLY SHOULD, you know?"

Mariah tossed out the comment that evening as she and Eden, now alone in the house with only their sisters' promises to return for Christmas to keep them company, sat curled on the sofa eating roast beef sandwiches from paper plates.

Eden frowned. "Do what?"

"Go to Italy. See the Sistine Chapel."

That Mariah was picking up a conversation begun two days before didn't seem in the least unusual to Eden. It had happened too many times over the years.

"I've never been out of Louisiana."

"All the more reason to go to Italy. Ah, Eden, there's a whole world out there."

"What's it like?" Eden asked, her face suddenly flushed with an enthusiasm usually reserved for the very young. For a moment, the features she deemed plain were transformed into a rare beauty. "The world. Not the Sistine Chapel."

Mariah giggled. "Big. And exciting." *And lonely.*

The thought came from nowhere, just as thoughts of pizza had punctuated the evening. She had heard Ford holler to two kids that there would be a pizza party after church that night. She could see all the gooey spread of cheese, hear all the laughter, feel all the camaraderie. Ford would be good with children. Wonder why he wasn't married with a household of kids to call his own? As always, the subject of kids, principally the subject of childbirth, left her uncomfortable. Childbirth was too easy a way to die . . . and left too much guilt behind.

"What?" Mariah realized she'd missed a whole segment of what Eden was saying.

"Is there anyplace you haven't been?"

Mariah considered the question. She'd been from the hot, arid plains of Africa to the lush, tropical forests of South America. She'd been from mountain to valley, from stream and fiord to the dust winds of the Middle East. She'd even once traipsed over the frozen earth of the Yukon on the last leg of the Iditarod Trail. Was there any place she hadn't been? Suddenly, the lyrics of a song came to her. Something about a woman who'd traveled everywhere, even to paradise, but she'd never been to herself. Like the woman in the song, Mariah thought, *I've never been to me*. Why? Maybe because there was too much guilt and fear residing there.

Eden smiled, clearly in envy. "If you have to think that hard, there isn't anyplace."

"What was she like?"

Though used to Mariah's abrupt turns in conversation, Eden, nonetheless, jolted from this jarring question. "Who?"

"Mamma." Mariah didn't analyze how the topic had come to her. Her mother had always seemed a natural segue from guilt and fear.

"She was..." Eden, who'd been eight at the time of their mother's death, thought a moment, trying to settle on just the right word. "She was soft. Everything about her was soft. Her hair, her eyes, her voice, her touch." Eden smiled. "And she felt so soft when you snuggled up against her."

Mariah smiled, as if she, too, was remembering soft.

"And she always smelled so good—somewhere between spice and perfume. And she baked great sugar cookies. And loved the wisteria on the arbor. That's why Daddy insisted on a cemetery lot large enough for a wisteria bush."

In the wake of such poignant memories, their smiles faded.

"He was never the same, was he?" Mariah asked quietly.

"No," Eden answered with a bittersweet smile. "When you love that hard and lose the one you love, you're never the same again."

Nor can you ever love what killed your beloved, Mariah thought, her taste for the sandwich suddenly gone. She lay the plate on the coffee table, slid her feet into worn Mickey Mouse slippers that looked ridiculous on a woman her age, and moved to stare out the living room window. The night was black, and she could feel its coldness trying to force entry through every crack and crevice.

Just the way her father's emotional neglect had forced entry through every crack and crevice of her heart. Strangely, though, she didn't hate him. Quite to the contrary, she loved him. Thoughts of Ben Calloway gave way to thoughts of Ford Dunning. Again, Mariah didn't search for the reason why. It just suddenly seemed important that it had been Ford Dunning who'd buried her father. Ford Dunning, whom she intuitively knew had capable hands.

Strong and gentle hands. Hands that felt warm and strong and gentle against her own.

"I've decided to stay for a while," she announced before she changed her mind.

For a moment Eden said nothing, then asked, "Are you serious?"

Mariah turned away from the window. She smiled. "I think so."

Tears filled Eden's eyes.

"I'll need a job, though."

"You can work at the mill. Oh, Mariah, I don't believe it. I really didn't think you would. I mean, I've asked you a thousand times before. Why? Why now?"

Why?

Mariah didn't honestly know. Maybe she was staying because, for the first time in her life, she had a crawl-back-in-the-womb feeling, a feeling that she'd traveled the world, even to paradise, and that maybe it was now time she booked passage to herself. Or maybe it was that another birthday was creeping up, bringing with it the old fear of dying young. Then again, maybe she was staying because of strong and gentle hands. Or maybe her reason for staying was as simple, as practical, as the answer she finally gave.

"I owe a man an IOU."

MILES AWAY, in a small, cramped but cozy trailer, a pair of strong, capable hands reached for a stomach tablet. Ford wondered if he was getting an ulcer. Heaven only knew he had a right to one. The only word to describe him was *intense*. Funny thing about the word *intense*, though. Sooner or later, the *in* part of it went sailing out the window and all you were left with was *tense*. He could never remember it being any other way; he could just remember its getting worse. Typically the son of a minister, a PK, or preacher's kid, was rebellious, a hell-raiser. He'd been no exception. He'd seen the inside of more principals' offices than many teachers and had run more punitive laps than the schools' track stars. Following high school, he'd enlisted in the army, against his father's wishes, which, of course, only made doing so more appealing. Right out of training, he'd been sent to Vietnam. It was there his life had changed—twice.

He could still remember the smell of being "in country!" The stench of open sewers, the black mud teeming with garbage and refuse. And he could still remember the total culture shock he'd felt. He'd realized within days what a sheltered life he'd lived. The witnessing of such wholesale death and destruction exposed his stupid juvenile pranks for what they were: stupid juvenile pranks. It did one other thing, as well. It slapped his faith across the face, leaving him to conclude that there was no God, or that He was in control of nothing. The best he could say for God, if He even existed, was that He was having Himself quite a laugh at the joke called Vietnam. Feeling that his father's life had been naively spent, Ford had vacillated between being an atheist and being angry with God. The feeling, so empty it made him hurt physically, had lasted nearly six months. Until...

Ford plopped two tablets into a glass of water, letting the fizzing sound chase away memories that to this day, almost twenty years later, were painful. As always, though, the memories, like gray clouds on a rainy day, insisted on hovering. Glass in hand, Ford padded his stockinged feet back into the trailer's living room, which was done in shades of brown and terra cotta in a style called masculinely cluttered. Unerringly, as he knew they would, his footsteps carried him to the picture nestled in the book cabinet. He stared at the enlargement of a photo ironically taken only minutes before his life forever changed.

The photo was of two men and a woman in a Saigon bar. One of the men was Ford himself, the other another American soldier. Both sported crew cuts, Army-green fatigues and silly grins. The woman was Vietnamese, dark-haired, dark-eyed, beautiful. Ford had his arm around her waist. She was staring up at him ... adoringly.

Mei-Lee.

The name still teased and taunted, the way shattered dreams always do. Unconsciously, Ford's free hand went to his shoulder, where he traced the scar that lay beneath the wrinkled shirt hanging out of his jeans. There was no way, though, he could rub the hurt in his heart. He downed the contents of the glass, hoping that they, at least, would ease the dull ache in his stomach.

Ford had walked away from the incident in the bar a changed man. He grinned wryly. Actually he'd been carried away on a stretcher. He had witnessed a perfect, unselfish act of love that had spoken volumes to his angry, atheistic heart. If there was a God, He was that feeling of unselfish love—and surely only God could create something that perfect.

He had returned home with a goal: to get a degree in psychology, a subject that had long fascinated him. He'd rushed through to a master's degree in an unprecedented four years, then on to a doctorate, and had joined the staff of the Veterans Administration Hospital in Shreveport, where he'd worked with troubled Vietnam vets. Somewhere along the way—he could never remember making a conscious choice in this direction—Ford had started working with drug addicts, prostitutes, gays, any and everyone who needed help. More and more, again with no real conscious design, he turned these troubled people on to his simple faith, which had little doctrine beyond "God Is Love." At some point, he'd found himself taking Bible courses for his own enjoyment. Two years ago, his dad, still a practicing minister, had asked him to fill in temporarily as pastor for a friend who, because of ill health, had had to give up a small, nondenominational church in Haughton.

Ford smiled. He could still remember his astonishment and his reply of, "You've got to be kidding. I'm not a preacher."

He could equally remember his father's answer. "Are you sure about that, son?"

Utilizing his father's advice of "Simply speak from the heart," he'd mounted the pulpit that first time, and he'd returned again and again because he slowly began to feel a calling that scared him as much as it delightfully challenged him. Except for a few Laurel Simmonses, who thought him too liberal and his methods too unorthodox, the church had accepted him. Amidst his growing pastoral commitment, Ford never once, however, slacked up on his counseling career. In fact, it continued to grow. Increasingly he was growing to wish there were more than twenty-four hours in a day. He knew he worked too hard, stretched himself too thin, drove himself to the very brink of collapse. He was also smart enough to analyze why. He was trying to justify surviving when two other people had died. He was trying to justify having someone sacrifice his life for his.

Ford gave a weary sigh and stepped back to the desk piled high with papers. He eased into the chair, set down the glass and checked the clock. It was ten-fifteen, and he still had a million things to do before he could call it a night. Raking his hand through his hair, he closed his eyes and forced his mind to relax, to let go of the past, to let go

of responsibilities and obligations, to just let go. He beckoned forward the image of anything pleasant.

Without hesitation, the image of Mariah Calloway appeared. Mariah Calloway who had hair the color of
moonbeams on snowbanks. Mariah Calloway who had a
voice like the wind. Mariah Calloway who, unless he was
mistaken, was a fourteen-karat-gold fraud.

CHAPTER FIVE

"CALLOWAY MILL. While you slumber, we'll cut your lumber."

"Mariah?" the caller asked tentatively. On the one hand, the throaty, near laryngitic voice was unfamiliar, while on the other, who else but Mariah would have answered a business phone with such a greeting?

A week had passed, during which Mariah and Ford had had no contact. She had worked Monday through Friday at the mill, from eight o'clock in the morning—"You've got to be kidding! You want me to start work at eight o'clock!"—to three in the afternoon. She had begged out of church that Sunday because of a cold that had left her sounding like Lauren Bacall and feeling like Lauren Bacall after a steamroller had had its flat way with her. It was now Monday morning, at ten minutes after the godawful hour of eight.

Mariah grinned, sniffing into a Kleenex. "Trying to herd up your lost sheep, Rev?"

Ford chuckled. "While your absence was conspicuous yesterday—no one waved from the congregation—that isn't the purpose of my call. By the way, you sound like you have a cold." She also sounded as sexy as all get-out, but he refrained from saying so.

Mariah gave a sudden sneeze, then a nasal, "Yeah? How can you tell?"

She could imagine his grin.

"Just a lucky guess."

She could also detect what she thought was the changing of the phone from one ear to the next. She wondered where he was. At church? At home? And what did his home look like?

"I hear you're staying in town awhile," he commented, not mentioning how much the news had pleased him. Principally because he wasn't certain why the news should have pleased him so.

"Looks that way. I had an IOU to pay off. I'm a woman of—"

"Honor."

She grinned. "Right."

"Well, that's what I'm calling about."

"My honor?"

His grin grew wider, though Mariah couldn't have said just how she knew so. Nor could she have explained why she, her nose drippy, her throat scratchy, her eyes runny, suddenly felt better.

"My money."

"You're sending Louie after me, eh? What's it gonna be? Break a finger, rip my nose off my face, tear my—"

"Actually, I was hoping to avoid anything that violent. At least for now. Instead, I have a proposition."

"Why, Rev, you sly devil," Mariah purred.

At this Ford laughed outright. "Nothing of a compromising nature, Miss Calloway."

"Oh, darn. Well, let's hear it, anyway."

"Look, I'm in a bind." His tone had gone from teasing to sincere, a fact Mariah noted. "I need someone to type up a test for the high school course I'm teaching."

Mariah burst into cold-clogged laughter. "You want *me* to type? The man who taught the course I took retired right afterward, and rumor had it that even after therapy he wouldn't go near anything that had keys on it. Not even Florida.''

''You can't be as bad as I am.''

''Believe it.''

''I buy correction fluid in the largest size.''

''I'll need a bucket of it.''

''I'll buy a bucket,'' he said seriously, thinking of how one mountain of work only gave rise to another. ''Look, I'm desperate. I'm so far behind I can't wag my tail fast enough to catch up.''

A provocatively interesting image jumped to Mariah's mind. She ignored it, however, for the gravity in his voice. ''When do you need it?''

''Tomorrow. So I can run it off and give it out Wednesday. And I just don't have time to type it tonight. I'm supposed to be in three places as it is. Oh, and by the way,'' he added, ''I'll need you to help me grade the papers Friday night.''

''Now, let me get this straight, Rev,'' Mariah said, still stalling, though she'd already decided on her answer. What kind of choice did she have when he was practically begging for her help? Moreover, what kind of choice did she have when she suddenly realized it had seemed forever since she'd seen him? Although why that should matter didn't seem quite clear. ''For an error-riddled typing of one test and the subsequent scoring thereof, I can nullify my IOU for $38.82?''

''Ninety-two. You owe me $38.92. And yes, that's exactly right. I'll lock Louie back up.''

Mariah sighed heavily. ''Then, I guess I have no choice, do I? But,'' she hastened to lie, ''I'm only agreeing to this because I'm in debt and comatose at this hour. And sick, to boot.''

"Great! Not about your being comatose and sick, but about your agreeing. Listen, do I need to pick you up?"

"No, I think I can get Eden's car."

"That's even better than great. Here's how you get to my place..."

THE TRAILER, small and definitely not new, sat amidst a copse of pine trees that stood tall and proud against the cold fire of wintertime. A carpet of pine needles, falling one by reluctant one until the ground lay covered like brown snow, smothered the sound of the station wagon coming to a stop beside the sleek, white sports car.

Mariah cut the engine and would have checked her watch, had she worn one. Which she didn't. In fact, she didn't even own one. Every time she bought one, she lost it, leaving her to have to function with no watch again, which she always managed to do. The pattern only proved her point about watches and time: watches were invented to make money for watchmakers, and the only real time that mattered was the last second dividing life from death.

Reaching for her purse—now, where was it? Ah, the back seat. Why was it in the back seat?—she opened the car door and slung her legs, encased in jeans, toward the ground. Red shoes, high and thin-heeled, found their footing amid the strawlike pine needles. She had to be on time, which was to say, it had to be near six, because Ford's instructions had been simplicity at its best. She'd gone to the church, then two miles past it to the first dirt road on the right. Another quarter mile and voilà: the trailer!

As she approached the steps, she noted the sunset spilling across the sky in colors an artist would kill for—purple, peach and not just pink but a melon color so ripe, she could taste its juicy sweetness. She'd seen sunsets all over the world, but couldn't honestly remember one more spectacular. Mariah didn't dwell on the philosophical implications of what one could find in one's own backyard. Instead, she concentrated on the light that burned within the trailer.

She knocked, which rattled the screen door back and forth. There was no answer. She tried again. Still there was no answer. She wedged open the screen door, turned the handle of the door beyond and hollered, "Hey, it's me!"

"Come on in! I'm dressing!" called out a voice, a deep, masculine voice, from what Mariah assumed was a bedroom.

She stepped inside and closed the door behind her. A cozy warmth, primarily issuing from a replica of an old-time, wood-burning Franklin stove, embraced her. Shedding the fur coat, she tossed it on a cream-and-rust-plaid sofa, crossed to the stove to warm her hands and looked around. To the left was a minuscule kitchen, sporting only a small stove, small refrigerator and smaller-yet sink. The dining room table was designed to accommodate four, provided each person was pencil thin. To the right, however, lay a more spacious area—the living room, most of which had been sacrificed to an enormous desk. The desk was piled outrageously high with papers, books, journals, magazines and a hundred other things, including a Bible, a typewriter, a calendar and a clock. Shelves, gorged with books and a smattering of odds and ends, filled the wall behind it.

"I'll be there in a minute," Ford called. "I got a late start. As usual."

"No problem," Mariah said, thinking it best not to dwell on the fact he was dressing only walls away. Somehow the realization was . . . unsettling.

"The test is on the typewriter. Best of luck reading my writing."

She laughed, moving to the desk and picking up the sheaves of ordinary notebook paper.

"I'll manage," she said as she began to read. She suddenly frowned as the questions jumped out at her.

1. Can a woman get pregnant if she doesn't have an orgasm?
2. Can a woman get pregnant by having her breasts touched?
3. Can a woman get pregnant from tongue kissing?
4. Can you get AIDS from kissing?

"What do you teach, anyway?" she asked, quickly scanning the following four pages. All the questions followed suit, ranging from yes/no questions to multiple choice to essay. All the questions dealt with sexuality and reproduction. Explicitly so.

"Sex ed," he said as he walked into the room.

Mariah glanced up. "Sex educa...tion?" The word cleaved into halves as he came into view. He was dressed totally in black, except for a champagne-colored tie that precisely matched his eyes. He was fiddling with the tie with both hands, as though unaccustomed, even uncomfortable, with this aspect of the male dress ritual. At the sight of her, both hands stilled.

As her eyes roamed the breadth of his ebony-clad shoulders and the length of his ebony-sheathed legs, two thoughts raced through her mind. One, the devil must have wept real tears when he lost this one and, two, every girl in his sex ed course no doubt had the most delicious fantasies.

Delicious fantasies. They were something she could manage one or two of herself—one or two dozen.

On the other hand, Ford was not altogether a stranger to fantasies. They were what flashed into one's mind at the sight of tight jeans, earrings in triplicate, and a red, clingy sweater, this latter which he knew intimately—as in, had once had it draped over his head. The fantasy really went wild as he wondered if the same bits of red lace, ludicrously called underwear, lay beneath the clothes. He thought it best to call a halt to the fantasy here and now, while he still had some presence of mind.

"Hi," he said, thinking it wasn't the cleverest thing a man had ever said to a woman.

"Hi," she returned, wondering if she couldn't have thought of something more original to answer. Then, again, it might have been a wondrously original response, considering her brain was filled with such lush, lustful images of jet black.

Both seemed to deplane their flight of fantasy about the same time.

"You, uh...you don't know anything about tying these damned things, do you?" Ford asked, once more giving his attention to the tie's crooked knot. All except for that portion of his attention which insisted on remaining back on red, glossy lips. Lips that had once—needfully—kissed his.

"As a matter of fact, I do," Mariah answered, stepping toward him and pushing his hands away. His big hands. His strong hands. Both of which she tried to ignore. "I didn't think you good guys could use that naughty word."

Ford had quite willingly allowed his hands to be pushed away by others promising more competence. "You mean the damn word?"

"Yeah," she said, concentrating on slipping fabric over fabric, rather than on the fresh smell of after-shave lotion or the smooth surface of a newly shaven jaw.

Ford grinned, magnetically drawing her eyes to his. "I've got an image to live up to. I'm God's bad boy."

Mariah grinned, too—and with a deliberate provocativeness that Ford immediately recognized. "How bad?" she asked, her head-cold-husky voice suddenly decibels lower.

He shrugged. "Depends on what member of the congregation you talk to. Some think it's an impishness I might outgrow. Others are praying for my soul even as I pray for theirs."

Both he and she were smiling widely now. His smile faded. "The truth is, I don't think God plays by all the rigid rules some think He does. I think He's bigger than petty rules. I think He's only interested in what's in our hearts."

"Fascinating religious concept," Mariah said "And just where does that place you, denominationally speaking?"

"I'm somewhere to the right of Hare Krishna and somewhere to left of fundamentalist Catholicism."

Mariah laughed. "A Zen-Baptist, maybe?"

Ford laughed, too. "Sounds as good as any label."

"And what if you're wrong about God not playing by rules?"

"Then I know I'm not wrong about His leniency. It's only us human beings who won't forgive each other. Or ourselves," he added softly, meaningfully.

This last comment zeroed its way into two guilty hearts. Mariah thought of her mother, Ford of a young man buried in Illinois and of a dark-haired, dark-eyed woman buried in Vietnam.

"There," she said patting the knot and stepping back, ignoring the guilt and the smell of after-shave, the latter which turned out to be far more potent than she ever could have imagined.

"Notice how I'm tactfully refraining from asking how you know so much about tying ties," Ford said. He, too, was pushing grim thoughts aside as his fingers appreciated the perfectly executed knot.

Mariah giggled, producing the sound of a soft spring breeze. "I used to wear one."

Ford's look said he was interested.

"When I worked as a croupier in Vegas. I wore black satin pants, a white blouse and a black tie." As she spoke, Mariah wandered toward the desk and propped a hip against the corner. It was the only space not covered with stacks of paper.

Ford grinned. "So that's how you travel the world. You're a croupier."

"Croupier. Bartender. Usually a croupier. Most people like living dangerously. Even if it's only by relying on the tumble of dice or the shuffle of cards." The gleam in her eyes, the careless toss of her white hair, said she was clearly one of those who liked—loved—walking the thin edge.

Ford noted the gleam. And the toss.

"Tell me something, Rev," she drawled, that gleam brightening, the toss growing more reckless until her hair was a thick mane of silver flowing down her back, "are you one of those who likes living dangerously?"

Provocative. Ford heard the word in her tone of voice, smelled it in the sultry fragrance of her perfume, saw it in the sensual pout of her lips. Everything about her was pointedly provocative. Studiously provocative. Purposefully provocative. Ford suspected she'd played the game so long, hidden herself so successfully behind it that she was no longer even aware of game playing. But buried somewhere was the woman who'd kissed him with a need so honest, so great, it had scared the living hell out of her.

Ford slid his lips into a grin no less suggestive than hers. The hand hiked at his hip held the same lazy provocativeness. "I don't know, Mariah Calloway. I guess I haven't given it much thought."

For the next few seconds that was primarily all either did—think about his sense of daring. It was a contemplation that might have gone on forever had not the phone at Mariah's elbow chosen that moment to ring. She jumped. Ford started. He then immediately assumed a serious demeanor. One that befit someone whose career always placed him on call.

"Hello?" he said, crossing the room and picking up the receiver as Mariah scooted out of the way. He held the cord up for her to pass under it. Her hair, a profusion of wildness once more held back by red lace, brushed the back of his hand. It felt as if a mild charge of electricity passed over him. "Yes, this is he. Yes, Mrs. Wilson?" The lines of his face tightened. "When? What kind of accident?"

At the word *accident*, Mariah paled, though she reached for the test and tried to read it.

"What do the doctors say? I see. Yes, of course, I can stop by. I can be there in about—" he checked the watch at his wrist. Mariah noted a crisp curling of dark hair, so brown it hinted at black, around the leather watch band. "In about an hour and a half. Maybe a little longer. What room is he in?" Ford stretched for a pen and pad, in the process causing splayed corduroy to do appealing things to one masculine anatomy, and jotted down a number. "No problem. I'll be there. And try not to worry, huh?"

"Is someone hurt?" Mariah asked as Ford hung up the phone.

"Mrs. Wilson's son—they belong to the church—was in a motorcycle accident." Ford folded the note and shoved it into the breast pocket of his shirt. Then he grabbed his black wool jacket and threw his arms into it.

"Badly?" Mariah asked, her throat tight. Accidents, blood, hospitals—they all elicited the same reaction.

"He'll live, but I don't think he'll be riding a motorcycle for a while. He shouldn't have been in the first place. Not without a helmet. It's too dangerous."

"Yeah, dangerous."

At the strangled word, Ford looked up. Mariah was as white as tissue paper. He swore softly. "I'm sorry," he said. "I didn't take this cold of yours seriously." He guessed he hadn't because he rarely took his own health seriously, especially colds. He just didn't have time for the pampering. "Look, if you don't feel well—"

"No, I feel okay. The cold sounds worse than it is," Mariah said, glad he'd misunderstood the cause of her distress. Rounding the desk, she seated herself in front of the typewriter.

"Are you sure?"

"I'm positive," she said, starting to roll paper into the cylinder. When he hesitated, she prompted, "Go, will ya, so I can read this pornography."

He grinned. "Look, I'll be at the Chateau Hotel—"

"Heavy date, huh?" she teased, strangely disliking the prospect. Wonder why his meeting someone hadn't crossed her mind before?

His grin grew. "Real heavy. I'm speaking on drug rehabilitation."

Mariah relaxed.

"Then I'm gonna run by Schumpert Hospital, then I'm going to a Christmas party at the VA. It'll be late when I get home. Just leave the typed test on the desk."

"Right."

"And if you have any questions..." he paused. "Don't. 'Cause I don't know how you could reach me. Unless you try tracking me down."

"I could probably find the president before I could find you. Besides, I'll guess at what I don't know."

He grinned again. "Good. Just guess."

"'Bye."

"There's coffee..."

"I brought my tea." She smiled sweetly and wiggled her fingers. "'Bye, Rev."

"The teakettle's..."

"'Bye."

"And I think there's some cookies..."

"'Bye," she said, arranging the test at a good reading angle.

He had reached the door, where he hesitated. Turning back, he said, "Mariah?"

She glanced up, huge emerald eyes meeting those of purest amber.

"Thanks."

He was gone before she could even begin to pick up her stomach from the floor where his grin had kicked it.

P-R-E-

g, g, g. Where was the g key? Someone kept moving the darned thing! Spotting it, Mariah triumphantly depressed it.

P-r-e-g-

She hastened to add n-a-n- She was on a roll. She could feel it! All she'd needed to do was get her fingers warmed up.

-d-.

There! Perfect! Perfecto!

P-r-e-g-n-a-n-d.

Pregnand?

Mariah groaned and reached once more for the bottle of white liquid eraser with a hand that looked like a casualty of war. Two long red nails had become two very short nails, both in need of filing because she'd been unable to find anything resembling a file or emery board, either in her purse or Ford's trailer. What did men do for such practical emergencies? The only thing the search had netted her was a look at Ford's bedroom and the drawn conclusion that he couldn't make a bed any better than she could. She also discovered that she felt...odd...standing in his bedroom, staring down at the place where he spent his nights.

Slathering the *d* with white liquid until it disappeared, Mariah breathed a deep sigh as she waited for the stuff to dry—which was what she'd spent much of the night doing. She glanced over at the clock on the desk. It was ten minutes after ten. At the rate she was going, the typing would take another couple of hours. She groaned at the prospect. And stood.

Tea.

She needed a cup of tea. She looked around for her purse, could find it nowhere, and was on the verge of saying the damn word that Ford was so sure God was lenient about, when she saw the black leather strap peeking out from beneath the fur coat. Stepping to the stove, she lifted the teakettle and, discovering it already full of water, situated it atop a burner. She placed her hands at the small of her back and arched. Aside from being stiff from sitting so long, she was alert, wide awake. She'd always been a night person, not coming fully into her own until the moon shone brightly. And she'd always made it a habit not to stay too long in one place. One had to see the moonrise from every vantage point.

Restless.

She'd long ago accepted the fact that she was restless. And that she bored easily. Boredom. It was the unpardonable sin. Beat her, skin her, fry her in a skillet, but don't—don't!—bore her.

As though just taking time out to think this through had bored her, Mariah began to prowl as she waited for the water to boil. She scanned the spines of the books haphazardly stacked on the desk. For all of the desk's chaos, she'd bet money that Ford Dunning knew exactly where everything was, just the way he probably knew where everything was in his life. The books represented an eclectic assortment of subjects: theology, psychology, sexual reproduction, and Sidney Sheldon's *The Windmills of the Gods*. A Bible, worn and frayed, lay nearby. Mariah flipped it open to the presentation page. It had been given to Ford by his father on a day almost twenty years before. For a reason Mariah couldn't explain, she liked the fact that Ford had not felt the need to replace the Bible with a newer one.

She liked, too, the way he'd scattered bits and pieces of his life amid the books lining the shelves behind the desk. There was a photo of an older man and woman—his parents, she presumed—plus diplomas and civic citations for service. There was also a framed quote of something. She picked it up and immediately recognized the name of the German poet Goethe.

"Until one is committed there is hesitancy, the chance to draw back, always ineffectiveness. Concerning all acts of initiative and creation, there is one elementary truth, the ignorance of which kills countless ideas and splendid plans: that the moment one definitely commits oneself, then Providence moves, too. All sorts of things occur to help one that would never otherwise have occurred. A whole stream of events issues from the decision, raising in one's favor all manner of unforeseen incidents and meetings and material assistance which no man could have dreamed would have come his way. Whatever you can do or dream you can do, begin it. Boldness has genius power and magic in it. Begin it now."

Carefully, thoughtfully, Mariah returned the framed verse to the bookshelf. Commitment. Ford was a man of commitment. She, too, was apparently a woman of commitment. She'd spent her life being committed to not being committed. Like the wind, one had to be free, with no shackles to attach or bind. One had to be able to pick up and go, to run, to roam, to see what lay beyond.

Didn't one?

That she'd asked the question at all startled her. That the whistle of the teakettle made no answer necessary relieved her.

Exactly two hours later, at ten minutes after twelve, Mariah finished typing the test. She felt as if she'd just crossed the finish line of the Boston Marathon—tired, but filled with the pride of accomplishment. She was also restless, as if she'd been caged too long. Placing the test on the typewriter, she had just reached for a pad on which to leave Ford a note when she saw car headlights cut a golden swath through the night. Instantly, she felt less tired.

"What are you still doing here?" he asked minutes later as he came through the door.

"I was just leaving," she said, noticing that he'd loosened the tie. Her guess was that he'd done it the first moment he could.

Ford suddenly realized that during a lecture, a visit to a hospital, inane party chatter and good wishes for the holiday season, his mind had been on silver-blond hair and crimson lips.

Mariah suddenly realized that amidst the impossible frustration of typing, whitewashing and retyping, her thoughts had been on a darkly dressed man with sun-tinted eyes. Those eyes now looked tired—dog tired. Curiously, that fatigue stirred some instinct that had been dormant until now. She longed to reach out and smooth away the deep wrinkles around his eyes and mouth. But she didn't. Instead she picked up her coat.

"How'd it go?" he asked, automatically stepping forward to assist, but she'd already shrugged into it by the time he stood beside her. He didn't honestly know whether he was disappointed or relieved that he wouldn't be touching her.

Neither did she.

"It was a piece of cake," she said in reply to his question. "It was just six hours of the most miserable torture I've ever been through. Did you know that someone keeps moving your *g* key?"

He grinned, temporarily smoothing out some of the weariness wrinkles. "You noticed that, too, huh?"

"It was hard not to," she answered, heading for the door. "Oh, by the way," she said, displaying her butchered nails, "you owe me the price of a manicure." Before he could respond, she asked, "Don't you even own a file or an emery board?"

"Sorry about the nails, and there's a manicure kit in the medicine cabinet of the bathroom."

"Oh. How thoroughly logical. No wonder I couldn't find it."

He opened the trailer door for her, then followed her through it, obviously intent on walking her to her car. The frigid night air rushed at them, breathing its chill down their necks.

"It's cold." Mariah shivered, her breath a frosty vapor.

"Yeah. They say it's gonna get colder."

He pulled open her car door, and she moved to get in. She didn't, though. Instead, she turned within the wedge of space. Ford stood at the wedge's width—tall, lean, dark. Their eyes met.

"Well, good night, adios, au revoir, ciao," she said with an impish grin.

He grinned, too. "Good night. And thanks."

"You're welcome. Oh, how was the kid?"

"Lucky."

"Good."

A fresh gust of wind came out of nowhere, tumbling Ford's near-ebony hair onto his forehead and wildly scattering Mariah's. Ford would have sworn moonbeams frolicked through the wavy mass. And not that he would have blamed them, for his fingers suddenly itched to make the same journey. Just as she wanted—desperately, she realized—to rake back the wayward lock giving the man of God such a devilish look.

"Well, night, Rev," she said again, this time with a grin that had gone from impish to sultry. "You behave yourself, ya hear?"

Ford's grin reappeared. "I hear."

At the smile that flashed brilliantly in the night, Mariah's eyes lowered to his lips.

Ford's eyes dropped to hers, a sweet confection in sinful scarlet.

She was aware that his eyes were on her lips. The realization caused a tiny little thump in her stomach. Just as Ford's heart rammed into a very masculine rhythm at the realization that her eyes were similarly on his lips.

Slowly, their eyes met again. Time seemed to stand perfectly still, measured only by rustling leaves and the exquisite silence of evening.

"I must be," Ford said at last, his voice low and so scratchy it could have manicured her nails. Right after it curled her toes.

"You must be what?"

"I must be one of those people who like living dangerously."

The kick in Mariah's stomach came again, this time more strongly. Conversely, her voice seemed robbed of all substance. "How dangerously?"

"This—" he bridged the distance between them and lowered his head "—dangerously." He had barely completed the word—in fact, she felt it instead of heard it—before his lips took hers.

Mariah had heard the word *meltdown* before, but had never truly understood its meaning until that moment when Ford's lips gently worked upon hers. Every bone in her body melted into a jellylike substance, making it the miracle of miracles that she remained standing. Perhaps she did so only because Ford's hands had found her shoulders.

His lips were soft, gentle, yet masculinely demanding, seeking angles of sensuality which pulled from her a reaction her woman's body was helpless to withhold. His tongue never touched hers, never breached the entrance of her mouth, and yet its sweet threat hung between them. It was the only time in her life that she could remember a threat being sweeter than reality. Instinctively, striving to lose herself in his heat, she eased her hips forward, meshing her thighs with his. Her hands tunneled beneath his jacket, her fingers curling themselves in the fabric of his shirt.

Likewise, a ribbon of desire curled within her.

As did something else as well.

The need to be healed. In places of the heart where she'd never realized she hurt. This man implicitly promised that healing—his strength, his tenderness, vouchsafed that promise—but for him to heal her, she'd have to show him her heart. Open it to him. Let him see the raw wounds of loneliness, of grief, of guilt. That she couldn't do, even though she wanted to, because it was altogether too dangerous. In compensation, she'd just concentrate on the sensual feelings he aroused in her, the feelings that caused her blood to boil, her skin to burn.

She stepped closer and teasingly, tauntingly, ran the tip of her tongue across his lower lip. Sparks of fire blazed and Ford raised his head at their shocking intensity. Both he and Mariah were breathing hard. Both pairs of eyes, hers those of a consummate temptress, were hazy and luminous. Ultimately, as though it was necessary for her to be the one in command, Mariah pulled herself from his arms. Wordlessly she slid on to the car seat. Wordlessly Ford started to shut the door behind her. Before he did so, however, she spoke.

"I was right, Rev," she said, her voice as thick as syrup, her eyes alluring. "You're sexy."

He had been right, too, Ford thought minutes later as he watched the taillights of the car disappear. Mariah Calloway was a fraud, hiding behind a provocative, bawdy facade. Oh, she was sensual. There was no doubt of that.

She'd responded just the way a woman should to a man, but what he wanted to see was what was behind that sensuality. He wanted to see the woman who lived behind the locked door.

For professional reasons? the psychologist in him questioned.

No, the truthful minister in him answered, the taste of the temptress's kiss still on his lips, he wanted to see her for the most personal of personal reasons.

CHAPTER SIX

"ARE YOU SURE about this?"

Ford, almost at the end of the essay question he was scoring, finished reading, then looked up. Mariah sat on the sofa, her feet, clad only in white socks with lace trim—the kind little girls wore—curled beneath her. She, too, was grading papers from the master Ford had provided. Once she'd completed her part, she passed the test on to him for his evaluation of the essay question. They made an efficient team. They were even making progress, despite all the provocative teasing the occasion, and Mariah's disposition, necessarily gave rise to.

Actually Mariah was in rare form, Ford admitted, his eyes taking in the sight of her. She was dressed all in white—white jeans, a white sweater that proved his libido was in working order, white heels, white lace in her hair, and two—not three—but two pairs of nonjangly demure earrings. All in all, she looked like purity personified. In reality, she was a summa cum laude graduate of the Sadie Thompson School of Destroy That Preacher.

She glanced up, too, their eyes meeting. His peered through black-rimmed glasses. She frowned. "How old are you?"

As though growing accustomed to her erratic thought patterns, Ford simply rearranged his hips in the chair he occupied, his socked feet propped across the desk's edge, and asked, "Which question first?"

"How old are you?"

"Thirty-eight."

"Thirty-eight? Isn't it wonderful what they're doing for the elderly in terms of bifocals these days?"

Ford grinned, wishing that he didn't see quite as well as he did—with or without bifocals. The white sweater cupping her curves to perfection, the white jeans hugging her hips to distraction, made him realize for the first time Adam's true plight in the Garden of Eden when Eve had so beguilingly tempted him. He'd never again be so quick to point an accusing finger at the poor man.

"Actually," she added, "I think the glasses make you look very masterful, very stern, very professional, very—"

"Sexy," they both finished.

Mariah giggled; Ford's grin widened.

"You're only saying that to make an old man feel good."

"Right. Gotta be nice to the elderly."

"So what am I sure about?" he asked, returning the conversation to the first question. "Better get me while my ancient brain's still functioning."

She rattled the test paper in her hand. "Are you sure that toes are an erogenous zone?"

"Yes," he said, reaching for another test paper.

"Well, that was certainly said with authority."

"Toes are an erogenous zone," he said matter-of-factly. A log in the stove popped, as if in agreement.

"I didn't know that, Rev."

"Too bad about your choice of uninformed partners," he said. He'd learned that the only way to handle Mariah Calloway was to tease as long and as hard as she. The only thing was he had trouble teasing about the lovers she'd had—uninformed or not.

Uncoiling one foot from beneath her, Mariah extended her leg and wriggled her toes. "Sorta like an adult version of This Little Piggy Goes to Market, huh? Tell me something, Rev, you ever kissed a woman's toe?"

Ford appeared totally unflapped by the question as he picked up his mug and took a sip of his tepid coffee. "No woman's toe that I care to discuss with you right now."

"Ah, c'mon, kiss and tell."

He peered over the top of his glasses. "I'd like to remind you that these papers need grading tonight."

Her leg was still extended. "You mean, if right this moment you were to kiss, then suck my toe—"

"We're not quitting until these papers are graded."

"—I'd fall into a rapturous state of sexual excitation?"

Ford crushed a sheet of waste paper in his fist and flung it at Mariah. It bounced off her lace-trimmed foot. "Grade, woman, grade!"

They both were grinning hugely. Likewise both were wondering just how erotically a piggy could go to market.

"Who's Jeff Simmons?" Mariah asked an hour later. It was, thankfully, the last of her one hundred and eleven test papers.

The name immediately snagged Ford's attention. "Why?"

"He calculated perfectly the woman's fertile days according to the rhythm method, which half the kids miscalculated by the way, but missed entirely the question about a woman being able to get pregnant even though she doesn't have an orgasm." Mariah frowned, teasingly. "You can get pregnant without having an orgasm, can't you? This isn't like the toes . . . something I've missed entirely?"

The fact that he ignored her teasing—he'd given her as good as he'd gotten all evening—alerted Mariah to his mood change. That and the fact he reached for the test. "Let me see."

She handed the stapled papers to him.

Silently, he studied the five-page exam. Including the essay question dealing with sexual responsibility. Finally, he exploded. "This is exactly what I've been trying to tell everyone about these kids! On the one hand, they know things I didn't know until I was thirty. On the other hand, they have a brainful of inaccurate street information. You're right, he figured to a day his partner's fertile period, but then thinks he's gonna get freebies if she doesn't have an orgasm. That's great, just great!" At this he dropped his feet to the floor and wearily combed his fingers through his hair. His shoulders drooped, as in defeat.

Not bothering to slip on her shoes, Mariah rose from the sofa. Instinctively, without questioning her actions, she moved to comfort him. "Hey, I'm sorry," she said, starting to massage his shoulders with her long, slender fingers.

Ford sighed at the pleasure permeating his oh, so tired body. "No, I'm sorry," he said. "I got on my usual soapbox. It's just that these kids are gonna drive me crazy. No, their parents are gonna drive me crazy. No, that isn't right, either. *Some* of their parents are gonna drive me crazy." He moaned as her fingers kneaded a bed of bunched muscles just to the side of his neck.

"What do you mean?" she asked, sensing his need to talk, sensing her genuine interest.

"Some of the parents, including Jeff's mother, who happens to be a member of my church, think that by teaching responsible sex, safe sex, that I'm encouraging promiscuity."

"Teaching a couple the rhythm method encourages them to try it out?"

"Exactly," Ford said, this time outright groaning at what Mariah was doing to his neck. He thought he probably could stand about a thousand years of this! "And, God forbid," he added, "I should mention condoms or spermicidal foams or the pill!" This last he said as though it were some heinous monster.

"I should think parents would be scared stiff with AIDS," Mariah said, "and that they'd want their kids to know all the facts."

"Trust me, some parents are perfectly content to bury their heads in the sand. AIDS is out there, but it couldn't possibly touch their kids. No more than it's going to be their daughter who gets pregnant or their son who knocks his girlfriend up. What are you doing?" he asked suddenly, closing his eyes and wallowing in the luxury of her thumb rubbing at the nape of his neck. Her thumb then trailed up to the base of his head.

"Anyone ever tell you you're tense?"

"They've probably tried to, but I've been too busy to listen."

Mariah laughed and did something wonderfully delicious behind each of Ford's ears with the pads of her thumbs. "We've established Jeff's mother's position. What about his father's?"

"He died two years ago."

Mariah pieced together Ford's quick interest at Jeff Simmons's name and the explosion that followed. "And you've been subbing, right?"

"Yeah, I guess you could say that. He's uh...he's a damned good kid. One any man could be proud of."

Mariah wondered again why Ford Dunning had no children, no wife. She also wondered why she kept wondering about that.

"So," Mariah said, letting the subject of Ford's lack of a family drop, "you're going to keep teaching sex ed to the Jeff Simmonses of the world."

"And the Megan Blakes. That's his girlfriend," Ford explained. "I just hope I can talk louder than their hormones."

"Ah," Mariah said in understanding, "we think piggies may be going to market."

"We think piggies may be going to market, or that Jeff and Megan are at least thinking about trying it, and I've got to get through to them that taking piggies to market, like everything in life, has a price tag attached. Being sexually active demands the acceptance of certain responsibilities. Ohhh, Mariah, that feels so good!" he groaned.

Mariah's hands had slipped once more to his shoulders, where they were rubbing in deep, thorough circles. Ford lolled his head to the left, giving her freer access. She took it. Leaning forward, she applied still even more pressure to his tension-tightened muscles.

Ford felt the steady rhythm of her fingers, a rhythm that had surely been born in heaven. He sighed, letting the pleasure seep into his flesh, cleansing his mind of everything—a rare occurrence at best. Sensation replaced thought. He was aware of the warmth pulsating from her touch, just as he was aware that tendrils of her hair danced along the exposed column of his neck. He felt, too, the occasional brush of her breasts against his back. None of these movements, in contrast to almost everything she'd done all evening, were calculated. The provocativeness she was now displaying was totally natural. It was also far headier than her usual faked form of seduction.

Gradually the pleasure he was feeling metamorphosed into a slow, heated pain. The kind of pain the male body experiences at times of arousal.

Mariah, too, was discovering new sensations. She was suddenly and acutely aware of his spicy after-shave, the way his muscles were firmly, healthily, corded beneath the fabric of his long-sleeved shirt, the way his hickory-colored hair curled ever so slightly at the nape of his neck, at the nape of his vulnerably exposed neck. She crazily wondered if the back of the neck constituted another erogenous zone.

Mariah's hands stilled.

Ford picked up the red pencil that had dropped from his fingers.

Their eyes met.

"I, uh..." He cleared his throat. "I need to get these papers finished."

"Yeah. Sure," she agreed, fresh out of suggestive comebacks. Mariah stepped back and hooked her thumbs into the front pockets of her white jeans. Her hands still tingled from the warmth of his skin.

"I'll only be another ten or fifteen minutes."

"No problem. I'll, uh... I'll just have some tea."

"The teakettle—"

"I know," she said, edging toward the small kitchen. "You want some more coffee?"

He shook his head. "No. I'll probably be wide awake from all the caffeine as it is."

"Wouldn't want you wide awake," she said. "You might just get into trouble."

Trouble.

It was what Ford had plenty of, trying to keep his eyes on the few remaining tests. Oblivious to his divided attention, Mariah prepared her tea, slipped into her high-heeled shoes, and, occasionally sipping, roamed the room. She finally settled on the bookcase behind Ford. Not seeing her, but simply hearing her, he found an even greater drain on his attention. He could hear a book ease from the shelf, could hear the sexy shuffle of her high heels, could hear her pick something up and put it back down any number of times. Any number of distracting times.

Mariah had just replaced the photo of Ford's parents when she noticed another photo. This one was of three smiling people—two men in military fatigues and dangling dog tags, one of them a very young Ford, and a woman. A Vietnamese woman. A beautiful Vietnamese woman. A beautiful Vietnamese woman who was staring at Ford with open affection. His arm was familiarly draped about her.

As Mariah stared at that arm, Ford, with a defeated sigh, pulled off his glasses and tossed them onto the ungraded tests. "I'll finish these papers later," he said, scraping back his chair and rising. Rolling down the cuff of his shirt, he turned. At the sight of Mariah holding the photograph, he stopped. Her eyes found his.

"You, uh...you were in Vietnam, huh?"

He resumed rolling down his cuff. "Yeah. 1968."

"I was but a child then."

"So was I."

"You, uh...you met the guy there?" Mariah had no idea why she was avoiding mentioning the woman; she just knew she was.

"Yeah. We were in the same unit."

"He, uh...he looks nice."

"Yeah."

"Have y'all stayed in touch?"

"He's dead," Ford replied. For long moments neither spoke. Finally, Ford added, "His name was Bill Michaels." Gesturing toward the snapshot still in Mariah's hand, he said, "The three of us—Bill, Mei-Lee, and I—"

The woman had had a name, Mariah thought. Mei-Lee. A pretty name for a pretty lady. A pretty lady who'd been in love with Ford.

"—were in a Saigon bar. Someone tossed a grenade in through a window. Bill threw himself on it to save Mei-Lee and me." He said the words so matter-of-factly that Mariah knew the subject contained a rainbow of emotions. All in dark colors. "She, uh...she died, anyway. I was the only one to survive."

Ford didn't mention that he'd thrown himself across Mei-Lee, but that the act hadn't been enough to save her. Neither did he mention that he'd spent two months in a military hospital recovering from his own wounds.

Seconds thrummed into seconds. Emerald eyes probed amber eyes. At the same time amber searched emerald.

"It's awesome having someone give his life for you, isn't it?" Mariah said.

Awesome.

It wasn't the word he'd probably have chosen, but nonetheless it was applicable. "Yes," he answered, "it's awesome."

Understanding, basic and pure, passed between them. It was an understanding that no one else had ever shared with either. In an explicable way, and though the burden could never be totally lifted, the sharing lightened the load. Both were a little surprised to discover that.

It was Mariah who shattered the serious mood. As though she'd had all the gravity she could stand, she grinned suddenly. "Well, Rev, is my IOU paid off?"

Ford grinned. "In full. As soon as I drive you home."

"I'm sorry I couldn't get Eden's car," she apologized again.

"No problem," he said, throwing his arms into a pumpkin-colored leather jacket that made him look more than intriguing. He reached for her fur coat.

Mariah set the photo back on the shelf, keenly aware that she hadn't asked what his relationship with Mei-Lee had been. She was also keenly aware why she hadn't. She hadn't wanted to hear his answer. Stepping forward, she slipped into the coat and flipped her lengthy silvery-white hair back over the collar. Her grin widened. "I don't suppose you'd consider letting me drive that little sports car of yours?"

In answer, Ford dug into his jeans pocket and tossed her the keys.

Mariah caught them and laughed—he thought a little overbrightly—before replying, "C'mon, Rev, let's live dangerously."

The car sang through the night.

It had been singing ever since Mariah, leaving behind a swirl of red dust, gunned the sports car from the dirt road onto the deserted country highway. Shifting gears and manipulating the pedals like a pro, she drove hell-bent for leather, as if Satan himself were chasing them. Ford knew, however, that Satan had better sense than to be traveling this fast on curvy roads.

Silently, sitting as casually as though he were at his desk, he watched the speedometer climb. Ninety-five...one hundred...one hundred and five... He lifted his eyes to Mariah. Her hair was wild, tossed hither and yon by the winter wind that had accosted them as they'd gotten into the car. She'd removed her coat, so that every movement of her body was visible—her long legs as she alternated between gas pedal and brake, her arms as she geared and guided the wheel, her shoulders and torso as they swayed to the speed. A smile danced at her lips, while a reckless light glinted in her eyes.

Reckless.

She embodied the word... and had done so ever since they'd shared the serious incident back at the trailer. He wondered if talking about her mother, which they'd obliquely been doing, was responsible for the mood. He also wondered why she hadn't asked about Mei-Lee. She'd wanted to, but she hadn't. Had he wanted her to? He gave it some thought—somewhere between one hundred and one hundred and ten on the speedometer—and decided he didn't know.

Mariah glanced over at him and grinned. "She's a beauty!" she hollered over the roar of the car.

Ford grinned back. "Yeah." He might have been referring to the woman rather than the car, however.

"I drove in the Grand Prix once."

"Did you kill anybody?"

Mariah laughed. "No. Didn't win, either. In fact, I was second from last, but I had a ball." Ford was just wondering how she would have had access to such a specially designed racing car, when she supplied the answer. "I drove a friend's car. Nick had broken his ankle and couldn't compete."

Ford couldn't have stopped the question even if he'd tried. "Nick?"

"Yeah. Nick Logan."

Ford waited for more. There was no more. This time he did stop the question. It wasn't any of his business if this Nick Logan was a friend or a *friend*. He wondered then why it should feel—and very much so—like his business.

Mariah effortlessly negotiated a hairpin curve without slacking the speed by as much as a degree. She smiled at the car's performance. "I can't believe this machine is owned by a minister."

Thankfully the comment drove away thoughts of Nick Logan. A grin split Ford's mouth. "That sounds like a prejudicial remark."

"You know what I mean."

Unfortunately he did. "Some of my congregation would agree with you. Jeff's mother, Laurel Simmons, for one."

"She sounds like your personal nemesis."

"You could say that."

"But you don't give a damn what Laurel Simmons thinks, right?"

Ford's grin widened. "I guess I don't. I don't remember ever reading in the Bible that a minister shall not drive a sports car. Besides," he added, "it's my only vice. Give or take."

"Well, we certainly wouldn't want you to go viceless," Mariah teased, taking the turn into her driveway at the same outrageous speed. Gravel momentarily spewed everywhere. Expertly, as a concession to the possibly damaging pea-sized rocks, she slowed the car, then brought it to a complete stop in front of her house. She cut the engine, turned in the bucket seat and ran her arm along its back in almost one motion. The earth hadn't even fully settled beneath them.

Ford, still a study in nonchalance, already leaned in the corner of the car, his arm, too, propped along the back of the seat. Deliberately, neither touched the other. Ford appraised the glitter in her eyes. She looked like a woman on the verge of orgasm, a woman about to climax on thrills.

"Did you have fun?" he asked calmly, his lips twitching.

"Yeah. Did you?"

"Let's just say I feel a lot more mortal."

Mariah laughed, a sound of pure exhilaration. Even as Ford watched, that exhilaration assumed sexual overtones. "Tell me something, Ford D-u-n-n-i-n-g, are you gonna kiss me good-night?"

The question was like a tiny explosion in Ford's gut—and directly below. "You want me to?"

"You want me to want you to?"

He chuckled. "I've been a psychologist for years, and even I wouldn't begin to try to analyze that. Besides, did you know you answer questions with questions?"

"Do I?"

They both smiled.

Hers faded, her mouth pouting sensually. She ran her red nail down the sleeve of his jacket. Deliberately. Provocatively. Even through the leather, he felt it. Keenly.

"You know, of course, that if you don't kiss me," she purred, "I'll just be forced to kiss you."

"That sounds...interesting."

Her mouth arced into a sassy smile. "Does that mean you're forcing my hand?"

"I wouldn't be at all surprised if that was what I was doing."

"It would probably have deep psychological implications if I didn't go through with it," she said, leaning forward and trailing her finger onto the curve of his shoulder.

"Probably."

"Then, again," she said, inching higher toward his neck, "it would probably have deep psychological implications if I did."

"Probably."

Her fingers slowly, sensuously made a fist in the collar of his leather jacket and tugged him toward her. "Then analyze this, Rev."

That was precisely what he did. Her lips were sweet and soft and... measured. As in calculated. As in in total control. Hers fit over his provocatively, but with a teasing flippancy. When she pulled away, her breath wasn't even disturbed. Her eyes gleamed not from passion, but from play.

"Well, what do you think?" she whispered, sirenlike.

"I'll tell you what I think. I think it's my turn now." Before Mariah knew what was happening, Ford had hauled her into his arms and smothered her mouth with his.

This kiss was just as measured, just as calculated. This time, however, the control was Ford's. He had but one goal: to reach beyond Mariah's game playing. His lips brushed, stroked, rolled over hers—gently and not so gently. His hands moved up her sweatered back, drawing her into him, so that his lips could begin all over again brushing, stroking, rolling over hers.

Mariah knew only that she'd suddenly been surrounded by Ford—his arms tenderly caging her, his leather-clad chest flush with hers, his lips... Oh, his lips! A preacher wasn't supposed to know how to kiss like this! A preacher was supposed to be dull and boring and sexless. A preacher wasn't supposed to know just what angle of mouth to mouth set a body aflame. He wasn't supposed to know...

Mariah moaned as his velvet tongue penetrated her parted lips. In that second she died just a little—died of a sensual explosion that blasted its way to the very core of her being... and beyond.

Bolder than sin, his tongue dipped, teased, swirled around hers. Its every orchestrated movement was to incite her tongue to join his. But her tongue didn't. Instead, confused by his mastery of her senses, even frightened by it—this man stripped away layers of her that she didn't want stripped away!—she tried to pull free.

"No," he whispered raggedly, his arms gently, but firmly, stopping her. He enveloped her closer. "No more playing at kissing, Mariah. Now we're gonna do the real thing."

Spearing the fingers of one hand through the savage tangle of her hair, his mouth took hers again, his tongue once more the instant invader, the clever conqueror. The silken rapier slid over, under and around hers—slowly, erotically. Heat spread everywhere through her body. Heat and languor and the most exquisite tingling. Mariah had no choice but to respond.

She whimpered.

And mated her tongue with his.

Tip to tip.

Greed to greed.

As if she suddenly could not get enough of the intimacy he was offering.

A deep moan issued from Ford's chest.

One more swirl, one more touch of tip to tip, and he withdrew his tongue, gentling the kiss from sensual to sweet. The kiss was almost—almost—chaste when he raised his head from hers. Mariah's breath was battered, her eyes hazy. Mariah looked startled, as if she'd lost a bit of herself and didn't quite know what to make of it . . . or where to start looking.

Ford, his breath little better, his own eyes less than clear, smiled to himself. While he still hadn't glimpsed the woman behind the locked door, he'd sure as hell jiggled the key in the lock.

SHE COULDN'T FORGET the kiss. It was as simple as that. And as complex. What she couldn't understand was why it kept gnawing at her senses. She'd kissed other men. Lots of other men, for heaven's sake! But Ford's kiss had been...it had been different. It was that simple and that complex.

It had also been days since Mariah had heard from him. Not that she was counting! Well, maybe she was. And that she couldn't understand, either.

Her job at the mill demanded a sizable portion of her time, while the Christmas holiday demanded another fair share. At first, she and Eden had decided, because of their father's recent death, to do nothing in the way of decorating. One evening, however, Eden had arranged fresh holly and bayberry-scented candles on the mantel. Mariah had placed the wreath on the door the following night. Two days later, she showed up, peeking through the branches of a fir tree that she said had called her name as she'd driven by the Christmas tree lot. She and Eden had spent all evening trimming it in ornaments Mariah could remember seeing as far back as she could remember Christmas.

She also remembered a kiss.

And wondered why Ford didn't call.

One by one, two by two, presents started appearing beneath the tree, while the aroma of sugar cookies and spice cakes filled the house. Mariah's contribution, in terms of cooking, was to stay out of Eden's way.

Two days before Christmas, Nick Logan, her old sometimes-roam-the-world-together friend, called to wish her a happy holiday and to announce that he might be stopping by to see her after the first of the year...if she was still going to be in Calloway Corners. Mariah surprised herself by saying she was. She also told him to hurry because she'd missed him.

Miss.

Did she miss Ford? No. How could she miss a dull, boring preacher? Except that he was everything but dull. Everything but boring.

Christmas Eve day, both Tess and Jo arrived home, Tess quietly and wearing a false bravado concerning her upcoming divorce, Jo with a bluster that said let's get this thing called Christmas over with and get back to business.

That night Mariah saw Ford. Though that was all.

The church, according to tradition, held a Christmas Eve midnight communion service which the four sisters, if they were all at home, just as traditionally attended. The small church glowed with lighted tapers that illuminated the stained-glass windows, while blood-red poinsettias, donated by church members, lined the altar. Two poinsettia plants had been given in loving memory of Grace and Ben Calloway.

When Ford, wearing a black robe with a now-white stole representing purity, took his seat before the congregation, his eyes unerringly found Mariah's. She started to wriggle her finger, but didn't. Instead, she just let her eyes hungrily search his...and his, hers. Throughout the short sermon, Ford deliberately averted his gaze, as if his attention couldn't afford such a severe distraction. Later, pew by pew, the congregation walked to the front of the church to take communion.

Mariah watched him out of the corner of her eye as he and a deacon approached her. From the deacon she accepted a communion cup of grape juice. When Ford stopped in front of her, a vessel of wafers in his hand, she opened her mouth to receive the symbolic host. Ford's eyes brushed hers. In his, she saw complete devotion, sincere passion for the God he served. Intuitively she knew he would have a similar passion for any woman he loved and, just as his love of God was sacred, so, too, would be his love for a woman. The realization unexpectedly warmed her...and troubled her, for he would demand the same passionate, sacred love in return.

Dutifully Ford moved on. After the service he started to approach her—that Mariah would have sworn—but interruption after interruption by holiday well-wishers kept him from her side. Even though it was after one o'clock when they arrived back at the house, Mariah had been certain Ford would call. He had not. She went to bed miserable and grew even more so during the sleepless night.

Christmas Day was blistering cold, with a wind that cut instead of blew. After the opening of presents, after a sumptuous meal of turkey and dressing and cranberry sauce, after the other three sisters had settled down for naps or quiet time, Mariah left the house. She had to do something to appease her restlessness, and walking might just fit that bill. Besides she wanted to see the pond. It was where, over the years, she'd often gone when life seemed a bit too much.

As Mariah was tramping through the winter-silent woods, Ford was putting down his dinner fork.

"You're not finished?" his mother, Jessie, asked.

Ford smiled. "Could I ever eat enough to satisfy you?"

"Probably not," the brown-haired woman replied, her smile very much like her son's. "It has something to do with maternal instincts."

"Well, tell your maternal instincts that I'm stuffed." He scraped back the modest dining room chair of the modest dining room, stood and walked to his mother. He bent and kissed a cheek that had remained unwrinkled despite sixty-nine years and a son who had always seemed unable to perform in expected ways. "It was good, Mom."

She patted his hand.

"Need some help with the dishes?" Ford asked.

"No, indeed," Jessie replied, talking now to her husband. "John, get the boy out of here."

Ford didn't point out that he'd long ago ceased to be a boy. Primarily because he'd long ago accepted that his mother and father would always look upon him as a boy. Their boy. Their only child.

"C'mon, Son, let's get outta here," John Dunning said, ushering Ford toward the door to the den. "Your mother is impossible to live with if she doesn't get her way."

John Dunning still stood tall with shoulders that sagged little from his seventy-two years. His hair, thick and bushy, revealed only minor strands of gray. It was only standing beside his son, when the comparison between ages was so blatantly obvious, that he appeared old. He could have retired years before, but he hadn't. Ford doubted he would until forced to. He also knew that God was going to have a hard time replacing this loyal servant. Few people were as pure-hearted as John Dunning. Ford hoped one day to be man enough to just stand in his father's shadow.

"You look whipped, Son," his father commented.

Ford dropped onto the sofa and, out of habit, ran his fingers through his hair in a gesture of sublime weariness. He smiled. "The holidays are rough."

"I know they are in the ministry and hear they're doubly so in the counseling field. Seems to me you're kinda getting it from both ends."

"I'm okay," Ford said, thinking of the many obligations he'd had during the past few days.

The holidays, normally hectic anyway, brought severe depression for many. Because he always made himself so accessible, his patients didn't hesitate to call him. He'd talked one woman out of suicide, while he'd tried to make a bevy of other patients see that life wasn't a black pit of despair. He'd offered them hope. Priceless hope. But it had taken its toll on him, along with a series of little frustrations that one by one amounted to little. Together, they spelled *potential ulcer*.

The first frustration had come the evening he'd dined with Ruth Doege and J. C. Hardcastle. What he'd seen were two people who should be married. They were in love. Practically, however, he couldn't push the issue. All he could do was watch them cherish each other in ways that many married couples had forgotten. He also listened with an open ear when they suggested establishing a more relevant senior citizens program at the church. Apparently not every senior citizen wanted to bingo his life away.

The second frustration had come when Jason Taylor, Seth Taylor's troubled son, hadn't shown up for any of the basketball practices as Ford was certain he would, while the third frustration had unexpectedly arisen when a chaperone for the New Year's Eve dance at the high school had canceled. Why had he volunteered not only to chaperone the dance, but also to be responsible for recruiting other chaperones, as well? The fourth frustration, and the pièce de résistance, came when the anonymous donor for the choir robes had to withdraw his generous offer because of a dramatic financial failure that had come out of nowhere. The bad news had come after the gowns had arrived and after the congregation was as proud as punch. Ford didn't know how to tell them that the robes, still in boxes in his church study, were going to have to be returned.

"...human."

Ford focused his attention. "I'm sorry, Dad. What did you say?"

"I said, give yourself a break. You're only human, you know."

Human.

He knew that all too well. He was bone-weary with a thousand things left to do. But he couldn't rest. He knew that all too well, too. He couldn't rest because he'd survived when others had died—one sacrificially. Now it was his turn to give fully to others. Oh, but he was tired . . . so tired.

He could imagine Mariah's hands massaging his sore muscles, could feel her lips melting against his, could see her eyes meeting his—pure emerald starlight that had momentarily and completely banished his fatigue.

Human? Yes, he was human! She made him feel it in every inch of his masculine body.

" . . . sink."

Ford glanced up.

"Let me go see if I can unstop that datburned sink for your mother. Be right back."

Ford checked his watch. Three o'clock.

"I'm gonna use the phone, huh?" he said, rising.

"Sure. You know where it is."

Ford walked to his father's study and dialed a number he now knew by heart. Unfortunately something pressing always prevented his dialing it. The phone began to ring.

Dear God, he thought, let her be home, because he had a real human need to hear her voice. Even as he waited, even as he remembered a kiss, he wondered if he wasn't just setting himself up for a fall.

Was it foolish beyond words to think that one could ever tame the wind?

CHAPTER SEVEN

"HELLO?"

Ford hesitated. It wasn't the voice he'd hoped to hear. "Jo?"

"Ford?"

"Yeah. How are you?"

"Fine. And you?"

"Okay," he said socially, feeling tired to the very marrow of his bones. "Merry Christmas."

"Same to you."

"Is, uh . . . is Mariah there?"

Jo, too, paused, as though surprised he was asking for Mariah. "Yeah, sure... No, wait, she walked down to the pond."

Disappointment flooded Ford.

"You want me to have her call you?"

Yes, he did, but he wouldn't be at his parents' house much longer. He'd promised to go by the VA. Some of the patients there had no families to spend the lonely holiday with. No one would be stopping by to visit with them but him.

"No," he answered. "Just tell her I called to wish her a Merry Christmas."

"Sure. I'll tell her."

"Goodbye."

"Goodb—Ford, wait a minute! Here she is!"

Her hand still on the knob of the front door, Mariah glanced up. Her eyes were bright from her outing, her nose chilled and red and threatening to run. She sniffed.

"For you," Jo said, holding out the receiver.

Mariah's heart accelerated with hope. "Who is it?"

"Ford Dunning," Jo answered, looking as though it remained the question of the century just what the good preacher wanted with Mariah.

Ordinarily Mariah would have had an outrageous comeback, but at the moment comebacks, outrageous or otherwise, seemed unimportant. She took the phone out of her sister's hand and put it to her ear. Once there, she hesitated, as if wanting to savor the moment. Finally, after Jo reluctantly disappeared back into the living room, she said, "Hello?"

Her voice was crisp with cold. Curiously, it washed over Ford like a heated wave. "Don't you know it's cold out, lady?"

He was grinning—she'd have staked her life on it!—and the power of that grin made her tingle. "Yeah, but warming up afterward, at least if you do it right, can feel so good."

Ford realized that her teasing, her brazen sultriness, was part of what he'd missed. Part. "Yeah," he said, making the one word sound every bit as suggestive as what she'd said.

Both hearts danced a little crazily.

"I just called to say Merry Christmas."

"Merry Christmas." There was a moment's silence before she asked, "Where are you?"

"My parents. In Shreveport. I'm stuffed," he added.

"Me, too."

Silence reigned again. "I, uh . . . I tried to get to you last night, but everyone kept stopping me."

"I know. I thought you might call when you got home."

"It was late. Past two."

"I stay up late. I'm a night person."

"I'll remember that." His voice had grown husky. "I've wanted to call before, but I've been so damned busy you wouldn't believe it."

"You sound tired," Mariah said, wishing more than she'd ever wished anything that she could reach out and comfort him, if it were only to massage the shoulders she knew were knotted with tension.

"I am." She was the only person he'd responded honestly to concerning that question. Usually he lied and said he was fine. "And I've got to go by the VA in a little while. Then I'm going home and actually sleep all night. Maybe."

"Unplug your phone."

"Believe me, it's tempting. Listen, I want you to do a couple of things for me."

"No," she said, grinning. "I will not do any more typing, and I will not grade any more monthly rhythm cycles."

Jo, who'd passed back into the hallway on her way up the stairs, looked up sharply. Mariah's eyes glittered with the delight of shocking her.

Ford chuckled. "I promise I won't ask you to do either."

"Then what?"

"I want you to help me chaperone a New Year's Eve dance."

Mariah groaned.

"C'mon, I'm desperate."

"You're always desperate."

"That's not the point. And I want you to organize a Senior Citizens group at the church."

"Oh, sure, right. I know how to do that."

"Just talk to them and help them plan some activities that appeal to them. It's your penance," he added.

"My penance?"

"Yeah, for making fun of my bifocals."

She smiled, then turned serious. "Ford, I don't know how long I'm going to be around."

The words knifed at him. Cruelly. Strange how cruelly, considering the short time he'd known Mariah. "Just do it for however long you're here. A week, two weeks, a month, whatever. Just help them get organized."

"Ford—"

"Please. It would take a load off of me. I know that's selfish, but—"

"I'll do it!" She would have done anything to lighten his burden. It was that simple, Mariah realized, though she couldn't make it appear so...even to herself. "But only because it's Christmas and I'm trying to be full of good cheer. And don't blame me for the chaos that may result."

"With you I'm fully expecting chaos," he teased. "By the way, I'll pick you up at six Thursday for the dance."

"I never said I'd chaperone."

"You never said you wouldn't." At her hesitation, he added, "C'mon, live dangerously. Spend the evening with teenagers. You'll even get to meet Laurel Simmons."

Mariah smiled. "Now how can I possibly pass that up? I might even volunteer to chart her fertile and safe days."

Ford laughed, more fully than he could remember doing in a while. "I strongly suspect every day's safe with Laurel. Look, I gotta go. I'm due at the hospital at four."

"You better hurry, then."

"Yeah," he replied, yet he made no effort to terminate the call.

Mariah, not wanting to, either, finally said, "Bye, Rev."

"See you Thursday."

"Thursday." Suddenly, even desperately, she said, "Ford?"

"Yeah?"

She heard the question coming. She couldn't have been more startled if it had been a freight train headed straight for her. "The woman in the picture..."

Ford could sense how tightly her hand must be grasping the receiver. Maybe that was because his was doing the same. "Mei-Lee was my fiancée," he said softly.

Nothing. Silence. Then, "I'm sorry. I mean, that she died."

Another silence. "It was a long time ago."

Her hand unconsciously relaxed its grip, but Mariah said nothing. She had no idea why his telling her that he was emotionally free from Mei-Lee, which, in effect, was what he'd said, could bring this kind of overwhelming relief.

"Mariah? Did you hear me?"

"Yes," followed by a typically breezy, "I'll see you Thursday, right?"

Uncertain whether to pursue the subject further, Ford ended up saying, "Right. Thursday."

Ford stared down at the recradled phone. Whether she would admit it or not—she probably wouldn't—the phone call, with its familiar undertones, with the tacit implication that each had missed the other, with her intimate question about his past, had subtly altered their relationship. Or, more to the point, it had established that they had one. At that realization, a warmth suffused him, momentarily ameliorating the tiredness of his body.

Mariah, too, stared down at the phone. A mixture of emotions, all inexplicable, all conflicting, poured through her. Then, because she hadn't a clue as to how to deal with them, she plastered on a bubbly smile and joined Eden and Tess in the living room.

"You should see the pond," she enthused. "It's absolutely gorgeous."

GORGEOUS. It was the only word that fit the woman standing in the doorway of the Calloway house. The red sweater-knit dress, its skirt pencil thin, clutched her hips like a worn glove encasing a familiar hand, while long sleeves perched at a jaunty angle in the middle of her forearms. The dress's neck garnered any leftover attention—of which there was little after one's eyes were finished with her hips—by mere virtue of the fact that there appeared to be little of it. At least that was how Ford interpreted the straight fold-over neckline that slipped off both her shoulders. Both her bare shoulders.

"You look—" his eyes made one last sweep of the high-heeled black shoes, the covey of earrings and the sprig of mistletoe in her fashionably ravaged hair "—gorgeous."

Mariah smiled, taking in his brown wool slacks, gold turtleneck sweater and tweed jacket, as honestly expressing her opinion of what she saw. "You don't look too bad yourself, Rev."

Ford lowered his eyes to the scarlet lips that could speak so softly, kiss so softly. "You ready?"

"For whatever you want," she answered with her usual suggestiveness.

His eyes darkened, though he said nothing. Reaching for her coat, he helped her into it and said a proper hello and goodbye to an apron-clad Eden, who'd just appeared out of the kitchen. Neither Mariah nor Ford spoke as they negotiated the sidewalk on their way to his car. They were equally silent, though their eyes brushed, as he opened the door for her and she, folding in her long legs, scooted onto the seat. He closed the door behind her, and she watched as he ducked under the low doorjamb and crawled in beside her. She expected to hear the thrum of the engine. Instead he inserted the key, turned toward her and, with not a single preliminary, took her in his arms. He kissed her— thoroughly, possessively, as though every moment since last they'd kissed was an eternity hellishly lived through. When his mouth left hers, her lips were warm and wet and parted. Surprise still echoed in the depths of her green eyes. Her misty green eyes.

Ford's lips, equally warm and wet, smiled. "You said you were ready for whatever I wanted."

Mariah grinned, making her appear a total vixen. Her voice flowed like heated honey when she said, "I love a man who knows what he wants."

For a moment they just looked at each other, smiles their only form of communication.

Ford's smile slowly faded, and he ran his crooked finger along her jaw.

"I missed you," he said candidly. Even as he spoke, he wondered if Mariah would play coy, if she would tease her way out of making a commitment. He even wondered if he'd been wrong about the phone conversation they'd shared a week before. Maybe he'd only wanted to believe she'd missed him.

"I missed you, too," she said, astonishing herself with the admission. She wasn't certain she'd ever told a man that before. Except for Nick Logan. But then, Nick Logan had always been special.

Ford's eyes delved deeper into hers before simply saying, "Good." He then withdrew his arms from her, started the car and, gearing it up, moved out into the night. For the duration of the journey, he deliberately lightened the mood.

When they pulled into the back lot of the high school, Ford had to search for a parking space. He finally found one, between two vehicles spilling forth giggling youths.

"So much for the chaperones being early," he said with a scowl.

"They're just eager to party."

"Or to pass around the bottle before we get here."

"Why, Ford Dunning, you suspicious little devil. Or is it experience you speak from?"

He grinned. "I plead the Fifth."

"Is that like a fifth of whiskey or the Fifth Amendment?"

Chuckling, he said, "Let's just say that preacher's kids are obligated to try everything."

Mariah, uncertain why she'd done so but unable to stop herself, had asked Eden—with an indifferent subtlety, she'd hoped—to tell her what she knew about Ford. Eden had told her among other things, most of which Mariah already knew, that he was the son of a minister.

"Everything?" Mariah teased.

"Close enough," he teased back, opening the door and flooding the interior with light. He started to get out of the car. "C'mon, let's go to work."

"Hey, Dunning," she called after him. He turned toward her. "I don't know much about chaperoning, but I do know not to show up wearing lipstick. Unless you're a woman."

He said nothing, though he let the door close, thereby closeting them in the dark again, except for the parking lot lights. He reached into the back pocket of his pants. To do so, he had to flex his hips upward. The action ensnared Mariah's attention. It also caused her heart to go pitty-pat.

Wiping the folded handkerchief across his lips, he asked her, "Did I get it all?"

She took the handkerchief from him and drew it across his bottom lip once, twice. Involuntarily her eyes went to his. His, just as involuntarily, went to hers. The car suddenly seemed warm despite the fact that the heater wasn't running.

"I suggest you get out, Miss Calloway," he said thickly, "unless you want to start wiping off red lipstick again."

The cold air worked wonders on two heated bodies.

"Hey, it's the warden!" some tall, strapping jock-type said as Ford and Mariah approached.

"The Gestapo!" someone else cried out, saluting Nazi-style.

"Does this mean the orgy's off?" another guy, his arm slung around his date's neck, called out.

Grins were slathered across teenage faces. Ford's face bore a matching grin as he ushered Mariah forward with a hand at her back. It was obvious Ford personally knew most of the kids, either from church or his sex ed classes at the high school.

"Let's keep the orgy down to a small one, huh?" he said.

A cat call, followed by two more, came from out of nowhere. "Who's Lady Bear?" someone shouted.

Lady Bear was the current slang for any good-looking woman. The phrase had gotten started as a play on the word *bare*. It had originated in the boys' locker room as a centerfold from a girlie magazine was being passed around. Unexpectedly, Ford had walked in on the scene, and two dozen male students had stammered to death on the spot. Ford had forever won over the two dozen students when he'd walked forward, casually unfolded the picture to its full impact, and announced, as though he were just one of the guys, "Great mammary glands." He'd made certain, however, that his next lesson dealt with respect for the opposite sex.

"Come on, men, a little decorum," Ford now said, adding, "And Lady Bear is your chaperone."

"She can chaperone me any time!"

"Yeah, I'm gonna need a lot of watching!"

"Hey, Lady Bear, you got a name?"

"She has a name and, if you animals will settle down, I'll introduce her."

Mariah took all the teasing in the spirit in which it was meant. She even teased back, much to the delight of the kids. When introduced to each, she extended her hand and gave that young man or young woman her full attention. Ford liked that. She was treating them as people, not awkward monsters trapped between youth and adulthood.

"And this is Jeff Simmons," Ford said, nearing the last of the doorway entourage.

"Hi, Jeff," Mariah said, looking into sensitive brown eyes. "Ford's said some nice things about you."

"Yeah?" Jeff said, looking past Mariah to the man behind her. There was more than a tad of hero worship in the young eyes.

Ford grinned. "I lied and said you were an okay kid."

Jeff grinned back.

"Mariah," Ford said, "I'd like you to meet Megan Blake."

Mariah's attention shifted to the brightest of blue eyes. Hair, its color defining auburn, streamed down the girl's back, highlighting perfect ivory skin and a smattering of delightful freckles. Although she was probably no more than fifteen or sixteen, Megan's ecru sweater molded a figure that an older woman might easily have envied. Mariah could immediately understand Jeff Simmons's infatuation. Megan Blake was beautiful, with the face of an angel, the body of a mortal temptress.

"Megan, it's a pleasure," Mariah said.

Megan smiled with an endearing shyness. "I, uh...I love your dress."

"Thanks," Mariah said, noting that Jeff slid his arm around Megan's waist, and that she slid hers around his.

"They like you," Ford said seconds later, dodging red and white crepe paper and clumps of colorful balloons.

The live band picked just that moment to launch into a song made popular by Wham.

"What?"

"They like you!" he shouted near her ear. His breath was warm and stirred her hair in a way she liked. The truth was, she was beginning to like everything about Ford Dunning.

"They're nice kids."

"Yeah. Uh-oh, Lauren Simmons at one o'clock."

Mariah shifted her gaze to the woman bearing down on them like a steamroller. She was probably in her late forties, but the scowl on her face, a perpetual scowl, if the depth of the creases were any indication, made her look older. Even with the frown, though, she was attractive with her short brown hair and dark eyes.

"Evening, Laurel," Ford said.

"Are you going to let them play that loud?" It went without saying that she meant the band.

"I don't think we have a choice. Otherwise we'll have a mutiny on our hands. Besides, it isn't too bad."

"How can you say that? I can't even hear myself think. Why I..." She suddenly noticed the woman standing beside Ford. It was the woman of the uncivilized six earrings.

"Laurel, this is Mariah Calloway. Ben Calloway's youngest daughter. Mariah, this is Laurel Simmons."

Since the Simmonses had lived in Calloway Corners only five years, what Laurel Simmons knew about Mariah Calloway was only hearsay. Her appraisal of Mariah suggested that everything she'd heard was true in spades.

"Mrs. Simmons," Mariah acknowledged.

Her eyes never really getting beyond the six earrings, Laurel muttered something, then muttered something more about having to stand watch over the punch bowl, so no one would spike it.

"She's crazy about my earrings," Mariah said when the woman walked away.

Ford laughed. As though it was the most natural thing in all the world, he reached up, tracing his fingers over a gold stud, then a diamond stud, then the lobe of her ear from which a gold loop dangled. He realized that he'd wanted to do this for a long time—touch the ears so prettily crowded with ornamentation.

Mariah felt his fingers glide over jewelry and flesh. She shivered as his thumb joined in, stroking the back of her earlobe. Hot sensation hit her like a flash fire. Her eyes raised. His lowered, the honey-colored irises bearing evidence that the same sensations were tearing through him. Equally obvious was that neither could understand how so little could do so much so quickly.

"Doesn't it hurt to have all those holes punched?" he asked, his voice deeper, darker. He couldn't pull his hand away. Not if his life depended on it!

"Pierced. Not punched. And, yes, it hurts a little," she answered, her voice of the same thick substance as his. "But then everything in life hurts a little, doesn't it? Being born hurts, dying hurts, loving hurts, being loved hurts, not being loved hurts. Even sex is pleasure-pain, isn't it?''

Ford said nothing; he just studied her . . . and her every word. The psychologist in him was mesmerized by her philosophy, the man in him simply by the warmth of her skin.

"Take, for example, your hand at my ear," she continued. "The pleasure is so acute, I hurt right down to my toes. But if you take your hand away, it's gonna hurt even worse."

It was the craziest conversation Ford could ever remember having. No, not crazy. Profound. Sexy. It was the most profound, the sexiest conversation he'd ever been part of. And they were standing in the middle of a dance floor with a hundred people milling around them. With him doing nothing more than touching her ear. For God's sake, he was only touching her ear! And yet the pain scoring his body was so painful it was taking his breath away.

"Hey, Lady Bear, you wanna dance?"

It took both Mariah and Ford a moment to realize that someone had spoken. At the sight of the burly football player, Ford pulled his hand from Mariah's ear. She'd been right. The pain increased. He felt it. He could see from her eyes that she felt it, too.

"You wanna dance?" the boy asked again.

"I, uh . . . I don't know if a chaperone . . ."

Ford interrupted her. "Go on. If you're not afraid the big klutz will step on you."

Even as Ford watched, he saw Mariah assume another persona. Her hazy eyes brightened. The lips speaking such profound and sensual things grinned impishly. "Why not?" she said, allowing the young man to lead her away. Over her shoulder, she said to Ford, "What's a little pain?"

Complex.

He'd never met anyone as complex as Mariah Calloway. One moment she'd appear to be a space cadet, the next, a sage prophet. One moment she was bawdy, the next naive. One moment, she'd honestly admit to her sexuality in a way he'd never known a woman to do, the next she'd pull deep within herself rather than express her wants and needs.

The only thing with any real consistency was his attraction to her. And the pleasure-pain still roaming his masculine body. Damn! He swore at nothing in particular, at everything in general. He headed his steps toward the refreshments, hoping as he did so that someone had sneaked past Laurel Simmons and laced the punch with something strong. Something good and powerfully strong!

"PROBLEM?" Mariah asked later in the evening when the clock read fifteen minutes to midnight and the new year.

"Could be," Ford responded, his hands tucked inside his pants pockets. "I haven't seen Jeff and Megan for a while."

"And you think they may be taking piggies to market?"

"The thought's crossed my mind."

Ford and Mariah, by silent agreement, had buried the earlier incident. More precisely, both had at least given it a whale of a try. Mariah danced occasionally with some of the students and bantered with them constantly. She laughed and grinned and tried not to remember how Ford's hand at her ear had felt...or how his lips felt pressed to hers. Ford tried not to remember, either, though he was careful to keep his hands to himself—as in, tucked securely in his pockets. His eyes were another thing, however. As she danced, he watched—the sway of her hips, the silver splash of her hair, the gentle motion of her breasts. Was she wearing a brassiere? He assured himself she was, because the thought that she might not be totally devastated him.

"C'mon," he said, "let's check the parking lot." He figured at the very least the cold air might cool down some of his hot thoughts. "You want your coat?"

"No," she said, equally hoping to benefit from the chill.

As they headed out into the night, Mariah involuntarily shivered. Ford slipped off his sports jacket and, careful to touch her sparingly, laid it around her shoulders. She was instantly surrounded by his warmth and the musky smell of his cologne. The coat negated everything the gust of cold air had done.

"What are we looking for?" she asked, ignoring these new sensations. She really didn't know what was wrong with her tonight. She could never remember feeling quite this way. As if she desperately needed something from this man. As if she desperately needed him to touch her... to stroke her... to caress her....

"Hell if I know!" Ford said—roughly, because the wind was scurrying through Mariah's hair with nothing less than a sensual invitation. He jammed his hands back into his pockets. "Steamed windows, I guess."

She let his reply snatch away her disturbing thoughts... as best she could. She tried the diversion of teasing. "The sight and sound of piggies being loaded for market?"

He looked down at her as they trudged through the parking lot. Would she be a verbal lover? Would she moan? Groan? Whimper?

"Look, let's divide up," Ford suggested, desperate to rein in his runaway thoughts. They'd already made one row of cars. "If you see anything, holler. Oh, and I think Jeff drives a blue Chevy."

Mariah was midway of the third row when she saw them. Or, at least, what she assumed was them. All she could really see was a couple in the back seat of a blue car. They were in the kind of embrace she longed for. She stopped, turned, headed back for Ford. When he saw her, she motioned for him to join her.

"I think I found them. Or, at least, I found somebody."

"Blue Chevy?" he asked, falling into step beside her.

"Yeah. I think."

"Damn! Should I ask how far it's gone?"

"They're at least upright."

"I'll take whatever good news I can get."

Mariah laid her hand on his arm. He stopped. "Ford, you can't just go thundering up to the car. You'll embarrass them to death."

"What do you suggest? That I phone ahead?" He was snapping. Why was he snapping? Because he was failing Jeff and Megan. And because he wanted to be doing what they were doing with the woman standing beside him. "Sorry," he said, dragging his hand through his hair.

He looked around. Mariah looked around. Suddenly, she stooped and picked up a sizable rock. "Here, try this."

Ford took the rock and pitched it as close to the car as he could. Instantly, the writhing figures inside drew guiltily apart. Ford started forward, but stopped when Mariah held back.

"I'll, uh . . . I'll wait here."

"No," he said, not even realizing he was taking her hand in his, "come with me."

Still, she balked. "Ford, I don't know what to say or do."

"And you think I do?"

"But—"

He tightened his hand, while his eyes pleaded softly.

In that moment she realized that she would have gone anywhere with him.

Seconds later Ford tapped on the fogged car window. Jeff Simmons, his hands in a flurry trying to rearrange his clothes and his hair, rolled down the car window in movements so jerky Mariah would have laughed had not the situation been what it was. Ford leaned in, unable to make eye contact with either Jeff or Megan because neither would allow it. All Mariah could hear was a lot of deep swallowing and the heavy sound of guilt and embarrassment. And the rustle of clothes.

Ford tried to ease that guilt and embarrassment by speaking calmly, noncondemningly. "Look, I know this is a lot more fun than dancing, but it's also a lot more dangerous. Why don't you both take a deep breath and let's go back in. Okay?" As he spoke, he pulled open the door and rolled the car window back up. He then stepped back, giving the young couple an opportunity to get out of the car. In fact, his no-back-down stance gave them no choice.

Reluctantly, his eyes still downcast, Jeff got out.

The degree of his excitement was clearly delineated against the fabric of his pants. Just as clearly, it was obvious that Jeff Simmons was mortified.

Mariah's and Ford's eyes locked.

Suddenly, her spirit as blithe as they came, Mariah stepped forward. "Why don't you guys go for a walk? I'll stay here and help Megan with her hair. This wind does wicked things to a woman's hair," she added, making it sound as if the wind and not Jeff's fingers was the culprit.

"C'mon, let's go," Ford said, slinging his arm around the young man's shoulders. "We'll meet y'all back inside," he called, his eyes again meeting Mariah's.

Mariah nodded and watched the men walk away. She turned her attention to the girl crawling out of the back seat.

If Jeff was mortified, Megan was ready to die. She hung her head low, her hair falling about her like a tangled curtain of red. A passion-tangled curtain.

"I don't have a comb," Mariah said, "but let's see what we can do, anyway." As she spoke, she threaded her fingers here and there, lifting and shifting. Putting her finger beneath Megan's chin and angling her face upward, she said, "There."

Blue eyes still refused to meet Mariah's. Mariah wasn't sure but she thought the beautiful blue eyes were glassy with tears. Wordlessly, making no big deal out of it, Mariah unfastened the top button of Megan's sweater and refastened it appropriately, a feat hasty hands had not had time for. When Mariah glanced once more into Megan's face, she saw a single tear coursing down her cheek. Mariah wiped it away.

"None of that," she said, smiling. "It'll ruin your makeup."

Megan sniffed.

"Ready?" Mariah said, the two starting off for the building.

Halfway there, Megan spoke. "Miss Calloway?" Mariah inclined her head toward the young girl. "I'm not... I'm not a bad girl. At least, I don't think I am. It's just... it's just that I love him. And it's so hard..."

Megan didn't finish. She didn't have to.

Mariah slipped her arm around Megan's shoulder. "I understand. I'm a woman, too, remember?"

Minutes later, when Mariah saw Ford, she was clearly reminded of just how much of a woman she was. He stood, Jeff at his side, on the outskirts of the dance floor, within the shadows of potted plants. He was standing with his feet spaced apart, his hands in his pockets. The look was pure male. He turned when he heard the women approaching. His eyes met Mariah's.

Within seconds, Megan and Jeff had moved onto the dance floor. Both Ford and Mariah watched as Jeff took Megan in his arms. The older couple's envy was a palpable thing. Ford wondered what it would be like to casually slide his hand onto Mariah's hips the way Jeff was presently sliding his hand onto Megan's. Mariah wondered what it would be like to have Ford intimately touch her breasts the way Jeff had obviously touched Megan's earlier.

"You, uh…you were wonderful out there," Ford said, keeping his hands deep in his pockets and far away from temptation.

"Funny. I thought you were." She was still huddled within the folds of his tweed jacket.

He gave a harsh snort. "Hardly." The snort was followed by a deep sigh. "I'm failing them. If they're not already having intercourse, they will be soon."

"You make it sound as if you're personally responsible."

His eyes found hers. "Aren't I? I'm his sex ed teacher, his preacher, his friend."

"I'd say you're up against some pretty stiff competition, namely, nature. The two of them are in love. Granted it's young love, but it's still love…and when you care for someone—" her voice dwindled to only a whisper "—you want to touch them…and be touched by them."

Ford's eyes darkened to a molasses-brown color.

Around them, people were shouting down the seconds to midnight, which noisily arrived on schedule. Horns blared, confetti rained, kids hollered and whooped. Everyone was kissing—much to Laurel Simmons's shock and dismay. Instead of "Auld Lang Syne," the band launched into Chris DeBurgh's romantic, sensual "Lady in Red."

It was Ford's undoing. Wordlessly, because he couldn't stand the barrenness another moment, he pulled his hands from his pockets . . . and Mariah into his arms.

CHAPTER EIGHT

FORD GROANED as their bodies made contact. Mariah sighed and slid her arms around his neck. Because his jacket was still wrapped around her shoulders, the conventional dance position was out of the question, but then both knew what they were engaging in was far from a conventional dance. It was simply an excuse. An excuse to touch and be touched.

Ford slipped his hands inside the jacket and splayed them at the small of her back. He thought her waist seemed incredibly small; she thought his hands seemed unbelievably large. Both thought they were still too far apart. He drew her closer. She went. Until his hard thighs molded her softer ones. Until their stomachs gently meshed.

Moving his feet slowly, rhythmically, he glanced down into her face. Neither spoke. Each just stared at the other. The male singer's gravelly voice filled the room, proclaiming that the lady in red had never looked lovelier than tonight. Ford knew that there were many nights of Mariah's life when he'd never seen her, yet he could not believe she'd ever looked lovelier than at this moment. Her hair was becomingly tousled, her eyes soft and dreamy, her lips sweetly parted. During the course of the evening, her scarlet lipstick had worn away, leaving her mouth nude and vulnerable.

"Damn, I want to kiss you!" he growled.

"I guess that would be totally unthinkable?"

"Totally."

Though the fronds of potted palms hid them from clear view, though they danced shadow within shadow, they were at the mercy of the crowded room. At the mercy of propriety.

"I guess it would be just as unthinkable if I kissed you?" she asked, her hands caressing the nape of his neck. The hair there eagerly curled around her fingers.

"Just as unthinkable."

"Then what are we gonna do, Rev?"

Their bodies swayed to the erotic beat, thigh brushing against thigh, belly against belly, need against need.

"What they can't see, they can't hang us for." His hands spread across her back, then pressed her closer. Reflexively she arched into him. Though his chest was hard with strength, her breasts, like fragile doves fitting into a nest, snuggled against it.

A burst of heat flared in Mariah's stomach, then drizzled lower into purely feminine reaches.

At the feel of her breasts, pear-shaped and firm, Ford hissed between his teeth. "You're not!" he grated.

"Not what?" When had speaking become so difficult?

"You're not wearing underwear."

"Yes, I am," she whispered. "Red panties."

Ford groaned, deep in a throat that felt raw from breathing hard. His hands, because he couldn't stop them, lowered onto the swell of her hips. His palms cupped the gentle flare.

"You like red, Rev?" she teased, her eyes mating with his.

"I like the feel of you," he answered roughly, hauling her hips up and toward him. His obvious arousal told her just how much he liked the feel of her. He rubbed her back and forth against him. Blatantly. She made a whimpering little sound and bit at her lip.

Ford uttered something that was both prayer and curse, then lowered his mouth to hers for that unthinkable kiss. He did have presence of mind to keep it quick, merely grazing her mouth with his. It only made them both want more. In reaction, like a lazy kitten, she inclined her head. He nipped her neck, then bit at the ear whose touch earlier had so inflamed his senses. This time her mouth sought his. And found it. His tongue darted forward, as if sipping at forbidden cream, before he hastily severed the kiss.

The illicitness of the kisses, the intimacies taking place beneath the sports jacket, only made the moment sweeter. And sexier. And sent sensations quivering through two bodies.

Mariah could never remember feeling as she presently did. Need had never been this great, nor this painful. Never before had her body felt on fire, from the inside out, from the outside in. At the shifting of Ford's hands, the fire blazed higher. When his knuckles caressed the sides of her breasts, the fire zigzagged like lightning through her hollowed tummy.

"Ford?" she whispered, her hands now clinging to his neck out of the need for sheer support.

The desperate calling of his name, the way her body had limply melted into his, sobered him. What were they doing? What was *he* doing?

Pulling his hands from beneath the jacket, he steadied her by digging his fingers into her upper arms. He deliberately distanced their heated bodies. They stared, he at an obviously aroused woman, she at an obviously aroused man. Finally she took a deep, settling breath. It was only then that Ford released her. Both suffered from the loss.

Neither knew quite what to say, quite what to do. At the distended condition of Ford's body, Mariah slid the jacket from her shoulders and handed it to him.

"I think you need this worse than I do," she said, trying to smile.

Ford took the jacket and wrestled his arms into it, thinking that he wasn't sure she didn't need it just as badly. Couldn't everyone see her nipples outlined by the knit of her dress? Or was he just preoccupied with the sensuous sweetness that had only moments before been nestled against him?

"Mariah, I..." He stopped, shoved his fingers through his hair and wished to heaven he wasn't who he was. Or what he was. He tried again, what he had to say going against every masculine instinct nature had bestowed. "Mariah, I can't give you what you want. What we both want." He longed to take her hands in his, but didn't dare. He wasn't strong enough. "I can't preach principles that I'm not willing to abide by myself. Certain things are expected of me. I have to set an example. I have— Ah, hell!" he growled, ramming his fingers back through his hair. He was having a hard time explaining why something was wrong when it had felt so consummately right.

He closed his eyes, conjuring up images of anything that might mellow out his body and mind.

"Does this mean we're not going to take piggies to market?" Mariah asked, an uncertain smile playing at her lips.

Ford opened his eyes. She was so beautiful! And he wanted, needed her so badly! "No," he said hoarsely, "we're not going to take piggies to market."

"Darn, and I was ready to load them up." Again she tried to smile, but it was only halfhearted. Smiling wasn't what she wanted to do. She wanted to make love. With this man.

"Mariah, I'm sorry. I shouldn't have let it go this far. It was my fault." Even as he apologized, Ford didn't really know if it had been his fault. It had seemed a matter over which he'd had no control. But he should have had. He'd always had before.

"Why do you always assume responsibility for everything?" Mariah said.

"Force of habit."

"Well, it's a bad habit."

Ford smiled slightly. "Just one of many."

"Tell me something," Mariah said. "What do ministers do? I mean, single ministers? Under these circumstances?"

Ford's lips quirked into a tease. "Run up a huge water bill without simultaneously running up a huge gas bill."

"The old cold shower, huh?"

"The old cold shower."

"Does it work?"

His teasing ended. "I have a feeling it won't tonight."

Suddenly Mariah, too, grew serious. Her feminine pride needed stroking. Almost as badly as her body. "If you were a doctor, a lawyer—"

"If I were a doctor, a lawyer, or an Indian chief, I'd have you in bed so fast, it'd make both our heads swim."

Mariah smiled, hiding once more behind the flippancy that had served her so well. "Where's an Indian chief when you need one?"

An hour later they drove home in silence. The air sizzled with tension. Ford kept his eyes glued to the road and his hands firmly planted on the wheel. Mariah stared out of the passenger window at the night-shrouded scenery. Both felt washed out from longing, yet curiously their bodies tingled as though each had never been more alive. And no matter how each tried to lose himself in other thoughts, neither had the power to override the feelings ruling two heated bodies.

Not even the radio cooperated, for the throaty voice of E. Z. Ellis, a rock singer renowned for his sexy lyrics, filled the car. And their souls.

"I have a need, baby. You have it, too. Lie here beside me until the night is through. Call my name when we both fall apart. Kiss me, hold me, make love to my heart."

Ford shifted in the car seat, seeking a position of comfort. He found none. Nor did E. Z. Ellis let up on his taunting.

"I have a need, baby. You have it, too. Lie here—"

Ford snapped off the radio. Mariah glanced over at him, he over at her. Neither spoke. Ford, who was a marginal acquaintance of E. Z. Ellis and one of the few people who knew that the singer had a cabin retreat on nearby Lake Bistineau, uncharitably promised to make the superstar pay for his present pain.

It was a pain that only grew worse.

Once the car had stopped in front of the Calloway house, the quiet grew louder, the tension thicker, the pain more . . . painful.

"You don't have to walk me to the door," Mariah said, cutting through the dark with eyes that unerringly found his.

"Of course, I'll—"

"You don't have—"

"I'll walk you to the door!"

But walk was all he did. He kept his hands buried in his pockets, as if there was safety in the fabric depths. Once at the door, Mariah turned. Starlight skipped across her ivory cheeks, while moonlight tunneled through her hair. It was all Ford could do to keep from groaning. It was all Mariah could do to keep from begging him to kiss her.

"Good night," he said hoarsely.

"Good night."

Neither moved.

"Tell me you understand," he said suddenly, fiercely, as though she had the power to destroy him completely.

"I understand." At the pleading look on his face, she laid her palm at his cheek. "I do understand, Ford." She smiled impishly. "You're a man of principle and I'm a woman of honor. We'll probably both be granted saint—" Ford brought her open palm to his mouth, where he delivered a slow kiss "—hood." The word trailed off into the night. It took Mariah's breath with it.

As though it was the last thing he wanted to do, Ford drew her hand from his mouth. Without another word, without the passage of another moment, he released her hand and thundered down the steps and toward the car. He was almost there when Mariah called out.

"Ford?"

He turned.

"Don't use all the cold water in town, huh?"

Twenty minutes later, Ford, his hands spread against the tiles, his head thrown back, stood naked beneath a spray of cold water. The pulsating shower struck him at the base of his throat, sending streams tunneling through the dark hair matting his chest and the lighter hair scoring his legs.

He sighed. If he had all the cold water in town and then some, he doubted it would relieve the ache consuming him. Irritated, aggravated, and definitely aroused, he shut off the shower, nearly breaking the faucet in the process, and stepped from the stall. He haphazardly dried off, turned out the trailer lights, then threw himself into bed. A cold bed. A cold bed that could have been warm if Mariah . . .

He groaned, jabbed the pillow and felt the ache move closer to unbearable. At 2:00 a.m., Mariah still on his mind, he swore. At 2:10, he contemplated another cold shower, but decided against it on the grounds that the last one had done little good. At 2:20, he swore more vehemently. At 2:30, quickly and clinically, he did what was necessary to end the ache. But it didn't ease the longing, which only seemed intensified by the lonely exercise he'd had to resort to.

At 3:00 a.m., he faced facts. He wasn't going to sleep, partly because he still physically ached for Mariah and wholly because he still longed for her.

BY 3:00 A.M., MARIAH had tossed and turned until her own bed looked like a war zone. She'd tried reading, warm milk and the cold shower she hadn't truly intended to take. Nothing helped. She still felt empty, achy, as if her blood flowed too near the surface of her skin. She was ready to climb a wall. Any wall. The Great Wall of China. It was one of the few places she hadn't been. She'd have to go there next. And soon. And also to Shanghai and Singapore and Sydney, Australia.

It was with a great deal of surprise, even discomposure, that she realized none of the above places had the appeal of Ford Dunning's arms. At that moment, at three in the slow morning of a long night, the only place she wanted to go was to Shangri-La.

HE WAS AVOIDING HER.

That she suspected by midweek, that she knew for certain by the end of the week. He didn't call. Not once. Her only communication was a brief note stating that the senior members of the church were meeting that Friday night to organize socially and to discuss alternatives to bingo. Could she be there around seven?

At ten minutes before the hour, dressed in a short, tight denim skirt and miles of booted leg, Mariah arrived. She had butterflies somersaulting in her stomach, from the possibility of seeing Ford or from the possibility of making a fool out of herself in front of strangers, she wasn't sure. The butterflies didn't seem to care about the reason. They just cared about somersaulting.

Entering by the side door, she instantly heard distant voices coming from the small recreational room at the far end of the hall. She started toward it. The butterflies became more agile. She passed by an ajar door marked Pastor's Study. The room was empty. The desk, like Ford's desk at home, was piled high. Across an open book lay his glasses. Mariah smiled, thinking back to the night they'd graded test papers. She remembered teasing him about his glasses, she remembered him kissing her, she remembered the New Year's Eve dance—his lips, his hands, his . . . She remembered. Everything. And too much.

She proceeded down the hall.

"Whatever y'all decide, just let me kn—" As if by telepathy, Ford glanced up. Brown eyes met green. Two hearts skipped an identical beat. Two half smiles, which in combination made a beautiful whole, followed. "Here she is now. So eager to be part of this group that she's early."

Mariah hesitated at the doorway, the butterflies in her stomach gone wild. His eyes looked like heated honey on a summer day.

Ford extended his hand. Mariah stepped forward and took it. He squeezed hers reassuringly. "Everyone, this is Mariah Calloway."

"Sure. Ben's and Grace's youngest," someone called out.

"Thought you were in Tahiti," another said.

"Oh, no, she's been home for weeks now."

"Isn't she just as pretty as can be? Looks just like her mamma."

Some of the dozen or more faces Mariah recognized, although it had been a long while since she'd seen them. All of the faces, even those she didn't know, were smiling.

"Hi," Mariah said awkwardly despite her usually extroverted disposition.

"If y'all need me, I'll be in the study," Ford said, releasing her hand. She suddenly felt adrift and looked back at him. He smiled, as if to say she could do it. "Oh, one more thing," he said, his tone grown serious. "I'm going to announce it this Sunday, but I wanted to share it with you first. I guess I'm hoping that the collective wisdom in this room will somehow come up with a solution."

He had everyone's attention. Even Mariah's. Whatever the topic, it was one he didn't take lightly. She could see the grim lines in his face; she could almost feel the coiled muscles in his shoulders.

"We're going to have to send the choir robes back."

"We're what?"

"Oh, no!"

"But I thought—"

"What happened, Ford?" J. C. Hardcastle asked.

"The donor ran into some financial bad luck. No one regrets what's happened more than he does."

"There's no way the church can absorb the cost?"

Ford shook his head. "Unfortunately not. We're still paying on stained-glass windows."

"How much are we talking about?" Ruth Doege asked.

Ford grinned wryly. "Choir robes aren't cheap. We're talking almost seven hundred dollars worth. We're talking minor miracle."

Someone whistled, which in and of itself was a miracle since most of the room's occupants wore dentures.

"Precisely," Ford said. "Look, you're not to get upset about it. Since y'all have known God longer than most, I thought you might like to toss up a prayer or two and see what falls down."

Everyone murmured in the affirmative.

"Well," Ford said again, this time looking at Mariah, "I'll be in my study."

When Ford exited the room, he paused in the hallway. She was nervous. Maybe he shouldn't have thrust this assignment on her.

"Look, I've never done this before. If y'all could just give me some idea of what you want?" Mariah asked.

"We want to do something besides play bingo," pert Ruth Doege, her woolen beret perched jauntily on her head, said. "Not that there's anything wrong with playing bingo. That's what we intend to do when we get old."

Everyone laughed. Even Mariah.

"What would you like to do, then?"

"Have some organized activity once a month. Something to look forward to," someone said.

"Like square dancing."

"Or clogging."

"You can't clog, James Shaffer."

"Well, I can sure as shootin' learn how!"

"Well, I tell you what I want to do," J. C. Hardcastle said.

"What?" Mariah asked.

"I want to go out to that race track when it's in season. I want to gamble a bit."

"Shame on you, J.C.," someone said. "When do we leave?"

Everyone laughed again.

Mariah relaxed. "Does anyone have a van?"

"J.C. does."

"Good," Mariah said, "What else do you want to do?"

"I want to travel. Maybe go up to the Passion Play in Eureka Springs, Arkansas."

Mariah nodded. "Where else?"

"Maybe Dallas to shop. And to hear the Symphony. Or to see one of those touring plays."

"Vicksburg to see the antebellum homes."

"Hey, Mariah, you know anything about traveling?"

"A little," she said, launching into how Eureka Springs was at its prettiest in the Fall when all the leaves were burnt orange and sunshine yellow.

Out in the hall Ford smiled—bittersweetly. Did Mariah know anything about traveling? He headed his tired steps back toward his study, keenly aware that the ache, the need, the longing was back. Soon, though, he wouldn't have to worry about her presence inciting them. Soon, like the wind, she'd travel on.

An hour and a half later, however, she traveled to his study. For long moments she stood watching him. Ford, unaware of her presence, was putting figures into a calculator, figures that obviously wouldn't come out the way he wanted them to. He had just dragged his fingers through his hair in total vexation when he saw her. His hand stopped.

"Is whatever it is that bad?" she asked.

He smiled. "Just trying to conjure up seven hundred dollars."

"Ten to one you're blaming yourself because you can't pull it out of thin air."

His smile broadened. "You're beginning to know me too well."

They both let the implications of that sink in. Neither pursued the subject.

"I'm sorry about the robes."

"Me, too," Ford said. "The congregation was excited about them." Nodding toward the rec room, he asked, "How did it go?"

"I had fun." Mariah was clearly surprised.

He smiled. "You're a natural people person."

She shrugged.

Neither seemed inclined to say more. Both just stared, Mariah at the way his hair tumbled onto his forehead, making him appear almost boyish. Almost. Ford stared at her flawless skin, her wide eyes, the trio of earrings that were beginning to seem natural.

"You're avoiding me," she said abruptly, and with her usual candor.

"Yes," he answered honestly. "I can control being with you. What I can't control is what happens to me when I'm with you." What he didn't say was that some elemental part of him was trying to save himself. He couldn't afford an emotional investment in a woman who was certain to exit his life at some point.

"Is what happens to you when you're with me so bad?"

"Not if I could do something about it."

"Can't we just be friends, then?"

Ford's eyes roamed over her—her face, the swell of her breasts, the flare of her hips. "What do you think?"

That it was the stupidest thing she'd ever suggested, because her body had grown warm solely from his look. The two of them would just be friends when Hell had harps. Mariah desperately wanted to say something witty, something that would ease the loneliness she was feeling. She could think of nothing, however. So she moved toward the door, intent on going.

"Mariah?"

She turned.

"If it's any consolation, I've missed you."

She said nothing. She just let his admission act as a salve to her bleeding feelings. She started on out into the hallway. There, she paused.

"You lied, Rev. Cold showers don't help at all."

THE IDEA CAME to Mariah that night as she, her mind crowded with thoughts of Ford, lay wide awake once more. The following morning, bright and early, she called J. C. Hardcastle.

"What do you think?" she asked when she'd outlined her plan for raising seven hundred dollars.

"I think the Lord works in mysterious ways. What time you want to kick this off?"

"Eight-thirty tonight. The church parking lot."

"We'll be there."

At precisely eight-thirty, Mariah turned Eden's car into the darkened parking lot of the church. As her lights went off, another set conspiratorially flashed on. A van crept from the shadows and stealthily eased forward. As it neared Mariah the door opened, and she, as though eaten up by the mammoth creature, stepped up on to the front seat. Glancing back down the length of the van, she peered into the eager, bright-eyed faces of the church's senior members.

"Okay, here's the plan..."

The dive that Duke Boyd had reluctantly recommended as having an on-going crap game in its furthermost back room was located on the Bossier Strip, a bawdy boulevard that had once spelled sin and iniquity. Through the years the city's vigilant vice squad, in conjunction with concerned citizens, had cleaned it up. As in most cities, however, one could still find a good time and plenty of booze. One could even find a little gambling action if one knew where to look.

Mariah glanced around as white-haired, white-browed J.C. negotiated the van into the crowded parking lot. A neon sign, missing every other letter, said they'd arrived at Bernie's Hideaway.

"Stay together," Mariah cautioned, "and let me do the talking."

As they neared the establishment's paint-peeling door, glossy, enticing pictures of female dancers jumped out at them.

"Those of you wearing pacemakers might want to adjust them accordingly," Mariah added.

When she opened the door, music, hard and harsh and with a seductive beat, practically blasted her back out. She saw several in her group reach to turn down their hearing aids. She wished she had one to turn down, too. Signaling for them to follow her, she bravely walked inside.

The room, chock-full of smoke, smelled as if it was in the middle of a three-alarm fire. The two women on stage, wearing short shorts and shirts tied just below their well-endowed breasts, could well have been the reason for the fire.

"Oh my!" someone in the group said as all the women's body parts moved in synchronization to the music.

"I'd forgotten everything could be so firm," Ruth said in awe.

"James Shaffer," his wife called, "wipe that spittle from your mouth!"

"You, too, J.C.," Ruth said, adding, "You know you shouldn't be looking with your heart problems."

"Oh my!" the first person said again.

A big, tough-looking ape of a man approached them. His expression said he'd just as soon bounce them as look at them. Perhaps even rather.

Mariah threw her head back, her hair blazing like heated silver behind her, and stared him straight in the eye. "Bernie's expecting us."

The ape looked doubtful, though he whispered something to the second ape in command. Within minutes the group was ushered into the seedy back room and the presence of a seedier Bernie. Bernie, wearing a tacky flowered shirt and the scent of yesterday's underwear, was a man who liked the color of money. Anyone's. Even money belonging to senior citizens. Senior citizens led by a class-looking dame.

"You Mariah?"

"Yeah," she said in her best moll voice.

"Ready to do it?"

"We're not here to dance."

One of the group who'd turned down his hearing aid asked in a whisper that scurried through the room, "Dance? I thought we were gonna play craps."

A friend shushed him.

It took exactly three rolls of the dice for tacky-shirted Bernie to realize that the classy-looking dame knew her way around gambling. Two more rolls and his ulcer began to gnaw at his stomach.

Mariah, pursing her moist, carnal-red lips in a way that every man standing around noticed, blew on the dice cupped in her red-nailed hands. "C'mon, baby needs a new choir robe." She tossed them, letting them fly onto the green felt table. A cheer went up from the church group, and Jim Shaffer tapped his cane in glee.

Bernie's ulcer took another bite.

An hour later, Ruth held seven hundred dollars in her age-spotted hands. J.C. stood protectively at her side, while Jim Shaffer, now brandishing his cane to remind everyone he had it and could wield it as a weapon if the need arose, stood to the other side of her.

Bernie, his stomach burning, waited to hear Mariah's pleasure.

"Let it roll," she said.

A collective gasp followed.

"But Mariah, we've got the money," Ruth said.

"It wasn't seven hundred even. There was sales tax, too. Besides, we need our initial investment back." Each member of the group had donated ten dollars—most of it from fixed social security checks. "One more time, baby," Mariah cooed, caressed the dice, then threw them upon the table.

A cheer went up. Mariah smiled. And held out her hand for the additional money. Just as it was being passed to her, the head Neanderthal burst into the room and spoke excitedly into Bernie's ear. Bernie blanched the color of the flowers in his tacky shirt.

"Raid? Hell, get this cleaned up!"

People started running like rats deserting a sinking ship.

The man with the low-turned hearing aid asked as he fidgeted with it, "What's going on? Where's everyone going?"

"Oh, dear," Ruth said, "do you think we'll have to go to jail?"

"Jail?" the man with the hearing aid asked. "We're going to jail?"

"No one's going to jail," Mariah said, hustling her little group toward the door. "Just take it easy. Watch out for each other. That's it, take each other's hands."

"I'm not playing bingo in the slammer," someone said.

"I want my lawyer," another said.

"You don't have a lawyer," someone pointed out.

They followed the route they'd taken earlier. Since drinking and watching women dance wasn't illegal, the gambling customers had spilled out into the main room. Threading through the crowd was like swimming in pea soup.

"Excuse us," Mariah called out. "Could you excuse us?" No one seemed to hear them above the roar of the music. Finally Jim Shaffer bopped someone on the head with his cane. The man turned quickly, angrily, but all he saw was Mariah's sultry, smiling face. "Excuse us, honey," she purred.

The man, rubbing his head and trying to figure out if he'd been hit or not, stepped back and allowed the entourage, chained together by their hands, to shuffle past him.

Once outside, Mariah cried, "Make a run for it!"

"Hey, I just found a cure for arthritis!" Jim Shaffer called, skimming along with his cane to anchor him. "Who would have thought getting raided would cure arthritis?"

"Hurry, hurry!" Mariah said, helping each to scramble aboard the van. Martha Shaffer's bad hip brought them to a halt until her husband picked her up in his arms.

"Ah, how romantic," Martha sighed.

Once all had boarded, Ruth hugged the money tightly as J.C. started the motor. At the precise moment he did, a cop car, its red light bubbling on top, pounced on the parking lot.

"Hit it, J.C.!" Mariah shouted.

J.C. floored the pedal, shimmying the back of the van before gaining control and scooting out into traffic. A cheer, along with victoriously raised fists, went up. Mariah was in the process of breathing a sigh of relief when she noticed the 300ZX that turned in behind the police. If possible, the driver of the sports car seemed in a bigger hurry than the vice squad.

Mariah whipped her head around and wailed, "Oh, no, it's Ford!"

Evidently he'd recognized the fleeing van and its familiar occupants just as Mariah had seen him. Squealing the car into a U-turn that A. J. Foyt would have envied, the sports car headed back out into traffic...right on the bumper of J.C.'s van.

J.C. summed up the situation best with, "Our behinds are in a sling now."

"What in thunder are y'all doing?" Ford demanded fifteen minutes later as he bore down on the disembarking van passengers. He stood with his feet apart, fire dancing from his eyes. He had exited the sports car so quickly that he'd left the motor running and the lights glaring. He'd also left the door open. A Bible lay on the seat, along with glasses folded into a case. There was also a newly purchased, already opened, roll of Tums antacid pills.

"What did he say?" the man asked, still trying to adjust his hearing aid.

"He said, 'What in thunder are we doing?'" a friend shouted into his ear.

The man nodded, then said, "What in thunder *are* we doing?"

"Well?" Ford said, his eyes fixed on Mariah. She'd taken the money, now cached in a support hose, from Ruth, as if so doing would place the responsibility squarely on her.

"Actually, we've already done it. We got the seven hundred dollars for the robes." Suddenly, she frowned. "How did you know we were there?"

"That's not important."

"How?"

"Duke Boyd. He was worried sick about you. As he should have been. Good grief, Mariah, don't you realize what kind of place Bernie's Hideaway is?"

"You have to go where the action is, Rev," she replied, her temper flaring as well. It was beginning to feel like a rough Saturday night. "You rarely find crap games in church rec halls! And how do you know what kind of place Bernie's Hideaway is?"

"They got dancing women, preacher," one of the men said. "With these skimpy little shorts on."

"And shirts tied just below their—"

"Shh!"

"Shh!"

"Did you call the cops on us?" Mariah asked.

"No, of course not! Duke got wind of the raid and called me."

"The preacher called the cops on us?" the man still adjusting the hearing aid asked in bewilderment.

"No, he didn't. Duke Boyd."

"Duke Boyd called them? Well, that low-life—"

"I didn't call the cops, Duke didn't call the cops, I don't know why they chose tonight to raid, but, dammit, that isn't the point!"

"That's right. The shirts are tied just below their pointed—"

Someone elbowed him. He gave a little grunt.

Ford threw up his hands and just stared at the Apple Dumpling Gang that looked as if it had run amok. No, it looked as though it had run amariah.

"Look, it was all my idea," Mariah said.

"Don't you go blaming this sweet thing," J.C. said. "We all knew what we were doing. And frankly I had the time of my life," he added, looking over at Mariah and winking. Mariah winked back.

Ford put his hands on his hips and sighed. "Y'all go on home. We'll discuss this tomorrow."

One by one, after hugs and pats had been delivered to Mariah, the elderly church members once more boarded the van. Mariah watched as it pulled away and into the night.

Her eyes came back to Ford's. She had the feeling his had never left her.

"You know, of course, that I can't take the money."

Mariah's eyes darkened. "Why not?"

"Why not? It's ill-gotten gains."

"Ill-gotten gains?"

"As in, won illegally."

Mariah marched over to his open car, grabbed the Bible and, waving it, shouted, "Show me!"

"Show you what?" His voice was rising as well.

"Show me where it says, 'Thou shall not buy choir robes with ill-gotten gains!'"

"You know damned well... That's not the point!"

"Let me tell you what the point is, preacher," she said, punctuating the air with a brazenly red nail. "A group of elderly people donated money they really couldn't spare with the possibility of losing every dime of it. Just so the church could have choir robes! That's the point!" She threw both the Bible and the support hose filled with money into his car. "There it is. You do whatever your holier-than-thou conscience dictates!"

Spinning around, she stomped off toward her car. She'd taken only a few steps when Ford grabbed her by the shoulder and whirled her around. Their fire-glazed eyes battled, while both were breathing hard and fast. Suddenly he jerked her toward him with a deep growl. She tumbled into his arms.

"Don't you realize how scared I was?" he groaned. "I could imagine all sorts of sordid things happening to you in that place. I could imagine...I could imagine..."

Inclining his head, he crushed her mouth with his. The kiss held no passion. It was simply punitive and placating. It punished her for the hell she'd put him through; it assured him that she was all right. But even as he sought to punish her, he gentled the kiss. Threading his fingers through her hair, he held her face within the brackets of his thumbs. Harshness became tenderness, anger a silky sweetness.

"You scared me!" he whispered, his mouth taking hers one more time before burying her face in his chest and cradling the back of her head with his hand. "What am I going to do with you, Mariah Calloway?"

Both knew what he'd like to do with her. Both equally knew it was out of the question.

That Sunday morning the choir wore its new robes, the Apple Dumpling Gang wore smiles, Mariah wore a look of supreme satisfaction, and Ford...Ford just hoped that God had a sense of humor.

CHAPTER NINE

FRIDAY AFTERNOON of the following week, Nick Logan, dressed in leather and aviator sunglasses, rode into town astride his Harley Hog. His arrival brought a smile to Mariah's lips—the first in days.

"Nicky!" she shouted, throwing wide the screen door, racing down the sidewalk and hurling herself at him. She'd only moments before gotten in from the mill. In fact she still held the note from Eden she'd found tacked to the refrigerator.

Nick barely had time to position the motorcycle's kickstand before Mariah tumbled into his arms. Whisking her off the ground, he whirled her around, planting a kiss firmly on the end of her nose as he settled her back to earth.

"How's life treatin' you, kid?" he asked, whipping off his dark glasses.

"Okay. Will you look at that tan!" she cried, cuffing his arm playfully. "Where've you been?"

"Cozumel."

"Scuba diving?"

"What else?"

"You turkey!" she said, wanderlust coursing through her veins.

He laughed. "You do look pale."

"Thanks," she said, cuffing him again, then falling into his arms for another fierce hug. They started up the sidewalk arm in arm.

"How long can you stay?"

"I'm leaving with the sun in the morning."

"Where you headed?"

"California."

"Can't you stay longer?"

"Gotta see the sunrise from the beach Wednesday morning."

Gypsy that she was, Mariah understood clearly why it was necessary to see the sunrise on a California beach Wednesday morning. Because she did understand, she didn't beg him to stay. That emotional latitude was the reason their friendship had lasted so long. And had been so strong. Neither pushed the other; neither demanded things that were undeliverable; neither pried into the other's life. If there were unshared secrets between them, and there were—Mariah knew nothing of Nick's family, not even if he had one, while he knew nothing about the father's love she'd always coveted—the acceptance of each other at face value bonded them more securely than all the shared secrets in the world might have.

"Then let's make the most of what time we have," Mariah said, tightening her hold on his waist. "Eden's gonna be sick she missed you," she added. "I've told her all about you."

"I take it that means she's not here?"

Mariah waved the note still in her hand. "You just missed her. She's staying the night with the Griffen twins. Their mother's in the hospital. She just had another set of twins."

At the mention of *twins*, Mariah thought she saw a cloud drift across Nick's affable eyes, but then, she rea-

soned, it was surely nothing more than a trick of the late-
afternoon lighting. A supposition validated by Nick's
laughter.

"You told her so much about me, she slipped out the
back door."

"Only you slip outta back doors."

"I do not. Going out a window is much faster."

Mariah giggled and squeezed him. "I'm glad to see you,
Nicholas Logan."

"I'm glad to see you, too, Mariah Calloway."

They spent the next three hours talking and laughing and
do-you-remembering. As the sun was setting and the moon
preening to wakefulness, they got on the Harley Hog and
rode. The air was chilled to a briskness that robbed Mariah of her breath. Her hair, which she recklessly refused
to shield beneath the legally required helmet, flew outward in chaotic disarray. The ride was exciting and exhilarating and all she thought about was Ford. Why hadn't
he called her? She'd expected him to. No, she hadn't expected him to. Something had happened in the parking lot
that Saturday night. His body had trembled, not out of
anger, but out of fear—fear for her safety. It was the first
time a man had ever cared that deeply for her well-being.
She liked the feeling, even as it frightened her. She feared
it because one could grow so accustomed to his protectiveness. As for Ford, the moment had shaken him as well.
She had intuitively sensed it.

"Hey, you all right?"

Mariah scrambled her thoughts back into a semblance
of order and laid her cheek against Nick's wide back.
"Couldn't be better," she lied, tucking her chin from the
wind's cold, frost-grizzled fingers.

They bought a hot, cheesy pizza, which Mariah snuggled close to on the return trip to the house. Still laugh-

ing, they got in just shy of nine o'clock. Mariah kept the pizza warm in the oven while Nick showered off the dust of a day's journey. It was taken for granted that he'd spend the night—they'd even shared hotel rooms on more than one occasion. If it had even crossed Mariah's mind that his staying, particularly with Eden out of the house, smacked of impropriety, it would have been the single factor that decided her in favor of insisting that he stay. She loved nothing better than causing a few waves in the sea of life, especially if the water sloshed upon staid and prim personalities.

"I feel almost human again," Nick said ten minutes later as he plopped down in front of the crackling fire Mariah had built in the hearth. His hair was damp, his feet bare. The shirt he wore was untucked from his jeans and only semibuttoned. The slit of fabric revealed a dark forest of hair.

"Here," Mariah said, handing him a gooey piece of pizza.

Abstractedly she noted Nick's appearance. Unable to stop herself, she made a comparison. Nick's hair was almost the exact color of Ford's, yet it was only Ford's that invited her to run her fingers through it. And while both pairs of eyes were brown, only the lighter shade of Ford's made her heart skip a beat. Their chests were equally wide, yet it was Ford's alone that spoke a sensual message to her. She wondered if he had hair matting his chest the way Nick did. And what would it feel like beneath her hands? Against her lips?

"Umm," Nick said in deep appreciation of the taste spreading throughout his mouth.

At the sound, Mariah corralled her runaway thoughts, but not before suspecting that the same "Umm" would apply to Ford's chest.

As the last of the meal was being consumed, Nick said, "Come to California with me."

Mariah's tongue halted in its sweep of her pizza-crumbed mouth. Her initial reaction was that she couldn't up and leave the following morning for California. The mill needed her. And so did Eden. On second thought, however, the mill was running without her before she returned home for her father's funeral. And as for Eden . . . well, Eden had been surprised she'd stayed to begin with. She certainly must be surprised she'd stayed this long. So why couldn't she go to California in the morning? An image of Ford flashed in her mind.

Ford.

But even with him, she thought, it made sense to go. They were headed in a direction that neither knew quite how to handle. And the bottom line was he was scaring her by making her feel emotions she'd never felt before, emotions she didn't want to feel now. So why not do them both a favor and just leave?

"Think about it," Nick said, sensing her indecision. He'd never before associated indecision with Mariah. Usually at the word *go*, she was packed and out the door. This new turn of events caused him to take a good hard look at his friend. "You're different," he proclaimed at last.

Mariah glanced up. "What do you mean?"

"I'm not sure. There's just something different about you."

"I'm wearing my hair exactly the same—"

"No, it's not physical."

She laughed, a bit nervously. "My emotional and spiritual natures have changed?"

Nick considered. "Yeah."

"Doo-doo, doo-doo, doo-doo, doo-doo. Welcome to the *Twilight Zone*. You have before you a young woman who looks the same, but her emotional and spiritual natures have changed. Was the lunar pull of the moon responsible, or was it the pepperoni on the Domino's pizza?"

Nick grinned. "You're crazy."

"Proves my point. I was crazy yesterday, I'm crazy today, I'm gonna be crazy tomorrow. Nothing's different."

Nick said nothing more, though Mariah could tell she hadn't dissuaded him. Which concerned her and left her with an unsettling question. Was she different?

Fortunately the subject had to be shelved. The unexpected ringing of the doorbell saw to that. Frowning, Mariah rose from the floor.

"You expecting anyone?" Nick asked.

"Un-uh," she said, her feet, sans the scruffy Mickey Mouse slippers, crossing the room and out into the hallway.

With a naive lack of caution, she pulled open the door. A man, tall and broad-shouldered, his hands buried in his pockets, stood in the smoky shadows, his features all but obscured in the moon's dim glow. Only his eyes, which seemed painfully haunted, were visible.

"Ford," she whispered, her heart bounding with a new and faster rhythm.

He didn't smile. Neither did he speak. He just seemed intent on absorbing the sight of her. She, likewise, soaked in his presence.

Finally he said, "I, uh . . . I was in the neighborhood."

A smile danced in one corner of Mariah's mouth. How easily this man inspired smiles! All he had to do was show up on her doorstep—looking like a million bucks waiting to be spent. "No one's ever just in my neighborhood."

Ford's lips quirked as well. "So I lied." Mariah stepped back; Ford stepped in. "I heard that Emily Griffen was in the hospital and that Eden was staying with the twins. I thought you might could use some com . . . pany."

The word faded into a whispered death as Ford's eyes connected with those of the man rising out of the cozy scene scattered before the fireplace. The man's hair was damp, his shirt was partially unbuttoned, his feet bare. Ford had the unChristianlike urge to punch him in the nose and ask questions later. Inexplicably, however, there was one question he didn't have to ask. He knew who the man was. He was . . .

"Nick Logan," Mariah verbalized the name in Ford's mind, "this is Ford Dunning. Ford, this is Nick Logan."

A quick smile spread across Nick's tanned face. He stepped forward, swiping a hand down his jeans. "Sorry about the cheese. We've just been doing severe damage to a pizza." He took Ford's hand in a forceful, friendly grip. "Ford, nice to meet you."

Ah, hell! Ford thought, *the guy is gonna be nice. I won't even be able to work up a decent dislike for him.*

"Nick," Ford acknowledged, turning his attention back to Mariah. "I, uh . . . I should have called."

"It's all right."

"Hey, man, come on in," Nick said. "We were just sitting here catching up on old times."

And doing what else? Ford wanted to ask, but didn't. *How could any man be with Mariah and not want to have his hands all over her?* He looked at her. Her face was flushed, her hair disheveled, her lips lacking their usual red. But couldn't the fire have rouged her cheeks? Wasn't her hair always disheveled, as though a man's hands had recently played through its silken strands? And couldn't she have eaten off her lipstick? Then again, maybe Nick

Logan had kissed off her lipstick. Then again, maybe he should just punch him out! Ford jammed his hands into his pockets.

"It was Nick's car I drove in the Grand Prix," Mariah explained, trying to tag her friend. She was totally unaware it wasn't necessary.

"Right," Ford said, and something in the way he said it—not rudely, but with an unnatural crispness—snared Mariah's attention. Was it possible... No, Ford Dunning would never stoop to jealousy. It was too ignoble an emotion.

"Ford has a 300ZX," she said, wishing, though, that he were jealous. Just a little bit. She liked the way Ford's being jealous of Nick felt.

"Great little cars," Nick said.

"When did you get into town?" Ford asked.

By an unspoken decision, the three moved into the living room. Nick began picking up soda cans, soiled napkins and the ravaged remains of the pizza—homey things that more than a mere acquaintance would do.

"This afternoon."

"He's been scuba diving in Cozumel."

"Any good reefs there?" Ford asked, attempting to be civilized, though heaven alone knew the effort it was taking.

"Yeah, great scuba-diving area. You dive?"

"Yeah," Ford answered.

"You never told me that," Mariah said, genuinely surprised, delightfully pleased.

Ford glanced over at her. "You never asked." She looked so beautiful in nothing more than jeans and an oversize sweatshirt! And the toenails peeking beneath the jeans had been painted red. He had a desperate urge to show her just how erotic toes could be. "Pardon?" he asked, realizing Nick had spoken.

"Have you dived any in the Caribbean?"

"No. Only in the US. Lake Ouachita in Arkansas and in Florida."

Mariah indicated for them to be seated. Nick sprawled back on the floor before the fire. Ford took the sofa. Mariah, coiling her feet beneath her, took the other end of the sofa. "What?" she asked, dragging her eyes from Ford's and back to Nick.

"I told him we met scuba diving. In Aruba." He turned his attention back to Ford. "We didn't know each other and had been partnered together. This little idiot used up all her air, then came begging me for mine. We had those older vests without backup mouthpieces, so we took turns with mine until we could reach the surface. We've been partnering together ever since."

"My hero," Mariah said, giggling. "Actually, Ford rescued me too, didn't you, Rev? Oh, did I tell you he was a preacher, Nick? And a psychologist."

"Well, I'm certain you two didn't meet in church."

Mariah feigned offense. "I've been good, haven't I, Ford?"

Ford was still reeling from Mariah being sixty to a hundred feet below the surface of the sea and carelessly allowing her air to run out.

"Well, relatively good," she amended. "Anyway, I was skunk drunk and Ford came charging in and rescued me."

"*You* drinking?"

"A girl has to be naughty occasionally," she replied, avoiding how her father's death had driven her to imbibe. "Doesn't she, Ford?"

"When, uh . . . when are you leaving?" he asked Nick. The question, though nicely put, was also bluntly put. It also came out of thin air and in no way answered Mariah's question. It was her tip-off that Ford was, indeed, jealous of Nick Logan. Elation filled her heart.

Nick Logan, having finally figured out how the wind was blowing, hid a smile. "Bright and early tomorrow. I'm headed for California."

"He's asked me to go with him," Mariah said, suddenly feeling a reckless need to push the issue.

Ford whipped his head around.

"What do you think I ought to do?"

Jump start his heart, put breath back in his lungs, anything to save a dying man. Instead he said, and in a voice he hoped was even, "I think you ought to do whatever you want to do."

The air was so thick that a knife could have done no more than chip at it. Mariah wasn't certain what she wanted him to do. Forbid her to go? Ford, on the other hand, used all of his willpower to keep from doing that very thing.

"Will you look at the time?" Nick said, shattering the silence. He faked a yawn and stifled a smile. "I hate to do this, but I've gotta turn in. I'm dead on my feet."

Ford and Mariah looked as if they were surprised to find someone else in the room . . . the world. Mariah started to scramble from the sofa.

"I'll get you a blanket."

At the mention of the word *blanket*, Ford had visions of Mariah's bed. The sheets were rumpled from lovemaking, a pillow indented from Nick's head. Would she crawl back in beside him later? Would they make love again? And was he going to be able to hold onto his sanity if he didn't let go of these crazy-making thoughts?

"Stay put," Nick said, having already risen and crossed to her.

Before Ford could do more than suck in a dry breath, Nick had tilted Mariah's chin and was lowering his head to hers. Ford was already asking God's forgiveness for ramming his fist into Nick Logan's handsome, tanned face when Nick's lips grazed the tip of Mariah's nose. Air flooded back into Ford's lungs.

Nick glanced over at Ford and grinned. "You're a class act, Dunning. Under the circumstances, I'd probably have decked you ten minutes ago."

Before Ford could do anything more than scowl, and Mariah smile, Nick Logan was marching out of the room and up the stairs.

"What does that mean?" Ford barked, his eyes raking Mariah.

"That it's obvious what you think," she said calmly. He was jealous. Ford was pea green with jealousy. Although the realization might tempt a woman to enjoy it to its fullest, the truth was she couldn't enjoy it, or anything, at Ford's expense. She wondered what that said about the depth of her feelings for him.

"Which is?"

"That Nick and I are lovers. That he's giving me what I want."

The world stood perfectly still.

"Is he?" The question was hoarsely, fearfully asked.

But boldly answered. "No. Nick and I have never been lovers. Just the best of friends. And even if we had been, he couldn't give me what I want now."

"And what do you want?" Ford held his breath, barely daring to hope.

"You, preacher man. I want you." The last three words were a guileless whisper. A whisper that echoed through the corridors of Ford's suddenly swollen heart.

Had he burned in Hell for it, there was nothing he could have done to stop himself from reaching for her. Mariah went willingly, wondering why his touch always felt so soft, so satisfying, so right.

Sighs and moans mingled as his mouth moved over hers. His hand speared beneath her hair, curved around the nape of her neck, and he exerted the pressure necessary to keep her lips aligned with his. Her hands worked their way up the front of his sweater, feeling his beaded nipples beneath the wool and the fabric of a shirt. Ford groaned and pressed her back into the sofa. He followed her down, his body blatantly pinning hers.

"Don't punish me by staying away," she breathed from her mouth to his.

He raised his head. His eyes were the color of molten honey. "Is that what you think I'm doing?"

"That's what it feels like," she answered honestly.

"No, no," he said, brushing his thumb across her bottom lip, "I don't mean to punish you. It's just that you make me crazy when I'm with you. Then again, I'm crazy when I'm not with you. Hell, you just make me crazy!"

"I won't make you crazy. I won't seduce you. I won't arouse y—"

Before she could even get this last word out, Ford urged his hips into her pelvis. He was fully aroused. It was a heady, exhilarating feeling to feel him full and strong against her. Typically Mariah, she also giggled at the promise she'd so soon broken. "I promise not to do it again."

His lips tweaked. "Liar."

"No, I promise. I do. I'll stay at arm's length. I won't say or do anything seductive. I'll wear a nun's habit. I'll...I'll...I'll die if you don't kiss me again."

Ford moaned as he pressed his mouth on hers. This kiss was slow, grindingly slow, and absolutely, positively carnal. Though he knew his body would pay, and supremely, he pulled out all the stops. The tip of his tongue flicked the corners of her mouth, moistening them with his warmth, before piercing her lips. She took him inside her mouth, caressing his tongue with hers. He went deeper, then deeper, coiling velvet flesh to velvet flesh. His fingertips, wantonly feverish, combed the column of her neck, memorizing the softness of her skin, the rapid beating of her heart and at her throat. Her fingers curled in the thick folds of his sable hair.

Finally, sensing a point of no return, he wrenched his mouth from hers. His eyes closed; he laid his forehead against hers. She closed her eyes, too. Their breathing laced together.

"You can tell Nick Logan he was wrong. While he was right about my not decking him, he was dead wrong about my being classy. I wasn't gonna bother decking him if his lips had touched yours. I was gonna go straight for the jugular."

Ford felt Mariah's smile curve along his chin. "I thought preachers were supposed to be nonviolent."

"I'm a psychologist, too, and we preach venting our feelings."

Her smile turned to laughter. It sounded like wind rippling across fertile fields of flowers. It sounded like wind gently blowing away years of his loneliness.

Ford raised his head and swallowed back the deep emotion tightening his throat. "Are you leaving with him?"

Mariah's eyes darkened from emerald to richest jade. "Tell me not to."

The woman behind the door. He was glimpsing the honest, vulnerable woman behind the door. Albeit it was only a crack, but she herself had opened the door to him. Intuitively, he knew that few, if any, had ever been so graced.

"Don't go," he ordered, his whispered voice the consistency of the roughest sandpaper. "Please."

Mariah let the words, the fire in his eyes, warm her. She had spent a lifetime being reckless and daring, but she had the feeling that what she'd just asked him to do was the most reckless and daring thing she'd ever done. For it set her on a journey she'd never traveled. A journey of self-exposure. A journey of dependence. A journey there might well be no returning from. Slowly, damning caution, she raised her lips to his. Once more she embraced recklessness. Once more she worshipped at the feet of danger.

"No," she whispered, "I won't leave."

THE NEXT MORNING, Nick left with the first light of dawn. As Mariah knew he would, he didn't awaken her. Saying goodbye was something they never did. It was another unspoken rule of their unique relationship. She knew, however, that soon she'd receive a funny card from the West Coast and that eventually their lives would cycle back until they were once more together—again with no questions asked, no goodbyes said.

Mariah, deliberately trying not to think about what had happened the night before—the part about promising she wouldn't leave—sat nursing a hot, honey-sweetened cup of tea when Eden, weary-eyed, arrived back home from baby-sitting the Griffen twins.

"I love children," she groused as she plopped into the chair beside Mariah and propped her elbows on the table, lowering her head to her hands, "but those two are certifiable monsters. I shudder to think that another set of Griffen twins will soon be unleashed upon the world."

Mariah wasn't misled for a moment. "You loved every second of their misadventures." After sipping her tea, she added, "You miss baby-sitting, don't you?"

Eden nodded. "But I've got to tend to the mill right now." This comment elicited a sigh. "I've gone over the books until I'm blue in the face, and I'm hanged if I can decide if we're doing great or lousy."

"Great, I'm sure. Daddy would have allowed no less." Actually what she'd meant, but didn't say, was that she was certain the mill was in the black with all the time Ben Calloway had devoted to it—to the exclusion of his family. This last hurtful thought she pushed aside with, "You should have one of your own."

Eden frowned. "My own business?"

"No, a child."

"I don't know whether you've noticed or not, but it takes two to tango."

"What about Dan Morgan?" Mariah, as indeed everyone in Calloway Corners, knew that the owner of the general store had had his eye on Eden ever since his wife had passed away several years before.

"I know he cares for me, but I also know he's looking for a mother for his children."

"Does his kiss make your heart do back flips?"

"What?"

"Does his kiss . . . forget it, it obviously doesn't. You marry a man only when his kiss makes your heart do back flips."

"I'll bear that in mind," Eden said with an indulgent smile.

"Speaking of a man who can make a woman's heart do back flips, you missed him."

"Him who?"

"Nick."

"Nick Logan?"

"Mmm," she murmured around a swallow of tea.

"Nick Logan was here?"

"Right here. Arrived yesterday. Left this morning."

"I'm sorry I missed him," Eden said quite genuinely. Suddenly she frowned. "You know, I think this happened once before. I mean, my just missing him."

"Hmm, I think you're right. You two seem destined to keep passing like ships in the night. Oh, by the way, he slept in your bed."

"Oh, dear, you did think to change the sheets, didn't you?"

"I did, I did."

"And you did pick up my gown—"

"I did, although that cotton sack you call a gown couldn't inflame a man who'd been in prison for years."

"That wasn't what I meant," Eden protested. "I just wanted the room picked up and tidy."

Something in the quick way Eden got out of the chair and went to the cabinet, where she started measuring out coffee, told Mariah that maybe her sister was wondering what it would feel like to have her gown run through the fingers of a drifter—a drifter who made women's hearts do back flips.

"You ought to get out more—" Mariah began, only to be cut off.

"Why did he leave so soon?" Eden asked.

"Wanderlust."

The coffee now set to perking, Eden turned. "Why didn't you go with him?"

It was a normal question, given Mariah's disposition. What wasn't normal was the way she suddenly lowered her eyes, as if truths were there that she didn't want revealed. "No special reason . . ."

"Mariah?" Eden said, easing to her sister's side.

Mariah glanced up. Nervously. "Ford asked me not to." She didn't explore the greater complexity of how she'd asked him to ask her not to.

"What's going on between you two?" Eden asked softly.

"I...I don't honestly know." Mariah rose, as if she could no longer sit still, and just moved to stand in front of the sink, her back to Eden, doing nothing. "I swear I don't know," she said in a small, confused voice.

"Does his kiss make your heart do back flips?"

For long moments Mariah said nothing, then turning, but not looking at her sister, she said, "I've got to go get dressed."

"Mariah—"

"I don't know," she said in answer to Eden's question. As she raked her fingers through her hair, she repeated, "I don't know."

It was a lie, though, and Mariah knew it. Ford's kiss *did* make her heart do back flips. In fact, even the merest thought of it did.

ALMOST TWO WEEKS later, on the last day of January, Mariah celebrated her twenty-sixth birthday. Ford gave her a pair of earrings, a twist of gold love knots. As he'd fitted them into her ears—she'd insisted that he be the one to put them on her—he'd noticed the brightness in her eyes. It was a brightness that worried him, for though her eyes shone with their usual impishness, their usual sensuality, they also glowed with something he couldn't explain. Something unnatural.

From the moment she opened the front door to him, Mariah had seemed wired with an energy that popped and hissed like the exposed filaments of an electrical cord.

She'd giggled and burbled her way through cake and ice cream. Then, as though she couldn't be still another second, she'd insisted they take a walk down to the pond. Ford thought Eden, who'd undoubtedly had to deal with this kinetic Mariah all day, had encouraged the trek. Ford had visions of Eden sighing in relief as they exited the kitchen door.

For a week the South had been in the clutches of freezing temperatures. Mid-week, snow had begun to fall. It had stopped only that morning, leaving its precious presence upon the earth like diamond dust. The afternoon sun glinting off the quiet landscape only enhanced this sparkling jewellike image. Ford now watched as Mariah, bundled in a fur coat and boots, stooped, fashioned a snowball and threw it at him. It went splat against his chest.

He feigned anger. "You're asking for it, Lady Bear." The name the guys had called her at the dance had stuck, and even Ford occasionally used it, probably because the image of her bare was never far from his mind.

"And are you going to give it to me?" she asked, her voice both bubbly and sultry.

"Maybe," he threatened, quickly bending and spraying her with a splash of snow.

The icy lace fell over her, flecks clinging to her dark coat and her pale hair. She cried out, giggled, then darted beneath the snow-laden limbs of a pine like a sylvan nymph. She disappeared from view, though Ford could hear her trampling toward the pond. He let her go.

From the night she'd asked him to tell her not to leave, their relationship had taken a new turn. One he could not fully describe. They spoke via phone each day now, and saw each other as time permitted, each accepting, if not liking, that they were destined to be sexually frustrated at meeting's end. He'd never taken so many cold showers in his life, and yet, he was helpless not to see her. Just as he sensed she was helpless not to see him. This, however, she would never admit to. Which was the reason he couldn't describe their relationship—he couldn't describe Mariah. She was fey, yet profound, young, yet old, and not only did she hear a different drummer, he suspected she heard whole bands which no one else could tune in on. Just when he thought he had emotionally caught her, she'd flee from his embrace, leaving him with nothing but a whisper of where the wind had been.

Just the way she had now fled from his sight.

"Are you always this excited on your birthday?" he called out, the question skipping through the snowy woods in search of Mariah.

She answered with nothing, though he knew she must have heard him. Okay, so he wasn't broaching the subject as cleverly as he'd hoped.

He found her in a clearing, the frozen pond behind her. She was just standing at its edge—staring. The way she seemed to stare at everything in life, with her eyes, but not with her mind.

At the sound of his soft tread she asked without turning around, "Do you think God gives you some special something in heaven if you die young?"

He picked up a twig and tossed it as far as he could out onto the glassy surface of the pond. The hollow sound told him what he knew already: that the pond wasn't frozen solid.

"I don't know," he answered.

Mariah glanced back over her shoulder. "Well, why don't you? You're a minister."

"Being a minister doesn't give you all the answers."

She accepted what he said as one of those things in life she had to, rather than as one of those things in life she wanted to. She turned back to the pond. "My mother died young. At thirty-two. That's young."

"Yes, it is."

"She, uh . . . she never even saw me." Mariah laughed. Not mirthfully. "For that matter, neither did my father." She, too, bent and picked up a twig. She started to throw it, then dropped it back to the ground. "My father despised my birthdays. He'd always give me this obligatory little gift, which I'm sure Martha or Eden picked out, then go to his room and get drunk."

"Martha?" Ford asked, curious at the name he'd never heard before.

"She was the housekeeper we had for a while. She lived in the apartment over the garage."

"Did you care for her?"

"I barely remember her. She left when I was seven or eight."

"Did you care for her?" Ford repeated.

"I don't know. I guess I did."

"You guess?"

Mariah shrugged. "No one can ever be your mother but your mother."

"Did you despise your birthdays?"

Mariah looked back at him. "What is this? Analysis time?"

"You brought it up." His eyes wouldn't release hers. "Did you? Despise your birthdays?"

Mariah severed their gaze. She stared back out at the pond. "Of course not," she lied. "What was there to despise? I got cake and ice cream and the gift Martha or Eden picked out."

The woods grew quiet. So quiet that the landing of a grayish-brown sparrow on a fallen limb seemed audible.

"Your mother's death, your father's grief wasn't your fault," Ford said softly, laying a hand on her shoulder.

She turned. "Wasn't it?"

Her eyes were still bright. In fact, Ford thought them brighter than ever. "No."

Suddenly the bright eyes seemed to explode with a fevered merriment, blistering him with their shards of heated green. "It doesn't matter. That was eons ago, millenniums ago, light-years and star-years away." She whirled, like an excited child, then stepped out onto the frozen pond. "Do you believe there's life on other planets?"

"Mariah, the pond's not frozen solid."

"Ah, c'mon, Rev," she said, beckoning to him as she walked out even farther, "you've gotta live dangerously to live at all."

"Mariah—"

"'Do not go gentle into that good night...'"

"With all due respect to Dylan Thomas, will you get your butt back over here?"

"You know Dylan Thomas?"

"Not personally. Now get back—"

"You know what I think? I think Dylan Thomas was a prophet. Maybe from the Pleiades...maybe from..."

The ice beneath her feet cracked.

"Mariah!"

"Antares..."

The ice cracked again, the sound ringing harshly.

"Dammit, Mariah!"

"Or maybe from Atlantis."

The ice split, Mariah cried out—both happened as Ford's arm snaked around her waist. Dragging her, he barely made it back to solid ground before the ice ripped wide open behind them. Angry, he crushed her against him even as he crushed the breath from her.

"What in hell are you trying to do? Kill yourself?"

Mariah's eyes gleamed with a macabre enjoyment, a frenzy born of both fear and elation. Suddenly, she kissed him hard and hurtfully, then tore free from his arms. With a laugh, she started back toward the house.

Ford watched her, his brow knitted in thought. He had felt the shivering desperation in her...and the fear. Like a victorious warrior, she had returned unscathed, but with the battle still coursing through her veins. Her blood still sang, her ears still rang, for she had just faced the mightiest opponent of all. She had just jousted, and quite deliberately, with death itself.

CHAPTER TEN

"MEGAN'S PREGNANT."

Ford glanced up sharply from the note he was writing himself. He'd been in the middle of preparing that Sunday's sermon when Jeff and Megan had shown up unannounced at his church office after Wednesday night Bible Study, asking if they could have a moment of his time. He'd suspected something was troubling them—it was written all over their young faces—but he hadn't been expecting this. His heart sank, though he tried not to show it.

"How far along?" Ford asked, laying the pencil down in mid-jot. He posed the question to Jeff since Megan, huddled in Jeff's jacket, seemed intent on studying every swirl of the grain in the hardwood floor.

Jeff Simmons squirmed in his chair as he looked at his watch. "About...about twenty-six hours."

Ford frowned. "I don't underst—" Suddenly he did, and he was torn between wanting to pull his hair out and laugh at their naïveté. "I see. You and Megan had intercourse last night."

Jeff lowered his guilty eyes, then, after a deep swallow, forced them back to Ford. Knowing what the gesture cost the young man, Ford couldn't help but admire him. "Yes, sir," he answered, quickly adding, "We didn't mean to. I mean, we hadn't planned to. It just...it just happened. We were kissing, then before we knew it, we were . . . It was all my fault."

"It was not!" Megan cried, looking up for the first time. "I wanted to, too. He didn't force me, he didn't talk me into it, he didn't . . . I wanted to, too." Her freckled face shone the same shade of red as her hair. Embarrassed though she was, she met Ford's eyes directly in defense of her lover. Ford remembered Mariah's comment about the couple being in love. He agreed.

"Let's don't even talk about fault," Ford said. "This kind of thing is no one's fault. Not when two people care about each other. When you care about someone, you want to touch them . . . and be touched by them. That's natural. That's the way God intended it."

Ford wondered what Mariah would say if she knew he'd borrowed her words. He also wondered what it would be like to know Mariah as intimately as Jeff now knew Megan. He dismissed the thought because it was inappropriate under the circumstances. It would also drive him crazy if he dwelled on it.

"God also intended for sex to work best within the framework of marriage, within the framework of commitment, within the framework of adulthood, for the reason that it does lead to children."

"We were going to get married, anyway," Jeff said. "We'll just do it now instead of later. I'll quit school and get a job—"

"No one's quitting school," Ford interjected. He knew that Jeff and Megan were juniors, that both were A students with promising futures. He had no intention of letting either quit school even if Megan were pregnant a dozen times over. Which he seriously doubted. "What makes you think Megan's pregnant?"

This time Jeff's cheeks colored. "I didn't...we didn't...use anything. We hadn't planned—"

"That's still no reason to believe—"

"She was ovulating."

As always, it struck Ford as incongruously ironic that the modern teenager knew nothing at times, yet at others could toss out the most technical of terms.

"It was her fertile time. I figured her cycle. Afterward," he added sheepishly.

Ford fought telling him that the rhythm method of birth control worked best if it were calculated before copulation. Instead, he turned to Megan. "When was your last period?"

Her face flamed as she told him.

In a matter of seconds, Ford had referred to the calendar and had arrived at the conclusion that Jeff's A in mathematics was well earned. "It's still no reason to go out and buy diapers," Ford said. "A woman's cycle isn't always predictable. You know that. We've discussed in class that that's why the rhythm cycle doesn't always work. Besides, fertilization doesn't always occur even when everything indicates it should. Sometimes couples try for years and still can't conceive."

Hope gleamed in Jeff's eyes. "Then you think she might not be?"

"I think there's a good chance she isn't," he said, standing and walking around the edge of the desk. "There is, of course, the chance she is, too. What you did last night makes babies. It's that simple. But let's wait and see what happens before we get excited. Okay?"

Relieved, both Jeff and Megan nodded.

Ford crouched down before them and, silently praying that God would lead him, he searched for the right thing to say. "You're playing with fire, kids." Even as he used the word *kids*, he knew in many ways the word no longer applied. "And fire, no matter how careful you are with it, can get away from you. I know it isn't easy to ignore the feelings you have, I know a lot of couples you know are having sex, but I'm asking you both to take a good look at what you're getting into."

Both young people kept their eyes downcast.

"It's not just yourselves you have to think about. It's your families, the child you could bring into this world. Sexual activity demands responsibility. I know you've heard this a thousand times, but it's true. You've got to act responsibly. You've got to abstain or take precautions. And even protected sex can get away from you. You've heard 'There's no such thing as a free lunch?' Well, lunches aren't the only things that aren't free."

Ford knew he was saying all the things he had to, yet he wondered just how realistic it was to tell these two not to express their feelings for each other again. Especially since they now knew how enjoyable that expression could be. If he'd experienced the sweetness of Mariah, could he turn his back on it? No. Unequivocally. Not even if he were going to be stoned to death.

"Should we tell our parents?" Jeff asked.

Ford focused his wandering attention. "What do you want to do?"

Jeff thought. "Mom would hit the ceiling."

That was possibly the understatement of the year, Ford thought. Blast the ceiling off the rafters was far more likely.

"The truth is," Jeff added, "I could live with Mom's flack. I just don't want her thinking badly of Megan. You know, that she's easy or something."

Ford was touched by Jeff's caring maturity. "Then, why don't you wait and see what happens. It could be that no one ever need know about this."

As the three of them rose in unison, Ford from the balls of his feet, Megan and Jeff from their respective chairs, Ford could tell that the idea of no one ever knowing was more than appealing to the couple.

"Let me know what happens," Ford said, walking them to the door.

Megan murmured a goodbye as she stepped out into the deserted hallway.

"I'll, uh . . . I'll be there in a minute," Jeff said to Megan, squeezing her hand for a moment.

"I'll wait in the car," she said, a small smile on her lips. Her eyes grazed Ford's and then she was gone, her ponytail and her hips swinging, the latter counterbalancing the innocence of the former.

When it was just man to man, Jeff was suddenly at a loss for words. He, too, seemed inordinately intrigued by the floor, just as his hands seemed determined to dig the bottoms from his jeans pockets.

"I, uh . . ." He glanced up, down, up. "I know you're disappointed in me." He spoke in a tone suggesting that Ford's respect was a thing of paramount importance to him.

"Whatever gave you that crazy idea?"

Jeff Simmons shrugged. "You'd just have to be...after last night and all."

"Would you be disappointed to learn I was human?"

"No, but—"

"Then, why should I be disappointed to learn you are?" A poignant silence followed. "Look, Jeff, we all make wrong choices. We all do things we wish we could take back, do over." He smiled. "Sometimes we even get lucky and make the right choices. The point is, we're all, adults and kids alike, struggling to do the best we can."

"But you wouldn't have let last night happen," Jeff insisted.

Ford thought of silver-white hair the texture of purest satin, of lips softer than the first red rose of spring. So far he'd been able to resist their temptation, the kind of temptation that entrapped you like quicksand and made you love every sinking moment. How much longer he could resist he had no idea. His body was growing tired of ethics, of morality. It just wanted some good ole basic satisfaction.

"I'm only human, Jeff. Don't make the mistake of thinking I'm something more." Finally, after one second became another, Ford spoke again. "If you love her, you owe it to her to protect her. Whether that's abstinence or birth control, I can't decide for you. I know what I want you to do—I want you two to wait because I think you're too young yet to handle this kind of responsibility—but ultimately it's your decision. Simply because it's *your* feelings."

Jeff gave a half smile. "Life ain't easy, is it?"

Ford grinned. "No, life ain't easy."

Jeff looked for all the world as if he could use a hug, though Ford knew that he, or any sixteen-year-old boy, would die before admitting it.

Instead, Ford tightened his hand on Jeff's shoulder. "Go. Get out of here. Your lady's waiting on you."

Jeff went. Midway down the hall, he turned, his tennis shoes squeaking loudly. "Thanks."

"Anytime. You know that."

"You, uh... you won't say anything?"

"What do you think?"

Jeff grinned. Like a boy, like a man. "G'night."

FORD KEPT HIS PROMISE. Later that night, stretched out on the bed as he talked to Mariah on the telephone, he didn't mention Jeff's and Megan's visit, though, strangely, he longed to. It would be nice, for a change, to share his burden, his concerns, with someone. Mariah, he realized with something of a start, would be his choice. He didn't analyze this realization—partly because he was too tired, partly because he didn't know if he wanted to face what he might find.

"Did you have a bad day?"

Ford hadn't even noticed until Mariah's soft voice came out of nowhere that a silence had fallen between them. It had been a comfortable, no-need-to-speak kind of silence, though.

"Yeah." His answer was weighed down with weariness.

Mariah heard his fatigue and wished she could massage the tension from his neck and shoulders, tension she knew she'd find bunched there. "Be still," she said, her voice little more than a whisper.

"What?"

"Be still. I'm rubbing your shoulders."

Ford closed his eyes and groaned. Even the thought of her hands kneading out the knots was therapeutic.

"Feel good?"

"Mmm. Lower."

"There?"

"Mmm."

"You're not," she said.

He was growing accustomed to her erratic conversational habits—or, at least, somewhat accustomed. "I'm not what?"

"You're not to blame for whatever happened today. Whatever it was."

"How do you know?" he asked, wondering if he were reaching any of the kids he taught, wondering if he were making even one iota of difference, wondering how you continued to live with the frustrating feeling of always climbing uphill.

"Because you're a good minister, a good counselor, a good teacher, a good man."

"You're just prejudiced because you have the hots for me. Could you rub lower?"

Mariah laughed. Ford could imagine the lights jumping in her green eyes. A week before, as he'd pulled her from the cracking ice, those same eyes had sparkled with fear and excitement. He hadn't spoken to her about it. The truth was he didn't know what to say. How did you tell someone that you thought she was so afraid of dying that she did everything she could to bring death about?

"You, kind sir, have the hots for me. Is that low enough?"

"No, lower. And, yes, I've got the hots for you."

"I didn't know ministers were allowed to have the hots. And if I go much lower, Rev, more than your name is gonna be revved up."

"Go lower and I'll prove to you that ministers have the hots."

The sexy repartee crackled, sizzled over the phone lines, singeing both Ford and Mariah.

"I want to hold you!" he groaned, rolling restlessly to his side.

Mariah's voice was throaty, reedy, silken like a siren's. "Then, why don't you just pull me down under you...pin me beneath you... and do all kinds of wicked things to me?"

Neither spoke for endless seconds as each envisioned, felt, the sensual scene as the imaginary woman massaging his shoulders was slowly drawn from his back to the flat of hers. His body would slide along curves and softness until he covered her completely, male to female, need to need.

At the powerful image, Ford's heart exploded like a canon, while a certain other part of his body longed for the same privileged expression. Mariah felt heat in places deep and secret.

"I think we'd better change the subject," Ford growled.

"And just when it was getting good," Mariah teased, though, she, too, was glad to leave the topic behind.

"Want to go to Florida the first weekend in March?"

It was now Mariah who groaned. "Why do I have the feeling you're desperate for my help again, instead of just being desperate for my body?"

"I'm desperate for your help in addition to being desperate for your body."

"Let me guess. You're taking a group of kids to Florida and you need another chaperone."

"Actually the kids will be chaperoning us." She could hear him shifting in the bed and wondered what it would be like to lie beside him. Beneath him. "I promised about twenty kids from school and church—these kids have maintained A averages all year—that we'd go to Florida in March. They want to do some snorkeling, some swimming and probably some heavy petting when I'm not looking. Which is the point...I need another pair of eyes. Other than Laurel Simmons's."

"Oh, no," Mariah moaned.

"What could I say? She volunteered."

"Well, she is good at sniffing out lust."

Ford chuckled. "Wanna go?" Before she could answer, he added, "Let me sweeten the pot. You and I could go scuba diving. There's a sunken ship there that's a great dive."

"Could we make it a night dive?" Mariah asked, a smile on her lips. "I've never made a night dive."

"Don't tell me there's actually something you haven't done?"

Mariah's smile broadened. "Two things. I haven't made a night dive, and I've never had my toes sucked."

"Well, why don't we see what we can do about one of them?" Ford asked huskily, deliberately leaving the choice in midair.

Mariah giggled. "When you put it that way, how can I refuse a trip to Florida? Besides, I'll get to ogle you in a swimsuit."

"Men are supposed to ogle women."

"We've been liberated. We now have equal job opportunities and the right to ogle men. Oh, by the way, do you?"

Another Mariah segue.

"Do I what? Ogle women?"

"No, silly. Keep up with this conversation. Do you have hair on your chest?"

"Does it matter?"

"No. I just don't know whether to fantasize you with the rippling muscles of Sylvester Stallone or the hair-matted chest of Tom Selleck."

"Do you fantasize about me?"

"I just said I did."

"Are the fantasies any good?"

"No, they're all bad. *Very* bad."

Ford laughed, a bit of Mariah's mischievousness slinking into his voice. "I don't think I'll tell you. About the hair. Or the lack thereof. I think I'll just leave you to wonder for the next two weeks."

Mariah grinned impishly. "Then, you leave me no choice but to retaliate. At this very moment, I'm wearing red lace underwear."

Ford groaned. She had lobbed a perfect shot. It was a shot that seemed an appropriate ending to the steamy conversation.

HE HAD HAIR on his chest. Tons of it. So dark and crisply curling that it literally took Mariah's breath away. Just, and for an entirely different set of reasons, as did the scar on his left shoulder, a scar that ran like a jagged bolt of lightning from his collarbone to she knew not where because it disappeared into the thicket of hair. She didn't have to ask where or how he'd gotten the scar. She just knew.

She knew, too, as she studied Ford from the striped towel spread on the white sand of the Florida beach, that he was the sexiest man she'd ever met. His body, lean and hard, was pure sensuality, as was his every movement. She watched as he, up to his waist in sky-blue water, instructed a group of kids who seemed more interested in just splashing each other. He was teaching snorkeling techniques. The afternoon sun glinted through his damp sable hair, leaving threads of black gold here and there before dappling its radiance about his bare shoulders. As always she was moved by his strength, his sureness, yet underlining both was the appealing gentleness she'd come to expect. He would be a memorable lover, the kind a woman couldn't easily walk away from. Which scared her a little bit because, more and more, especially after the single red rose had arrived on Valentine's day, she realized that she didn't want to walk away from Ford Dunning. Ultimately she'd have to, though, because she couldn't stand still in life. She couldn't stay put. She couldn't commit to anything but moving on.

But for right now, for this afternoon in the Florida sun, she'd think only of a hard, lean body, only of gentle amber eyes, only of a sexy chest with tons of sexy hair.

The lean, hard body, the gentle amber eyes, the sexy chest sloshed through the water and, grabbing up a towel which he ran through his hair, Ford started up the beach toward her. He didn't stop until he stood directly above her, his feet planted slightly apart. He had carelessly draped the towel over his right shoulder, leaving rivulets of water to run heedlessly through the hair on his chest.

Mariah, her body oiled in sunscreen lotion, propped herself on her elbows and with a lazy, catlike grace dragged her enormous sunshades down the bridge of her nose. Emerald-green eyes peered over the rims in blatant admiration. Without the slightest apology, she ran her gaze over his hair-dusted legs, up his moist swimsuit that knew just where to cling, up his broad, broad—from this angle it was so broad!—chest and, finally, to his eyes. Eyes that were just as candidly studying her.

What he saw was no less riveting. The simple, severe-cut white bathing suit, which she'd bought the day before, only hours after arriving in Florida, plunged at the top and on the thighs, so that her breasts were noticeable swells of ivory, while her legs seemed to go to the far side of forever. The swimsuit had unquestionably taken a year off a shocked Laurel Simmons's life. Ford suspected it had taken the same year off his, though the reason had nothing to do with shock. Now, he followed the lines of the one-piece suit back to Mariah's face, which was sexily dewed with perspiration. Her hair, frizzed from the water and the wind, was wild, while her lips and her toes appeared to have been dipped in the reddest of cherries.

He stretched his hand down to her and said roughly, "Help me get something out of the van."

They had borrowed J. C. Hardcastle's van, along with the van of another church member. Ford and Mariah, plus Megan and Jeff, had driven down in the 300ZX. They were now set up at a motel complex that opened onto the beach.

Wordlessly she took his hand. He yanked, drawing her up to stand before him. Their eyes met again, then, again wordlessly, they started off for the van, which was parked nearby. Mariah noted that he didn't let go of her hand, even though Laurel Simmons, her neck cricked to the side, was clearly watching them from beneath the shade of an oversize umbrella.

Beneath Mariah's feet, the warm, grainy sand turned to hot concrete, while around her the full sun gave way to the faint shadow of the van. Leading her to its far side and out of view, Ford, without preamble, pulled her into his arms. He nestled her to his wet chest even as his lips captured hers. She moaned and slid her arms around his neck. The kiss was deep and spicy, and Mariah thought she was drowning without the benefit of water. It had been a week since they'd seen each other, a week Ford had spent in Cleveland at a psychology conference, a week Mariah had spent hating psychology conferences. Ever since he'd picked her up, their kisses had been stolen. Just as they were now stealing bits and bites of this forbidden fruit. Tilting her head back, he lightly ground her lips with his, parting her mouth in an intimate, wet way. Sighing, surrendering, she tightened her arms around him. Seconds later, when thought had to be given to breathing, their lips broke contact. Foreheads nuzzled against each other.

"What do you have to get out of the van?" she whispered accusingly.

He grinned naughtily. "I lied."

"I thought lying was a sin."

"It is. But it's a bigger sin to let such lovely lips go un-kissed. Especially since I missed them so damned much. Ah, Lady Bear," he groaned, "I missed you!"

His next kiss was as light and simple as misty drops of spring rain. Mariah felt drenched in its tenderness. Beneath her fingers, which she'd placed upon his bare chest, ran the scar she'd earlier noticed. Instinctively, naturally, her lips still fastened to his, she traced its raised surface with the pad of her finger. The scar slanted across his tanned flesh, then flowed into the dark, curling hair, hair that moistly, teasingly tugged at her finger. The healed serration sliced across his coin-shaped breast, stopping only millimeters from the nipple. Her fingernail, however, brushed the pointed knot.

Ford sucked in his breath. Mariah, acting only on instinct, used the moment to draw her mouth from his. She began planting tiny kisses along the white line of the scar. When her mouth touched the nipple as her fingernail had, Ford thrust his fingers through her hair.

"Sweet heaven," he whispered, dragging her mouth back to his. His tongue had just speared forward when he heard a scratchy noise. His head jerked upward. Stunned by the sudden loss of his lips, Mariah's eyes flew open.

"I...I'm sorry," Jeff stammered. "We were just...I didn't know...we can come back." With that, he rounded the hood of the van, towing an equally startled Megan behind him.

"Jeff?" Ford called.

Jeff Simmons, as red as a beet, halted.

"It's all right," Ford assured the teenager in a voice that Mariah envied. It sounded husky, but strong. Had she had to speak that moment, nothing but air would have seeped out. "We were just...we were just kissing," Ford admit-

ted with a grin, nonchalantly wiping the lipstick from his
mouth with the towel that still dangled over his shoulder.
Mariah tried to edge away from him, but he kept her securely within the crook of his arm. He leaned back against
the van, crossing one leg over the other at the ankle, as if
it was every day he got interrupted in the middle of kissing a woman.

"I, uh . . . I just wanted to talk to you," Jeff said. "But
we can come back."

"No, go ahead," Ford said.

Jeff hesitated, looking from Ford to Mariah, then back
to Ford.

Sensing that the young man wanted some privacy, Mariah said, "I think I'll go soak up some more rays." It was
said so tactfully that Jeff would never have suspected that
sunning took a poor second to what she'd really like to be
doing. This time when she pulled away from Ford, he let
her go. But it was with obvious reluctance.

"We leave at nine for the night dive," he called after her.
She nodded in acknowledgment.

Megan fell into step beside her, glad for an excuse to
leave. "I think I'll sunbathe, too."

"Great!" Mariah said, adding, "Do you have trouble
tanning with your fair skin?"

"Yeah, sort of, but I use this stuff called . . ."

The two men watched them go. Their eyes then met.

"Megan got her period," Jeff said, cutting to the chase.

Ford smiled. "I'm glad."

"We've talked about it . . . about sex, I mean . . . and,
uh . . . we've decided we're too young for that kind of responsibility."

"I think you're acting very maturely, very wisely," Ford
said, allowing himself the luxury of believing for just a

moment that maybe he could make a difference, that maybe he had in at least one instance.

"I want to do what's best for Megan," Jeff said. "Even if I don't know how I'm going to. I mean, it's going to be rough...you know, not touching her. But I have to do what's best for her. I love her."

"I know you do. And I know it's going to be tough," Ford said, sliding his arm around Jeff's neck in a gesture of age-old camaraderie. They started off toward the beach. Neither spoke.

Ford thought, though. He thought that the kid beside him was now more man than kid. And that he'd just learned one of life's painful lessons. Sometimes you had to sacrifice yourself for those you loved. He, too, one day soon, would have to sacrifice himself. He'd have to let go of Mariah, simply because she, like the wind, could not be held. He frowned, asking himself a question he'd never allowed himself to ask before.

Would the sacrifice be made in the name of love?

BOTH THE NIGHT and the sea were black, as though the world had been tossed into a chasm of ebony velvet. Only bright, sparkling stars, which rode so low one was certain one could touch them by standing on tiptoe, relieved the severity of the dark sky. Inside the small boat that bobbed with the tides, beacons flashed, sending golden shafts of light over the three people aboard.

The guide from the local dive shop, a man whose hair had been bleached by the sun and whose body had gone from tanned to bronzed, was making final preparations to escort the couple to the sunken ship, a dive he'd made a hundred times before. Careful divers used a guide in unfamiliar waters, just as a careful guide always checked out the certification and experience of his customers. Both the man and woman—a good-looking couple—were qualified divers. The woman, a knock-your-socks-off blonde, glowed with excitement.

"The ship's down about sixty feet," the guide explained. "She went down about twenty-five years ago. A series of explosions in the stern bottomed her. Left a lot of jagged metal in that area, so it's best to stay near the bow. Fish have set up their usual habitation. Might even find a moray eel, so watch where you stick your hand. And watch the netting. It's easy to get tangled up. Let's all stay together and—" the man smiled "—enjoy."

All three were suited up—flippers that made them look like sea creatures trapped on land, rubber vests worn over swimsuits, and tanks of air heavily hunched on their backs. Everyone was still adjusting face masks and mouthpieces. Through the latter, each would breathe that precious commodity, air.

Ford tapped Mariah on the shoulder.

She turned. Within the shield of her face mask, her eyes glittered. Ford wasn't certain he liked the degree of glitter. It reminded him of the afternoon she'd walked on too-thin ice.

"Play by the rules," he said, the tone of his voice suggesting that she'd be sorry if she didn't.

His admonition seemed to be the spur she needed. Grinning hugely, she said, "Playing by the rules is the surest route to boredom." With that, she inserted the mouthpiece and, flashlight in hand, flipped over the side of the boat and into the water.

The guide looked stunned.

Ford cursed.

The cool water swallowed Mariah, immediately enveloping her in a world of silence, immediately filling her with a sense of freedom. Being suspended undersea was very much like flying, like soaring to the heights of the sky, as though she were a winged beast to whom God had given the gentle gift of flight. Along with the freedom, she felt a restless energy purling just below the surface of her skin. This energy led her to paddle her feet in a rapid descent. Her own breathing, escaping in silver bubbles that streamed surfaceward, was the only sound she heard.

Within the arc of her light, life burst into being. Sea animals, accustomed to their inky surroundings, flashed in startled movement. Schools of shrimp warily viewed the intruder, while luminescent plankton shimmered like fireflies in the disturbed water. Lobster eyes glowed like hot coals from the sandy bottom.

Suddenly something gripped Mariah by the ankle. She buckled, whirled, and stared into Ford's face mask. The face behind it was not overjoyed. For a reason she couldn't explain, his displeasure only made the restless energy inside her flow more swiftly. He let her go, making it patently clear by jabbing the water beside him that she was to stay close.

The guide taking the lead, he directed them to the sunken craft in only minutes. It lay on its side like a wounded behemoth. The three, their flashlights cutting through the murky stillness, moved in closer. Each found his own treasures of interest.

Little by little the restless energy tugged at Mariah, drawing her farther and farther away from the men until the forbidden stern loomed before her. Holes gaped like mouths frozen in the act of screaming. The salt sea had corroded the jagged edges until they looked like teeth ready to strike out at the nearest prey. In some grotesque way, there was a beauty to the stark scene. Compelled by a force stronger than she could resist, Mariah swam closer...
closer...recklessly closer...

At first, she thought it was Ford who had once more ensnared her ankle. Feeling a giggly giddiness, she twisted, expecting to see his disgruntled face. Instead, she saw her flipper tangled in a mesh of net. The giddiness faded, though it wasn't replaced with any real sense of panic. That began moments later when it became obvious that she couldn't affect her own release. The net, like the tentacles of an octopus, had wrapped around her flipper and had somehow gotten caught in the flipper's fastener. Still, the incident should have caused little concern—after all, she was with other divers and each diver carried a knife for just such an occurrence. She told herself to take it easy. *Just take it easy!* But even as she tried to calm herself, Mariah could feel the panic growing, rushing at her from all sides. It was the first time in her life that she could remember not being able to move when she chose to. It was the first time she'd ever been trapped. Adrenaline coursed through her body, causing her to thrash about madly.

She wanted loose! Now!

In her frenzy, the hose of her air tank scraped against the serrated opening of a hole. As sharp as a razor, as though they had been waiting for twenty-five years for just such a sacrificial victim, the teeth bit into the rubber tubing. Immediately Mariah's supply of air ceased. With it came a feeling of absolute terror. Out of instinct, she reached for her auxiliary mouthpiece, located on her vest.

Disbelievingly, she realized it, too, had been severed. Both hoses flapped mockingly. Desperately, she tugged at her ankle. Desperately, the net tugged back. And all the while, her air bubbled into the dark sea...and not into her lungs.

The truth came tripping like an ugly, nighttime beast. She was going to die. Here. Now. Young. The way she always knew she would. She'd confronted death before, but always they'd played the grim game by her rules. This time, however, death was calling the shots.

CHAPTER ELEVEN

OUT OF THE NIGHTMARE came two hands.

Frightened, disoriented, Mariah fought them. Flailing, she struck out, sending the flashlight to the bottom of the sea, where it peered back like a glaring evil eye. All the while she struggled. She yanked at her captured foot until the net cut into her flesh. She didn't notice the pain. She didn't notice anything except the burning in her lungs...the panic that had her in its angry arms...the feeling that a forever blackness waited just for her. On some subliminal level she wondered if it was easy, painless, to suffocate. She didn't think so. Because already a horrible heaviness had set in, a heaviness that was crushing her chest.

The intruding hands were persistent. They shoved hers aside, pinning them hurtfully out of the way when all else failed. Ford's free hand tried to remove the impotent mouthpiece from between her lips, but Mariah, unable to think clearly, clamped it between her teeth, as a starving babe a mother's breast, unwilling to let go of the only thing that even promised sustenance. Pointing to his own mouthpiece, he tried to explain that he'd exchange hers for his. Still, Mariah held fast to her own. Finally Ford ripped it from her mouth. Mariah looked startled. Scared. Desperate. She fought to free her hands. She fought to free her foot. She fought.

Taking a deep breath of air, he offered his mouthpiece to her. At first, she didn't seem to understand. He roughly thrust the life-saving device between her lips, gesturing with his mouth for her to blow out in a necessary clearing of water from the tubing. Instead, she greedily sucked in, receiving a mouthful of seawater. She choked. Naturally clearing the mouthpiece. Sweet air sang against her lips. She again looked startled, as though surprised beyond measure to discover that air existed anywhere in this dark universe. Then, ravenously, she breathed again, gasping in an insatiable frenzy that caused Ford to shake his head.

Slowly, he was saying. *Breathe slowly.* This she could understand, but she didn't care what he was telling her. She simply wanted air—lots of air—quickly!

She gulped, gulped again, then choked once more, sending giant air bubbles bursting in the water. It was only when Ford threatened to remove the mouthpiece that she earnestly tried to obey him. Ultimately, he let go of her hands. She hurried them to her mouth, pressing the rubber to her lips as though it were priceless. She was only vaguely aware that someone—the guide?—was working with her foot. She saw him unsheathe his knife. Seconds later, she was free.

Free!

Air and freedom. What more could anyone want? Except maybe the abatement of the panic that didn't seem to be lessening despite the air flowing into her lungs. Ironically, if anything, the panic seemed to be growing. She just wanted out of the water.

Now!

She kicked, starting upward. Once she'd eaten up the short length of hose connecting the mouthpiece to Ford's tank, she was jerked back. She tried to flee again. Ford grabbed her by the waist, hauling her flush to him. Face mask rested against face mask. Eyes leveled with eyes. Hers, he noted, shone with fear, not an excited fear this time. Just fear. His tried to reason with her, to remind her that she couldn't surface quickly, that she'd burst her lungs if she did. She didn't seem to care about burst lungs. She just cared about getting out of the water.

Ford pinned her struggling body to his, forcing her to go at his speed. In trapping her, though, he couldn't get to his vest to make use of his own auxiliary air supply. Calmly, he expelled the air in his lungs, since the volume and the pressure of the air naturally increased as he ascended. With the guide preceding them, holding both his and Ford's flashlight, the three erupted onto the surface. Totally depleted of air, Ford heaved in a huge breath. Mariah, spitting out the mouthpiece, gasped, as well.

"I...I'm dying!" she cried, clinging to him as if her life depended on it.

"You're not dying."

"I can't breathe! Ford, I can't breathe!"

"You can breathe," he assured her. "You *are* breathing."

"I can't breathe! I don't want to die. Ford, I don't want to die. I want to live!"

"Is she all right?" the guide asked in concern, dragging himself into the boat.

"She's having an anxiety attack. Here, help me get this off her."

Working quickly, the two men divested a frantic Mariah of her tank, mask and vest. All were haphazardly tossed in the bow of the boat.

"Pull her up," Ford ordered.

The guide tugged, bringing a panting Mariah aboard. In the process, one of the flippers was knocked from her foot and was sucked back into the water. No one seemed to care.

Mariah's breath was a rasped sound against the silence. "I...I can't..." She no longer even seemed capable of saying she couldn't breathe. "Ford..." she whispered pitifully.

"Are you sure she's all right?"

"Positive," Ford said, ripping off his air tank, along with his mask. Levering his hands on the side of the boat, he hauled himself inside. With dispatch, he removed both his vest and flippers. He reached for Mariah, who lay huddled on the floor of the boat, fighting to breathe. Her eyes were wide with fear.

"Come here, baby," he said soothingly, sitting down beside her and pulling her onto his lap. "Hand me that towel," he said to the guide, adding, "and do you have a sack, a bag, anything she can breathe into?"

"Ford, I can't br..." One breath was following another so quickly that she was reaching a state of overoxygenation. "Ford...I feel dizzy...I...I'm gonna...die..."

"You're just hyperventilating. You'll be all right. I promise."

"...promise," Mariah repeated, holding on to the word as she held on to him.

"Here," the guide said, producing a small canvas bag that held sundry seagoing necessities, all of which had been unceremoniously dumped on the bottom of the boat.

"Breathe into this," Ford demanded, holding the bag to her mouth and nose. She twisted her head. "Mariah, breathe into this!"

The authoritative tone of his voice, coupled with the fact he held the bag to her face, thereby giving her no choice, forced Mariah to do his will. She drew the air in hastily, just as hastily expelling carbon dioxide. In a short while, the carbon dioxide, which now saturated the air she was breathing, had washed out the overabundance of oxygen.

She began to breathe more slowly. Another minute and she was breathing without the bag.

Ford felt her wilt against him, her cheek and hand cradled against his chest. Her hand formed a fist against the dark matting of hair. He pushed the wet strands of her white hair back from her sea-damp face. Her eyes were closed, the lashes, golden in the lamplight, fanning across her pallid skin. Mascara, a rich brown, had streamed down her face despite its waterproof claims.

"That's it, baby," he whispered, picking up the large towel the guide had produced and draping it about her. He could feel her body beginning to tremble in the aftermath of fear. He hugged her close, bringing his mouth close to her ear. "You're all right, sweetheart."

Her cheek nuzzled closer, as though he were the center of the earth, the essence of all life.

Noticing that she still wore one flipper, he bent and took it from her foot. He frowned as he investigated the rope-like burn encircling her ankle. It was clear evidence of the magnitude of her fear.

"Fishing nets," the guide explained when he, too, saw the bloody bruises. He had started the boat toward shore. When he spoke again, the sound of his voice carried above the thrumming motor. "They get caught on wrecks. Generally they're just a nuisance, but the possibility's always there for what just happened. Still, if she hadn't panicked..." He let the sentence trail away.

"Yeah," Ford said, suspecting that for the first time the wind hadn't been able to blow at its whim. For the first time ever, free-spirited Mariah hadn't been free. The degree to which she'd fought for her freedom—the bloody degree—concerned him. Like a trapped animal, she'd been willing to sacrifice a limb just to escape captivity. "Yeah.

If she hadn't panicked,'' he repeated to no one but the night.

Mariah's now even breath whispered through the brown hair damply curling on Ford's chest. He felt it as one would feel a breeze singing across a summer-fevered body. Beneath the towel, her hand began to move—unconsciously, slowly. The fist unfolded, her fingers restlessly delving through the coils of hair. Beneath the lush growth was taut, strong skin, which her fingertips seemed intent upon knowing intimately. Again without conscious knowledge, Mariah found the scar and followed it downward, searching out the crest of his breast. She drew the pad of her finger across the hardened peak of his nipple.

Ford stilled her innocent hand by placing his atop it. He wanted nothing more than to tilt her head and take her mouth with his. Thoroughly. Completely. Until neither one of them could breathe! In fact, it was a compelling urge that fairly shouted to be satisfied. For that reason, Ford was relieved when the boat finally made shore.

Within minutes, the 300ZX, under his guidance, drove through the Florida night. The speedometer said he was moving fast, sports car fast, while the watch at his wrist seemed to be standing still. The hands didn't appear to budge past the hour and minute of 10:28. Mariah, the towel still draped about her, sat huddled in the passenger seat. She was crying. Somewhere along the way, trembling had turned to crying. He knew the catharsis was good for her, that it would cleanse away the residue of dark emotions, and yet the sobs chipped at his heart. He said nothing, did nothing, except repeatedly glance her way, because if he did what he wanted—if he stopped the car and took her in his arms—they'd never make it back to the hotel. So he let her cry. And tried not to notice how his heart hurt.

At 10:42, stopping on a dime, Ford pulled the car into
a parking slot in front of the block of rooms set aside for
the group. Cutting off the engine, he wordlessly threw
open his door and, rounding the back of the car in a flash,
wrenched open Mariah's door. Reaching past her and into
the back seat, he grabbed a pair of jeans he'd intended to
change into before driving home if the evening had turned
out as he'd planned. Instead, he'd simply worn the wet
swimsuit back. As had Mariah. Foraging through her
black handbag, he found her room key. He then scooped
her, again wordlessly, into his arms and slammed the car
door with a swing of his hips, He gave little or no thought
to the kids, or Laurel Simmons, who'd planned to take in
a movie at a nearby mall.

Flipping the light switch on, he closed the door to the
motel room. He lowered Mariah's feet to the floor, noting
that her crying had given way to only random sniffs.

"You okay?" he asked.

She tried to smile, but didn't quite succeed. "I don't
know."

"Here," he said, snatching up a white silk robe lying on
the foot of the bed where Mariah had carelessly abandoned it, "get out of that wet swimsuit."

As though the adrenaline had weighted her limbs, Mariah slowly reached for the robe. She pulled the strap of the
swimsuit from one shoulder, then the other strap from the
other shoulder, before realizing that maybe she should step
into the bathroom. When she padded her bare feet in that
direction, Ford's heart began to beat again.

As soon as the bathroom door closed, he shed his wet
trunks. Quickly, not even bothering with underwear, he
pulled on the jeans. He was in the process of zipping them
when the bathroom door opened. His hand halted, leaving the jeans unbuttoned.

They just stared at each other.

Ford saw a woman whose hair was totally bedraggled. Her face bore not a trace of makeup, and her eyes were red and swollen. The tears had completely obliterated the mascara. Her lashes looked bare and pale, giving her the appearance of absolute vulnerability, an image enhanced by the fact that she hugged the lapels of the robe tightly to her.

Mariah saw a man whose hair was damp and in need of straightening. Several strands strayed onto his forehead, where they leisurely reposed with no threat of being removed. His chest was bare, his jeans unfastened. In the triangular vee surrounding the swirl of his navel grew the same rich, dark-brown hair that carpeted his chest. His eyes shone with an intense and obvious concern. His arms looked strong and sure and . . . safe.

Suddenly the only thing in the world that mattered was being held by him.

Suddenly the only thing in the world that mattered was holding her.

"Come here," he said thickly.

Mariah went to him and entered his waiting arms. Her hands splayed wide across his bare, muscle-bound back, while her lips breathed hotly, harshly, into the hollow of his throat. One of his hands was flattened across her back; the other cupped her head, its fingers speared in the moist tangle of her hair. His strength pulled her to him; his warmth melted away the chill of the sea, the chill of fear, the chill of death.

Death.

She had thought she was going to die and, although she'd always accepted as fact that she would die young, she'd discovered a curious thing. She wasn't ready to die . . . didn't want to die . . . in fact, was adamantly opposed to the idea. She wanted to live. Live! To know again the wonder of Ford's arms, the brilliance of his kiss.

"Live," she whispered, her lips coming alive. She planted a soft kiss at the base of his throat before feverishly stringing them along the column of his neck. "I want to live . . . live . . ." Her mouth, in an increasing pattern of feeling, traced the underside of his chin, the slight dent punctuating it, the severe line of his chiseled jaw. "I don't want to d—" Pressing on tiptoe, her mouth took his, forever silencing the word *die*.

A need exploded within her. The need to reaffirm life's victory over death. She didn't question her body's dictation of what form that reaffirmation took. She simply did what felt right . . . natural.

Her tongue pierced the slit of his lips, embedding itself in the heated moistness of his mouth, where it began to move in a way that was blatantly provocative, highly suggestive. Even if Ford had wanted to deny a response, his body, already weary from denial, wouldn't have allowed him to.

Groaning, he sucked her tongue deep inside him, then deeper and deeper, before mating the velvet of his with the velvet of hers. The hand in her hair tightened, holding her head in place, as though it would be a loss too great to bear should their mouths be parted. The hand at her back slid onto her satin-sheathed hips, nudging her intimately against him. The unbuttoned button of his jeans dug sensuously into the filmy fabric of her robe, into the softness of her belly.

She whimpered as desire claimed her, making its throbbing presence known in a spot that rested against his masculinity. His hard masculinity.

Ford swept her up in his arms and put her on the bed, telling himself that all he'd do was place her there, that he'd end the kiss, that he'd stop himself while he still could. But when he put her down on the bed, he followed her there, bracketing her head in the shelter of his arms, deepening an already deep kiss.

Scared. He'd been so scared when he'd seen her trapped in the net, her air hose cut and bleeding oxygen! He couldn't lose her. Not before he'd ever really had her. At the thought of possessing her, on any level, his kiss turned fierce and hard. She'd walk away from him. One day, she'd walk away from him, and he'd be left with only the memory of what it was like to hold her, to kiss her, to—

"Make love to me," Mariah pleaded. She wrapped her arms about him, urging him closer, closer. Suddenly, she pulled her mouth from his and once more began to deliver kisses to the whole of him. Frenziedly, frantically, her lips touched his closed eyelids, his nose, his jaws and chin. Inclining her head, she kissed his neck, scooted lower and splashed kisses on to his shoulders, the muscles bulging in his arms, his chest. Her mouth found the nub of one breast. She kissed it before flicking her tongue across it.

Ford drew his breath in sharply.

At the sound, Mariah sought his mouth again. As ravenously as she'd once gulped in oxygen, she now took in the taste of him.

Both were breathing hard, the sound bouncing off the motel walls and raining down upon them.

"Easy, easy," Ford whispered, but he was kissing her with no less savagery. He'd almost lost her. *He'd almost lost her!*

His mouth took hers, his tongue now perpetrating the libertine actions that hers had earlier initiated. She opened her mouth to him, responding honestly to the emotions he created within her. When she sucked the tongue wantonly plundering her mouth, the way he had hers, he groaned...and thought he'd die from the heat building in him.

It was his mouth that now feverishly bestowed kisses along her neck, her throat, and in the vee of the silken robe. With all the unbridled movement, the robe had slid open until the swell of one breast lay partially bare. Not thinking of who or what he was, not thinking at all, but rather just feeling, Ford lowered his head, kissing the crest through the silk.

Mariah's breath hitched and, unconsciously, she arched into the magic of his mouth. The robe slithered away, leaving the ivory orb in full view. The areola was a rosy brown, the nipple darker and beaded to a point. Ford's mouth closed over it.

"Ohhh," she sighed, tunneling her fingers through his hair. She was going to die, after all. She was going to die of pure pleasure!

Ford swirled his tongue across the distended bud, then, with a growl, rushed his mouth back to hers. He kissed her. Roughly. Tenderly. Without restraint. As he kissed her, he filled his palm with her breast. She thrust against it, begging him to take more and more and more.

The robe opened completely, one side falling away to reveal her long, slender leg, her shapely thigh. Ford ran his hand the length of her. Her skin was warm and sweet—oh, so sweet!—and she the perfect assuagement of the sensual pain pulsing through him. Somehow, someway, her legs parted and he slid his hand between them, cupping the mound hidden secretly behind the silvery blond nest of curls. Mariah whimpered and, before either he or she knew what was happening, he'd removed his hand and replaced it with his body. It fit so deliciously, so naturally, within the cradle of her legs that he pushed, pushed himself against her, his body seeking what he'd cruelly denied it.

One hand lost in his hair, Mariah eased the other down the sloping curve of his back and into his jeans. She realized that he wore no underwear. Her hand spread wide, feeling the hard muscles of his buttocks. Under the stress, the zipper of his jeans gave slightly, affording her more skin to touch. She took what was offered. Their bellies brushed; the hair in the vee of his jeans brushed against the hair curled between her thighs.

Mariah cried out as his manhood, sheathed in denim, rubbed against her.

Instinctively Ford began to thrust forward. Over and over and over. Long, deep, intimate thrusts that simulated an even more intimate act. He was lost, feeling only her heartbeat, hearing only her cries, sensing only the rightness of giving her what she so desperately wanted, needed—what he so desperately wanted and needed.

The kids returning from the show, loud and laughing, boisterously in search of their rooms and saying a thousand giggly goodnights, shattered the idyll.

Responsibility.

He was a man who'd accepted certain responsibilities.

With a wounded growl, with every ounce of willpower he possessed, Ford rolled away from her and off the bed. Instinctively Mariah reached for him. She caught only air. When she was able to focus properly, she saw him standing before the draped window. One hand was propped against the wall, the other at his waist. His head was lowered, his shoulders sagging in dejection. She could see him fighting to catch his breath, to gain control. She fought the same battle.

Finally, Ford took a long, steadying drag of air into his lungs. He turned his face heavenward, as though beseeching God to end his pain. Something in the tilt of his head, something in the agony emanating from him, spoke to

Mariah as nothing else ever had. His pain became hers. She felt it settle heavily in the region of her heart. She clearly, astoundingly, recognized that she'd never hurt this badly for anyone before. It was as though she'd never truly looked beyond herself until this moment. Had she always been self-centered? Mariah considered the question. Yes, maybe she had been, she concluded finally. Maybe she'd always been so tormented that there'd been no time to register anyone's pain but her own.

Until now.

Drawing her robe closed, she rose from the bed and padded her bare feet to Ford. Banding her arms beneath his and crossing them over his chest, she laid her cheek against his back.

"It's all right," she whispered, wanting only to comfort him, for, curiously, in his comfort lay her own.

He made no reply. Her response to his silence was to tighten her arms and to nuzzle her cheek. They stood thus, both absently listening to the outside noises. The kids, reluctantly, were calling it a night. Shut doors opened to emit one last giggle, while girl-boy voices, low and whispered, vibrated lovers' messages.

"Jeff," Laurel Simmons called, admonishment strong in the single word.

From right next door, there came the muffled sound of Jeff saying something to Megan. It sounded like "I love you." Then there was the closing of a door, followed by another, followed by quiet. At last Laurel Simmons shut her door.

Taking Mariah's hand in his, Ford pulled her around him and nestled her in his arms. He rested his chin atop her head. His breathing had slowed, but his heartbeat, though steady, still rammed against his rib cage. And he was still aroused. Firmly. Boldly. He made no pretense otherwise.

But then, she was still aroused, too. Her body still ached, her breasts still tingled, her femininity still moistly throbbed.

As a woman, she knew the power she owned at that moment. All she had to do was push the issue, and she could have him as her lover. If she just moved her hips against his, if she only raised her lips to his, if she but begged him one more time. But just as she knew that she could have him, could make him abandon his principles, she knew, too, that come morning he'd hate himself. And possibly her. No, not her. Never her. As always, he'd assume the full responsibility and let the rest of the world go scot free.

Raising her face to his, she stared into his eyes. And smiled gently as she placed her palm to his cheek. "It's all right," she repeated.

"No, it isn't," he said, adding, "I want to be inside you." The admission was dark with feeling.

"I know. I want you there, but we both know it can't happen."

"It could if I wasn't what I am."

"Ah, but that's the rub. You are what you are. Just as I am what I am. And if you were anything but who and what you are, I wouldn't have the hots for you."

A look of amusement skittered across Ford's face. "When did you get so smart?"

"I'm always smart when I've got the hots," she said with a small grin.

His grin, though restrained by emotion, widened. "If that's the case, you're talking to Einstein."

Her smile broadened to join his. Abruptly her smile disappeared, along with her bravado. She swallowed. "Will you hold me until I fall asleep?"

A long while later, though her body was weary with physical and emotional exertion, Mariah still lay awake in Ford's arms. He was propped against the bed's headboard, she against his bare chest. The room had been snuffed of light except for that trailing from the bathroom door, which had been left ajar. Her robe had been securely closed, his jeans securely fastened. Neither had spoken for a long while.

"Why do you think God would refuse to answer a little girl's prayers?" Mariah asked, breaking the silence.

The hand at Mariah's back stopped its gentle massage. "What did the little girl pray for?"

Mariah's fingers wove their way, not sensually, but with a detached quietness, through the hair on Ford's chest. "Her prayers weren't silly or petty or frivolous the way a child's prayers often are. All she wanted was for her daddy to love her."

The poignancy in her voice ripped at Ford's heart. "Maybe God didn't have to answer the little girl's prayer. Maybe her daddy already did love her."

Mariah raised her head. "No, he didn't," she said with certainty.

"Oh, Mariah," Ford said, raking the dry, straggled hair back from her forehead, "your father loved you."

"No, he didn't," she insisted. "It's all right now that he didn't, but then it mattered very much."

Ford suspected—no, he knew—that it mattered just as much now. Maybe even more so. He wished he could say something that would ease her pain. All that came to mind were his conversations with Ben Calloway. "Why would he have told me he wished you'd come home more often if he hadn't loved you?"

There was surprise in Mariah's green eyes. "He said that?"

"He definitely did. More than once."

Mariah settled her cheek back against Ford's chest, mulling over what she'd just been told. Mulling it over and holding it close.

"He loved you. He just didn't know what to do with you. You reminded him too much of someone he'd loved and lost."

Mariah said nothing. She simply tested the shape, the form, the content of this hope that Ford had offered her. Was it possible that her father *had* cared?

"The two of you are a great deal alike," Ford offered moments later. "Both eaten to the core with guilt. You just chose to deal with it differently. He pulled into himself. He became an emotional recluse. You just try to kill yourself."

She raised her head. "Kill myself? That's ridiculous. That's—"

"Is it? You tell me then why you walk on ice you know is too thin. You tell me why you went over the edge of that boat tonight without waiting for me and the guide. You tell me why you went to the stern of that ship when you were warned against it."

"I...I—"

"There's only one person who wants you to die. And that person's not your father or your mother. It's you. Out of some convoluted sense of atonement."

Was he right? She honestly didn't know. Was self-punishment behind all the reckless antics she'd engaged in? But tonight she'd learned, and clearly, that she didn't want to die.

"I don't want you to die," Ford whispered fervently, echoing her thoughts as his finger smeared over the fullness of her bottom lip.

"No," she whispered against his fingertip, her tongue tasting the saltiness of his skin.

A tension, wholly sensual, once more entered the room. Eyes sought eyes, then lips. Ford sighed raggedly and settled her back against him. "I do want you to go to sleep, however, before you drive me crazy."

Mariah smiled against his belly and closed her eyes. She tried to contemplate all he'd said tonight, but she was too weary to make any headway. When she spoke again, her voice was riddled with sleep.

"Ford?"

"Hmm?" The clock read 2:40.

"Before tonight I wasn't certain there was a God."

It was a curious remark at best, one Ford couldn't possibly let pass. "What changed your mind?"

"When you touch me, I feel him," she said simply.

Ford would forever remain grateful that the woman in his arms soon fell asleep. If she hadn't, he feared he would have made love to her despite the principles he was so diligently trying to hold on to. Her comment about his touch had moved him that much. It had been a beautifully honest thing to say... just as his physical need for her was beautifully honest. Making love to her not only seemed the right thing to do, but it seemed as natural as breathing, eating, sleeping. How could anything that felt that right be wrong? How could God possibly care if they did what he so obviously wanted them to?

He closed his eyes, letting the curves and contours of her body imprint themselves on his. Her arm was slung across his belly, while the softness of her breast pressed against his chest. One leg, peeking from the robe, intimately entwined itself with his. It was the leg whose ankle bore the bruise marks from the net. The purplish-red marks reminded him once more of just how close he'd come to losing her. Even now the thought made his stomach empty of feeling.

Like lace and lightning, like sweetness and storm, the realization came. He was in love with the woman cradled in his arms. He was in love with Mariah.

Mixed emotions raced through him—elation, happiness, despair. Despair because the bruise also reminded him of how hard she'd fought to gain her freedom. How could he have gone and done something as foolish as falling in love with the illusive wind? And yet, even to save himself the pain he knew would one day come, he could not wish he didn't love her. The feeling in his heart was that beautiful. That precious.

An hour later he was still holding her. Simply because he had not been able to let her go. But he had to. Because morning would soon claim the sky.

Easing her arm from around him, he slipped from the bed, allowing her body to settle against the coolness of the sheet, her head to settle in the softness of the pillow. She moaned, then called his name. She tried to open her eyes.

"Shh," he whispered, tucking the cover up over her. "Go back to sleep, my Lady Bear."

Helpless to do otherwise, she did as bid.

Ford waited until her breathing was once more even, then prayed that he could find the strength to leave her. God must have been listening. Closing the door of her room behind him and making certain it was locked, he still barefoot and bare chested, headed for his own room four doors down. To get there, he had to pass by Laurel Simmons's room. So tired was he, so preoccupied with the wondrous feeling inside his heart, that he didn't notice the fluttering of the blinds as he passed by. Five minutes later, he was sound asleep . . . with visions of Mariah dancing in his dreamer's head.

CHAPTER TWELVE

FORD HAD READ all about the Salem witch trials. He now knew how those accused of witchcraft must have felt.

Although it was Laurel Simmons's voice he heard indicting him, it was the collective stare, the denouncing stare, of a dozen or so pairs of eyes that he felt. No, that wasn't quite true. There were several pairs of eyes that had been asked to join the group simply because they were on the church board, although the group was primarily made up of those who opposed Ford at every curve and turn. One pair of those friendly eyes, those belonging to the eldest board member, J. C. Hardcastle, looked as irate as Ford felt.

It was the Wednesday following the trip to Florida. Ford had thought Laurel particularly quiet, contemplative even, during the second half of the vacation. He now knew why she'd been. She'd been planning her strategy. She had initiated her attack immediately following the week's normally scheduled Wednesday Night Bible Study. Concurrently running with the witch trial was a meeting of the senior citizens, presided over by Mariah. Ford, who'd been cornered in the sanctuary, hoped that Mariah, in the rec room, didn't get wind of what was going on. One of them being humiliated was enough. And he sensed—*had* sensed ever since the word *Florida* had sanctimoniously left Laurel's lips, that humiliation was the object of the evening.

"I knew the moment we started with all this sex education that we had a problem," Laurel intoned. "Ford, Reverend Dunning, is just too forward thinking for a conservative church like ours, for a conservative community like ours. For heaven's sake, he's teaching these kids the rhythm method of birth control when he ought to be teaching them the morality of abstinence!"

Ford said nothing...just the way he'd said nothing since Laurel had begun her harangue. He simply sat before his accusers doing a silent seethe, accompanied with some uncharitable thoughts regarding Laurel Simmons that he'd ask God's forgiveness for later. Maybe.

"Well now, Laurel," another friendly pair of masculine eyes said, "that's not quite right. I have a son in Ford's sex ed class and he does teach abstinence. Besides, sex ed isn't a pulpit from which to preach morality. And I was on the high school board committee that voted to institute some form of sex education in the classroom. If Ford didn't teach the course, someone else would."

"I still maintain that the classroom is no place for sex!" Laurel said.

At her choice of words, a couple of people hid grins.

Ford's defender said, "Well, then it sounds like your grievance is with the school board, not Reverend Dunning."

For the first time Laurel appeared flustered. But only slightly. And only for a moment. "The whole subject of sex ed has little to do with what we're here for."

"Then what are we here for?" J. C. Hardcastle asked impatiently.

Ford shifted his attention to his friend. J.C. looked tired. Ford wondered if he felt well, and thought that the last few times he'd seen the man he'd seemed older. Ford made the mental notation to talk to J.C. about his health,

to remind him that maybe he should slow down in deference to his heart problems.

"Florida," one of Laurel Simmons's allies said, his head
perched at the angle of arrogance. His name was Dave
Kellerman, his disposition that of a tart lemon. "That's
what we're here for."

"What in tarnation is this about Florida?" J.C. asked,
impatience now bordering on downright irritability.

Laurel Simmons drew herself up to her full five feet,
three inches and edged her pointed chin forward. Even
under the circumstances, Ford noted that she wouldn't be
a bad-looking woman if she'd give up trying to police the
world. The stress of always searching out wrongdoing had
pinched her face, a face which the years had otherwise
been kind to.

"It pains me to report this," Laurel said, though everyone in the room knew she relished every word, "but I
think Ford, Reverend Dunning, acted with great impropriety when we were in Florida last week." To her credit,
she looked Ford full in the face when she made the charge.

He said nothing, wondering what she'd seen, or what
she thought she had. Was it possible she'd seen him coming from Mariah's room? If so, hanging him from the
nearest tree wouldn't satisfy her.

"Well?" J.C. prompted.

"Give her time," one of her cohorts said.

"Yeah, give her time," another chimed in.

"From the moment we left here, the Reverend and
Mariah Calloway were . . . friendly."

Ford's eyes darkened.

"So?" J.C. asked.

Laurel's chin climbed. "They left the group—the group
they were supposed to be chaperoning, I might add, leaving me to patrol those kids all by myself—and went out

alone. At night. On some kind of dive. And I can assure you Miss Calloway was wearing a swimsuit that would have inflamed a saint."

A bolt of anger shot through Ford. When he spoke, though, he admirably held the feral emotion in check. "Miss Calloway's swimsuit is not an issue here. And for the record, she and I were accompanied by a diving guide."

"And did that same guide accompany you to Miss Calloway's motel room, where you stayed until 3:43 that morning?"

Laurel Simmons had the look of a soldier who'd just gotten off his best shot.

Ford had the look of one who'd been hit by that best shot. The wound, however, exploded with rage rather than pain. This rage, fresh and full, streaked across his amber irises, tinting them the color of a rising storm.

"What are you suggesting, Laurel?" J.C. asked, his anger matching Ford's.

"That Miss Calloway and I are having an affair," Ford said, his voice filled with a quiet fury, "but I think she's doing much more than suggesting it."

The sanctuary grew so quiet one could almost hear all the prayers ever prayed there.

Finally Laurel asked, "Well, have you nothing to say for yourself?"

"No," Ford answered, coming to his feet.

Laurel had clearly expected the accused to deny the charge, or to at least say something on his behalf. His absence of a defense flustered her once more. It was only for a moment, however. "In that case, I have something I want everyone to hear."

With that she moved to the back of the small church and called for someone to enter the sanctuary. The someone was Jeff Simmons, who looked as though he'd rather be anywhere on earth but where he was. As he walked up the aisle, his eyes met Ford's, then he looked away, as though ashamed of what his mother was doing and the role she was forcing him to play.

"Tell them what you saw," Laurel ordered when they'd once more joined the group—the jury.

Jeff said nothing.

"Jeff," his mother insisted.

"I, uh...Megan and I, we, uh..." Still the betraying words wouldn't come.

"What Jeff's trying to keep from saying is that he and Megan Blake caught Mariah and me kissing."

All eyes found Ford. Even Jeff's, which were filled with an apology.

Ford smiled at the young man. "It's all right, Jeff."

"She asked me if I'd ever seen you and Miss Calloway together," the boy-man said, the words tumbling over themselves in explanation.

"I understand," Ford said. "I wouldn't have wanted you to lie." Ford's eyes shifted from Jeff to the group at large. "I have kissed Mariah Calloway. If that is improper, then so be it. As for the other allegation, it's none of this august body's business. If, however, you have no more faith in your preacher than to make the allegation in the first place, then I respectfully suggest that you spend the rest of your time together this evening voting me out and a new minister in." With that, he turned on his heels and exited the room.

He plowed full into an angry-eyed Mariah.

"You're not going to let them get by with that, are you?" she asked, green fire blazing from emerald irises.

Her meeting had broken up early and she'd gone in search of Ford. When he hadn't been in his study, she'd started looking around. The unscheduled meeting, which

J.C. had been dragged out of the senior citizen's group for, had intrigued her. Particularly since Laurel Simmons was spearheading it. The accusing tone of the voices in the sanctuary alerted her that something was wrong long before she was close enough to hear the specific allegations being leveled.

"C'mon," Ford said, brushing by her on his way to the study.

"Well, if you're not—"

"C'mon!" he said, catching her arm and hauling her behind him. Her red high heels, with which she wore lacy white socks, struggled to keep up with him.

The instant the study door closed, he released her...and she started talking. "Look, I couldn't care less what they think of me—in fact, the worse, the better—but I won't stand by and let them drag you through the mud."

"Yes, you will," Ford replied evenly, but firmly.

"Watch me," she dared, whirling and reaching for the doorknob. Ford's hand snaked out and flattened against the wood. The door, which had opened a fraction of an inch, slammed shut again.

Mariah pivoted, her body unexpectedly rubbing against his. Unbidden came a plethora of memories poignant enough to stagger her where she stood. As always when around him, she felt a rushing tide of need. It was a need which had never been assuaged...and that was what made Laurel Simmons's accusation so damned galling!

"For the love of heaven, Ford, they think we slept together! Which, if you ask me, is what Laurel Simmons needs—a good lay!"

At the nearness of Mariah, Ford's body did what it always did. It reminded him that he was a man. It was a reminder he couldn't take too much more of. "Yeah, well," he said, removing his hand from the door and stepping back where he could breathe, "a good lay would benefit a lot of us."

Two pairs of eyes smoldered.

At last, Ford, who felt himself burning to a cinder, raked his fingers through his hair, turned and walked toward the window. Outside, the night was black. Black like the shirt he wore. Black like his grim expression. Black with a dirty accusation.

"Nothing you could say would make any difference," he said. "Laurel and the others have already made up their minds. Besides, our sleeping together is just the tip of the iceberg. This group has been trying to hang me with something ever since I accepted the pastorate. They don't like the church music I sanction, they don't like my teaching sex ed, they don't like the sports car I drive. Like they said, I'm too liberal for their conservative taste."

"Then to hell with them and their conservative taste!"

He turned. Mariah's hands were splayed wide at the hips barely covered by the denim miniskirt, while her hair, as usual, looked sassy, as though it had been caught in a tumbling whirlwind and she didn't care that it had. At her she-tiger posture—even the snippet of red lace in her hair seemed to say cockily, "Yeah, buster, you wanna make something of it?"—Ford grinned.

"It's my job to keep them out of hell," he reminded her.

"I'm not sure they deserve to be kept out."

"That's not for me or you to decide."

"And it's all right for them to decide we're sleeping together? For them to force you out of the church on that colossal lie?" The jingle-jangle of her earrings evinced just how angry she was.

Ford didn't answer... at least not right away. When he did, his reply was unforeseen. "I'm not so sure it is a lie."

Mariah blinked. "Excuse me, did I miss something last weekend? I could have sworn you crawled out of bed just when things were getting good. Tell me, did I have a good time? And if I did, why do I feel like a saint? And why am I still so hot and bothered every time you're in the same room with me?"

Her last comment stoked a fire in Ford that never truly went out anymore—night or day. The only thing he could compare the yearning to was that of his restless adolescent years. Then it had simply been a matter of surging hormones. Love, which had increased the physical need a billion times, hadn't been involved.

"The bottom line, Mariah, and we both know it, is that if you'd pushed, I'd have thrown every principle I ever had right out the window."

She didn't play coy. "Maybe. But it can never be proven one way or the other."

"No, but we could make a pretty fair guess, couldn't we?"

"So you're going to let them hang you because of something we didn't do, but might have done if I'd pushed?"

"Technically it makes me as guilty as if we had made love."

Mariah exploded. "You're so frigging noble, Ford! And so frigging hell-bent on wallowing in guilt! And you know why?" She didn't give him the opportunity to answer. "Only because you lived when your friend and fiancée died."

"What is this, dial-a-shrink?"

She ignored him. "Because you had the audacity to live when others died, you work twenty-six hours out of every twenty-four trying to save the world in order to prove to it 'that you were worth saving. And if you can't save it, then you're going to assume the blame for not being able to.''

''What does this have to do with Laurel Simmons?''

''And in the meantime,'' she said, obliquely addressing his question, ''you're going to let the Laurel Simmonses of the world do their number on you. Watch my lips, Ford,'' she said, moving toward the desk and planting her hands wide on the flat surface, ''nothing happened in Florida! We did not make love. Because we chose not to. *We*, Ford! *We!*''

''Well, I may be trying to save the world,'' he said, splaying his hands on the desk in a similar fashion and leaning toward her, ''but at least I'm not running from it!''

''What the hell does that mean?''

''Just what I said. Talk about me wallowing in guilt—''

''Here we go again,'' Mariah said, referring to the conversation they'd had the weekend before.

''You're so riddled with it, and fear, you can't be still. You're a walking advertisement for seeing twenty-one countries in ten minutes.''

''I travel because I enjoy traveling.''

''You don't travel, you flee.''

''Flee? That's the most ridiculous thing—''

''And I guess you could stop running—''

''Traveling . . .''

''—anytime you wanted to?''

''Certainly.''

''Then do it!'' he shouted. ''Stop running and marry me!''

''I . . .'' She halted when what he'd said registered. ''Marry you?'' she asked, her sails crumbling from the sudden loss of hostile wind.

''Yeah. As in, till death do us part.''

She laughed. "I don't believe it. You want to get married so we can morally, in the eyes of God and Laurel Simmons, go to bed?"

"No, I want to get married because we're in love."

Love. The word, coupled with *marry,* took Mariah's breath away. She had the same empty-lung feeling she'd had the weekend before when she'd been trapped beneath the surface of the water, her oxygen seeping into the salty sea. She also experienced the same fear, as if the words had shackled her as securely as had the net. She swallowed, then breathed deeply—or tried to.

"No," she whispered, shaking her head in denial. "No."

Unable to stand the heat in his eyes, the heavy fear in her heart, she turned on her heel and made for the door. Somewhere deep inside she realized she was doing precisely what Ford had accused her of doing—fleeing.

Like an avenging knight in pursuit, he rounded the desk. Grabbing her elbow, he jerked her around and pinned her between him and the door. His usually gentle eyes burned like boiling, bubbling honey. She tried to look away, but he gripped her chin in his hand and forced her eyes back to his.

"Tell me you love me," he ordered. When she hesitated, he added roughly, "Say it!"

"Ford—"

"Say it!"

"I...I want to go to bed with you," she said, hedging to keep from admitting what she knew to be the truth.

"Say it!"

"I can't! Ford, I'm not into commitment. I'm—"

His lips took hers. Punitively, persuasively, he drove his mouth into hers until she had no choice but to part her lips for his sensual invasion. His tongue cut a pathway as if pushing aside her denial, slashing her resolve in half. At the fiery feelings that ripped through her body, a body already ravaged by need, she whimpered and her knees buckled. When she sagged, Ford pressed his body more fully into her, anchoring her against the unrelenting door.

His tongue swirled boldly in her mouth, sapping the last of any renegade resistance. She gasped when his mouth left hers for the column of her neck.

"Say it!" he ordered, tonguing and kissing her throat in fevered alternation. His forearms, his hands, now levered against the door, crawled higher as he nudged his hips forward. He ground himself into her, the hardness of his masculine body imprinting the softness of her feminine one.

She made a low, mewling sound.

"Say it!" he commanded, stroking the hollow of her throat with his moist tongue before settling his mouth against the sweet indentation.

"I...I..." The words she'd said before—that she wanted to go to bed with him—were in her mind. She tried to speak them. But they wouldn't come. Another set of words was fighting to be expressed. Words that explained why she wanted to go to bed with him. Words that explained why she wanted to go to bed with no one else but him. "I...I love you," she said harshly.

Ford's lips stilled, his breath hot and heavy against the spot that had vibrated with her silken disclosure. His eyes met Mariah's. Hers were awash with tears.

"But it still doesn't change anything," she whispered, the pain in her heart almost too great to be borne. "I'm still not into commitment."

"I'm only asking you to commit to loving me," Ford replied, a sense of dread already negating the beauty of what she'd admitted. Deep in his soul he knew what was coming. But he also knew he had to fight. He had to be able to tell himself later, when he was alone with nothing but a nightful of memories, that he'd done all he could to keep her at his side.

"No, you're not. You're asking for a lot more. You're asking me to give up my freedom." As though the word gave rise to the need, she pulled from his embrace. He let her go. And wondered where he got the strength to do so. As he watched, she moved to stare out the window.

"You can't be truly free, Mariah, until you commit yourself to something or someone."

She recognized the sentiment as Goethe's. It was a paraphrase of the framed quote she'd seen in Ford's trailer. Weeks before. A lifetime before.

"I am committed to something. I'm committed to not standing still." She turned, her eyes begging him to understand. "Ford, I'd die having to stay in one spot. I'd suffocate in Calloway Corners. I couldn't stand the boredom."

"Of being a minister's wife?"

"I don't know. Maybe that's part of it," she answered, pulling no punches. Even as she thought about it, however, Mariah realized that she'd never been bored with Ford. A lot of other things, wonderful other things, but never bored. "Besides," she added, "I'm not minister's wife material. Laurel Simmons would hardly embrace me, a bartender and croupier, as your wife."

"To hell with Laurel—"

"My marrying you wouldn't be fair to you. You need someone who can give you children. Someone who's willing to. I'm not sure I am. Just the idea of getting pregnant frightens me. I know it's crazy, but I equate pregnancy with death."

"I'm not asking you to have my baby—"

"Well, you should be!" she interrupted, unwilling to let him settle for something, someone, with so little to offer as she.

When Ford spoke, his voice had risen as well. "This isn't about having babies! It isn't about passing Laurel Simmons's test for a minister's wife, which matters little since I'm probably going to be ousted on my own dubious merits! This isn't even about boredom! It's about fear. Your fear. Fear of death. Fear of loving." His voice thickened; his eyes shaded to the color of sun-kissed whiskey. "Stop running, Mariah. Or if you have to keep running, run somewhere inside my heart."

For measured heartbeats, they just stared at each other. He was silently pleading, she begging, each for different and opposite things. He pleaded with her, for once in her life, to take a real chance—not the reckless kind she'd always taken on dying, but a chance on living, on loving. She begged him to understand that what he asked was impossible.

Into the quiet, tension-filled impasse came the hurried knock upon the study door. Without waiting for an answer, the door was flung open.

"Come quick!" the man who'd supported Ford at the witch trial said. "I think J.C.'s having a heart attack."

HOSPITAL WAITING ROOMS all have one thing in common: they demand that one wait. And wait. And wait.

Which was exactly what the group of six were doing—and had been doing for hours. At some point, night had given way to the trembling, fretful hours of early morning. In a little while, a new dawn would gild the world with promise. The question that everyone—Laurel, Ruth, Ford, Mariah and two of J.C.'s oldest and closest friends—was asking was, would J.C. see that dawn?

Doctors and nurses had been in and out of the intensive care unit of Schumpert Memorial Hospital in Shreveport like ants scurrying to and from a hill. The only thing they'd reported was that J.C. was stabilized. Whatever stabilized meant.

Restless, Mariah stood. "Would anyone like coffee?" She glanced around her. Ruth, her mouth puckered with concern, shook her head no, as did Laurel, whose mouth, for once, wasn't puckered. The younger woman sat holding her mother's hand with such affection that Mariah wouldn't have recognized her as the hard-nosed woman she'd heretofore seen. Laurel Simmons did have heart. It was just buried deep.

Mariah looked at the two older men, each of whom indicated he didn't want coffee, either. At last her eyes came to rest on Ford. He sat on the leather sofa, his arm negligently thrown across its back, his legs masculinely crossed in a square. A stubble of beard shadowed his face, making him look, Mariah thought, more handsome than ever. His eyes, which met hers directly, were scored with fatigue and rimmed with sadness. It was a sadness she knew she was responsible for.

"No. No, thank you," he said quietly, his eyes adding, *I want more than coffee from you.*

Please understand that I can't give you more, she silently begged.

Finally one of the other men looked up, curious to know what was delaying her departure for the coffee machine. Only then did Mariah realize she was just standing and staring at Ford. She turned and went down the hall.

She and Ford had engaged in no intimate conversation since the announcement of their friend's heart attack. By tacit agreement, what had transpired in the study was shelved. Each knew that their personal lives had to take second place for the time being. Besides, what more could they say?

She poured coffee that looked more like Mississippi mud than a beverage into a Styrofoam cup. The thick, jet-black liquid had just touched her lips when she realized she didn't drink coffee. What was wrong with her?

Yeah, one side of her brain demanded, *what's wrong with you? The man you love just told you he loved you. And you're acting as though the end of the world's just been announced.*

He wants to tie me down, the other side of her brain responded, as she threw the coffee away. *I can't be tied down. I've gotta be free to go, to blow like the wind across sea and land.*

Her heels clicking hollowly in the hallway, Mariah headed once more for the waiting room. She wasn't certain but she thought she saw the first rays of morning begin to lighten the sky.

"Out of coffee?" Ford asked as he noted her empty hand.

She smiled sheepishly. "I forgot I don't drink coffee."

He grinned, too, adding as she sat back down on the sofa, her thigh brushing his—a fact both registered with an increased heart rate—"Why don't you go home? I'll call you as soon as we hear anything."

It was a suggestion he'd made more than once. As always, her answer was what it was now. "In a little bit."

Mariah honestly didn't know what she was doing hanging around a hospital. In the past she would have gone to any lengths to avoid its austere, sterile halls. But for some reason she couldn't leave. One reason for staying was because she cared deeply for J. C. Hardcastle, the other reason... The other reason was that, fundamentally, in some innermost part of her, she wanted to be by Ford's side—to somehow lessen the burden he was carrying.

"In a little bit," she repeated.

In a little bit you can run away, the self-preservationist part of her mind added.

For right now, the other part of her brain pleaded, *just close your eyes and rest.*

Mariah came awake suddenly. She was aware that Ford's arms cradled her in their strength—had she sought them out, or had they sought her? Or had it been mutual? In tandem with the realization that Ford held her came another realization. A tired-looking doctor stood before them. Quickly, as though given the signal simultaneously, everyone rose.

"I think he's going to be all right," the physician said, adding with a crooked smile, "that is if we can quiet him down. He refuses to sleep until he's seen a Ruth and a Reverend Dunning."

Tears of relief had gathered in Ruth Doege's gray eyes. "I'm Ruth," she said.

Ford stepped forward. "I'm Reverend Dunning."

"If you two will follow me, I'll try to get my patient settled down."

Ford, his eyes meeting Mariah's, slipped his arm from her. She suddenly felt cold and alone. Unbearably cold. Desperately alone.

"Tell him hi," she whispered.

Ford nodded and smiled. The smile died. "Wait for me."

The arm that had sheltered Mariah now encircled Ruth as the two stepped down the hall toward the intensive care unit. Mariah watched as Ford bent and said something to the older woman. Sensing someone's gaze, Mariah turned. Ruth's daughter, Laurel, was studying her. There was still censure in the woman's eyes—Mariah would have been a fool to think otherwise—but the censure was diluted. At least for the time being.

"Thank you for waiting with Mother. It meant a great deal to her. She told me so."

"Your mother and J.C., they're nice people."

Laurel Simmons made no response. She and Mariah just continued to exchange looks. Finally Mariah started down the hall in the direction Ford and Ruth had taken. She knew she couldn't enter J.C.'s room, but something drew her toward it. Ford, perhaps, for already she missed him. Suddenly she stopped and looked back. Laurel Simmons was still watching her.

"About Florida, things aren't always what they appear to be," Mariah said, then resumed her trek down the hallway.

Laurel Simmons said nothing.

Despite the tubes, despite the beeping monitors, despite the gray pallor, J. C. Hardcastle still looked vital. It had everything to do with his blue eyes, which shone with purpose.

"You old codger," Ford said with a smile, "what in Hades do you mean scaring us this way?"

Ford had discreetly allowed Ruth and J.C. a few moments alone. The time had passed with lowered heads and whispered words. Ruth now held onto J.C.'s hand with a grip that threatened to cut off the blood supply. J.C. didn't seem to mind one bit.

"Just checking with God...to see if he was ready...for me," J.C. said, his voice curiously both weak and strong.

"It appears he isn't," Ford said.

J.C. may have nodded. Ford wasn't certain. He was certain, however, that his friend seemed restlessly intent on saying something.

"I want you to do... something for us."

"Anything," Ford answered.

"Better wait till you hear," the gray-haired man teased.

"I like the sound of it already," Ford said, grinning back.

"Ruth and me... we don't want to get married legally... all that property of hers and mine... we don't want to mix it in a legal tangle... want to keep it just as it is for our kids... but..." He stopped to rest. Talking had become an ordeal. The doctor, a young man who wore jeans and a stethoscope and had stood in the back of the room, moved closer.

"We want to get married," Ruth said. "Not legally, but in the eyes of God. Which we figure is all that counts, anyway. I had a proper, legal marriage once before," the older woman shared, "and all it brought me was pain. Jed Doege was a good man, but a hard man, a man who insisted you do everything his way. God love Laurel, she's just like him. Can't see beyond the tip of her pious nose. Anyway, I'm tired of doing what I'm told to. I have a mind of my own. And I'm of the opinion that those proper, legal marriages don't mean doodly-squat."

By the time she'd finished, Ruth's chin had elevated to a level that flaunted convention and dared anyone to disapprove. She reminded Ford of Mariah. But then, nowadays everything in life did.

"Well?" J.C. whispered. "You want to upset those church conservatives again?"

Both men knew that behind the teasing query was a serious threat to Ford. Those trying to hang him might well use this break from protocol to string him up higher. This might well be the point that proved he was too liberal for the likes of their small church. That is, if they were willing to give him the benefit of the doubt concerning his alleged affair with Mariah. Both also knew that it was Laurel herself who might protest the loudest.

"As soon as you're out of here—" Ford said, only to be cut off.

"Now," J.C. said, looking up at Ruth. "We've waited long...enough."

Without a second thought, Ford glanced toward the doctor. "Could you find us a Bible?"

Within minutes a plain black Bible lay on J.C.'s gowned chest. His hand and Ruth's, both lined in veins, both dappled with age, lay atop it. Ford's, tanned and sure of purpose, lay across theirs.

"Do you, Ruth Doege, take this man to be your law...to be your spiritually wedded husband, to live together in love and harmony, in pleasure and in peace, in sickness and in health?"

"I do," the older woman said with a confidence that shook the room—and the heart of Mariah, who stood at the doorway watching.

"Do you, J.C., take this woman to be your spiritually wedded wife, to live together in love and kindness, in laughter and in tears, in good times and bad?"

"I do."

Ford lowered his head and closed his eyes. Everyone else followed suit. Except Mariah. Who couldn't have pulled her eyes from Ford had her life depended on it.

"Lord, you who reads each heart, who knows the goodness therein, read the love and commitment contained in these two and sanction this union with your precious blessing. I pray, O Lord, you will shelter their souls in your loving grace, that you will bind them now, and eternally, as man and wife, that you will instruct the angels to sing glad songs throughout the Kingdom of Heaven in honor of this, their marriage. This we ask in the name of Jesus, who taught us all to love." Ford raised his head. "By the spiritual power granted me by God, I pronounce you husband and wife."

For a moment no one spoke. No one moved. The only sound in the room was the warm, golden blazing of the morning sun.

Finally Ruth laid her hand along the jawline of her husband. She smiled with all the contentment of a new bride. "Now, will you go to sleep, you old coot?"

Both the doctor and Ford grinned. Ford's grin vanished abruptly as he turned and saw Mariah. She was standing at the door, a tear streaming down her cheek. Her eyes were a hazy, sad green, a viridescent shade that said, I'm damned if I do, damned if I don't.

"I want that kind of love," he could hear her silently saying, "I crave it, need it, would sell my soul for it, but I can't cope with the commitment it demands."

He took a step toward her.

As though his nearness scorched her, she stepped back.

Don't run! his heart screamed. *Except to me. Let me hide you somewhere inside my heart.*

Yet, even as Ford watched, he knew he'd lost her. As, indeed, he'd known all along he would.

Swirling, a desperation gleaming in her eyes, she started off down the hallway.

"Mariah!" he called from the doorway.

She didn't look back, but only increased her stride until she was literally running.

Helpless, Ford watched. He watched her run down the hallway, watched her run from her personal demons, watched her run from his lonely life.

CHAPTER THIRTEEN

"WHERE TO?" THE TICKET AGENT at Shreveport Regional Airport asked two hours later. The overhead clock said it was thirty-five minutes after the hour of ten.

Mariah looked up at the friendly faced, blue-suited woman. "What?"

The friendly face repeated, "Where do you want a ticket to, ma'am?"

"Oh," Mariah responded, hauling her black leather handbag onto the counter and searching through for her wallet. Her hand closed about a tin of tea, a toothbrush, a red silk nightie, but no wallet. At the delay, the man behind her cleared his throat in displeasure, while the man behind him gave a deep, appreciative stare at the blonde dressed in high heels and tight jeans. Mariah noticed neither man. Finally, the wallet located, she pulled out all the bills, counting them as she did so. She then put down all the coins in the change compartment. She shoved the currency forward and answered the ticket agent's question of "Where to?" with, "Wherever $201.15 will take me." She spied a copper penny hiding within the fold of the gown and plunked it down on the counter as well. "201.16," she said, as if the extra coin made all the difference in the world.

The ticket agent frowned. "I don't understand, ma'am. Where would you like to travel to?"

"Flee," Mariah corrected.

"What?"

"Where would I like to flee— Never mind. I'd like to go anywhere $201.16 will take me. Provided the plane leaves within the hour."

There was really no hurry, she knew. She'd already said goodbye to Eden, who hadn't been all that surprised by her departure. Not even at the unexpectedness of it, since Eden had long ago accepted that she rarely could make sense out of anything her youngest sister did. The only thing Eden had seemed perplexed about was why Mariah, on her way out the door, refused to take Ford's phone call. Ford. He was the basis for the urgency she felt. She didn't want to face him again. She *couldn't* face him again. Her heart already hurt too much. Because not facing him again was so important, she'd made Eden swear that, if he called back, she wouldn't tell him that she was going. And Eden wouldn't break her promise. Still, there was this urgency...

"Several planes leave within the hour. There's one bound for Denver via Dallas. Another flies to St. Louis, another to Chattanooga. Both of those stop in Atlanta. Another plane is bound for Washington, D.C., while another—"

"Anywhere," Mariah said. "It doesn't matter."

"But, ma'am—"

"Anywhere."

The agent tried to appear as if choosing a passenger's destination was something she often did. "Yes, ma'am. Round-trip?"

"No!" *I'm not coming back. Until I can face Ford. Which may be never.*

In minutes, and to the relief of the impatient line that had formed behind her, Mariah had received her ticket and her change, had checked her luggage and was making her way for the escalator and Gate 10. She felt tired, weary, as though she hadn't slept all night. She smiled wryly. She *hadn't* slept all night. Once aboard the plane, she'd curl up, hug the news close about J.C.'s recovery, and drift off. Maybe. If she could get the image of Ford out of her mind. Ford's arms . . . Ford's lips . . . Ford's—

"Pardon?" she asked the woman X-raying her carry-on bag.

"Could you open that?" the woman asked. "The machine shows something large and metal."

"A tin of tea," Mariah said.

"Could you open—"

Mariah opened the bag and produced a tin of tea. She smiled. "Darjeeling. I never leave home without it."

The woman looked as though she was sorry she couldn't detain someone for strangeness.

Because the plane was scheduled to leave in fifteen minutes, the waiting room of Gate 10 was packed. Mariah spotted an empty seat way to the back, next to a serviceman in green. She made her way toward it. Sitting down, she leaned her head against the brick wall. She was so tired!

". . . headed?"

Mariah opened her eyes. The young serviceman repeated his question. "Where you headed?"

Mariah shrugged. "Nowhere."

The serviceman frowned. "But you've got a ticket."

"To nowhere," Mariah repeated.

"You, uh . . . you visiting someone in nowhere?" the guy teased at Mariah's charming, fey answer.

"No," Mariah said evenly, "I'm running away."

At some point during the long night, she'd accepted the fact Ford had been right. She *was* running away. It was what she'd always done. It was how she'd always coped.

He was equally right that she was running from fear. And—give the man a prize!—he had even pieced together what she was afraid of. She was afraid of dying. But, more than that, she was afraid of living... and loving. How curious that the one thing she'd wanted so desperately all her life—love—was the one thing she was so afraid to take a chance on now. She knew why, of course. One didn't have to be a psychologist to analyze her crystal-clear motives. She wanted love so desperately that she was afraid to embrace it, for fear she would lose it again. And having had it and lost it, the pain would be all the greater.

No, she'd just keep moving, keep running. That way, she would go on surviving. Alone. But, nonetheless, surviving.

And what of J.C. and Ruth and the other senior members of the church? They wanted to go to the race track, to Eureka Springs, to the dozen of other activities she'd helped them plan. But they could go without her. Couldn't they? Certainly. They'd understood from the beginning that she wasn't going to stay, and yet... And yet, strangely, she felt a sense of commitment to them. It was a commitment, though, that she'd more likely than not have been unable to keep even had she stayed. She and Ford had been accused of fornication, which was a serious accusation coming from a church membership. Would they have been so eager to make it had she herself been less radical? Probably not. Which only proved how wrong she was for Ford. Their lives were worlds apart. Their personalities worlds apart. He was sure and confident, she only precariously feeling her way around the jagged cliffs of life. He was the organized type who always knew where everything was, from his car keys to his faith to his opinion. She, on the other hand, was lucky to remember where the car was parked, she always managed to get God's answer-

ing machine rather than God himself and, as for her opinion, what time of day was it?

The young man beside her smiled, liking the lady's off-
beat style . . . and the way she looked. She was easily the
sexiest woman in the waiting area. "Well, sometimes that's
the only thing to do," he said. "Run away, I mean."

"Yeah," Mariah agreed ruefully. "Sometimes. What
time is it?" she hastened to ask.

He checked his watch. "Ten minutes till boarding."

"Good."

"In a hurry to run away to nowhere, huh?"

"Yeah." *In a big hurry.*

Relief flooded Mariah when the flight was finally announced. Standing immediately, she hefted her handbag
onto her shoulder. A line materialized out of nowhere, but
it seemed to be moving quickly, with passengers already
proceeding down the ramp. In a few moments she'd show
the stewardess her boarding pass, walk down the tunnel to
the plane and her seat and soar away into the sky where
she'd be free.

Free?

Would she ever truly be free again?

Maybe she never had been. Maybe Ford, and Goethe,
were right. Maybe to be truly free you had to be committed to something or someone.

*And maybe I'm going to go crazy if I don't stop think-
ing!*

The flight attendant smiled and held out her hand for
Mariah's ticket. Mariah had just thrust it forward when
she heard a familiar, throaty voice.

"Weren't you even going to say goodbye?"

Mariah's head whipped around, her eyes clashing with
the deep amber of Ford's. Just as she had the first time
she'd seen those eyes, she questioned how any irises could

be that rich whiskey color. She also questioned how he
could still be standing on his feet. He looked dog tired, as
though he hadn't slept for ages. And his face looked as
though he hadn't shaved in days. She had the sudden,
overwhelming urge—one, to cradle him from his weariness and, two, to feel the dark bristle of his beard against
her face, her neck, her breasts...

"Eden promised," Mariah said, her voice husky, her
breasts tingly.

"Don't blame Eden. I badgered her."

"Ma'am?" the other woman said, her hand still extended for the boarding pass.

"In a moment," Ford said to the airline hostess, dragging Mariah out of line. The strength in the hand clasping
her upper arm gave her no choice in the matter. But then,
neither did the whiskey-shaded eyes.

"You weren't even going to say goodbye?" Ford repeated, the question clearly reflecting his hurt.

"I thought it would be better this way." A fine trembling had set in at the sight of him, a trembling that weak-
ened both knees and resolve.

"Better or easier?"

She shrugged, admitting, "Easier, I guess."

"I'm not going to make it easy for you, Mariah."

"No," she said in a scratchy whisper, "I can see that."

"Where are you running to?" he asked, his choice of
words not going unnoticed.

His question prompted a silent question of her own.
Where *was* she going? Glancing down at her ticket, she
checked her destination. "St. Louis."

"Ah, St. Louis. A great little town to be alone in."

Alone. Both keenly felt the limitless perimeters of the
word. It left both empty, gutted, in need of communion.
In search of that succor, Ford's eyes searched Mariah's,

restlessly wandering the emerald fields before dropping to her lips. Her shiny red lips.

Mariah's trembling accelerated.

"Don't," she breathed.

"Don't what?"

"Don't kiss me."

"Why?"

He received no answer.

"Why, Mariah?" he repeated, dragging his crooked finger across the crest of her ivory cheek. "Because if I do, you might be reminded of what a good thing we have? Because if I do, you might feel how lonely St. Louis is going to be?"

At his touch, at his words, Mariah closed her eyes. "Don't," she repeated, no longer certain what she was pleading for.

"No, look at me," he growled softly. "You look at me when you walk out of my life."

Mariah opened her eyes, but only because his voice compelled her to. His image had become hazy. She vaguely wondered if she, who rarely yielded to tears, was crying. "Ford—"

"I love you," he whispered. "You can't run far enough or fast enough to escape that fact. I . . . love . . . you. Now and for always."

"Ford, don't—"

"I'm only a phone call away. Call collect. Night or day."

Plump tears gathered in her eyes and dropped from the corners. "Find someone worthy of—"

"And when you get tired of running, when there's no place left to hide, I'll be waiting for you. I'll hide you inside my heart."

"Ma'am?" the stewardess called. "Ma'am, we're ready to depart."

In the background, Mariah could hear silence—the waiting room had emptied, all the passengers now seated aboard the flight. In the foreground, she could hear her own tremulous heartbeat. The rhythm grew wildly erratic when she saw Ford lower his head.

"Don't—"

He kissed her. As gently as snow drifting aground. As gently as rain drizzling against satin hills and silken plains. As gently as a child's prayer uttered at nightfall.

When his lips first touched hers, Mariah silently begged that he not kiss her in passion. She could not withstand passion's assault. And yet, the longer his mouth lingered tenderly at hers, the more fervently she wished for passion, for the gentleness of his kiss threatened to drown her in its bittersweetness. This tenderness was all the more devastating, contrasted as it was against the roughened stubble of his midnight-tinted beard. Against her own wishes, her hand reached for, and cupped, the side of his cheek. Just one touch. She'd take just one touch to ward off—

"Ma'am?"

—the coldness of a thousand lonely nights.

"Ma'am?"

Ford released her, his eyes, hazy with emotion, seeking hers.

"I love you," he whispered. "Don't ever forget that."

"Ma'am, we have to go."

Mariah pulled her hand from his cheek. The absence of him tore at her senses. And then he blurred entirely from view. In that God-granted moment—maybe she could leave him if she couldn't see him—she whirled around and, not even bothering to show the stewardess her pass, raced down the tunnel and out of sight.

She found her seat, though heaven alone knew how. It was a window seat midway back in the plane. Neither suited gentleman whose laps she'd had to crawl over seemed to notice her moist, red eyes. Neither seemed to notice that she'd died a few moments before. Huddling in the seat, her purse clutched to her chest, she turned her body toward the window. Outside, the sun beat down merrily.

Sun.

She would stay in St. Louis a few weeks, find a job tending bar, save her money and catch a fast jet to some Caribbean island where the sun hotly bathed a white beach. She tried to imagine the grainy warmth beneath her bare feet, the solar fever blanketing her shoulders, but all she could feel was the heat of Ford's arms, the fire of his lips.

His was a fire that could rage with gentle persuasion, however, for her mouth still tingled from his tender caress. The thought caused her to amend her plan. She'd go somewhere where soft winds blew endlessly, letting them dance across her skin the way Ford's touch danced across her soul.

Or maybe she'd climb a mountain as high as Ford could carry her spirit.

Or maybe she'd race a car as fast as Ford could race her heart.

Or maybe she'd swim an ocean as deep as her love for him.

She swallowed, feeling another rush of tears. The truth was, no place beckoned her the way Ford's love did. And yet, she was still afraid. Afraid of so many things. Afraid, perhaps, of everything. She had been afraid as far back as she could remember. Seemingly, at least for her, fear had come with the territory of life. She'd been afraid her father didn't love her, afraid she would be made to pay for her mother's death, afraid her sisters, like she herself, blamed her for taking their mother away. Afraid. Always and forever afraid.

Mariah felt the gentle rock, the roll, of the plane as it prepared to leave the terminal and taxi for the runway. Swiftly, with the strength of a slicing sword, fear gripped her. This fear was new. Different. Desperate. This fear put all the others she'd ever known to pitiful shame.

Ford stood at the vast expanse of window, waiting for the plane, and Mariah, to leave. He knew it was masochistic to watch her go and yet, he needed this poignant, positive proof that she would be gone. He had hurt before—hell, he'd thought he would die after Mei-Lee's death!—but the hurting had never been this brutal. Maybe it was because he was older, maybe it was because he understood more thoroughly just how precious love was, maybe it was because he knew, with a certainty he didn't question, that he'd never love again.

The plane began to move, a slow creeping from the terminal. Ford's hands began to shake. To still them he plunged them into the back pockets of his jeans. Suddenly the plane stopped, then, curiously, the craft rolled back toward the terminal. A delay. No! Please no! he prayed. If she was going to leave him, let it be now. Don't drag it out into an endless agony. As though God heard his prayer, the plane, in barely a minute, and with Ford holding his breath every second of it, began once more to depart from the terminal. This time it taxied out for clearance. In heartbeats, in heartaches, the plane was racing down the runway. Ford, his heart empty, watched the nose of the plane tilt upward before rising from the ground and slipping into the waiting blue sky.

Empty? No. His heart wasn't really empty. Inside it were memories. Bitter memories. Sweet memories. Memories that, even though they hurt, he would never willingly part with. For they were all he had left of the woman he loved.

Please, God, he prayed more fervently than he'd ever prayed, *watch over her.*

A breeze.

As crazy as it seemed, he felt a breeze blow across the back of his neck. It was a soft, caressing breeze, a gentle breeze, a breeze that carried a kiss.

Ford turned.

Somehow knowing what he'd find. *Who* he'd find.

Mariah, her silver-blond hair rippling about her, her eyes dewy with tears, stood only feet away. "It seems I've developed another fear," she said, the words only a notch above a whisper.

Ford, hardly daring to believe she was more than a mirage seen through his glassy tears, pulled his hands from his pockets. They were still shaking. More than ever.

"I'm afraid—" She stopped, trying to gain a semblance of composure. Still, however, her lips trembled. "I'm afraid if I run this time, I'll never find you again...that I'll never feel again what I feel in your arms."

Ford tried to speak. He couldn't.

Mariah smiled quickly. "I, uh...I don't know anything about being a minister's wife. That is, if the proposal still stands."

Despite the emotions choking his speech, Ford managed to say, with a hint of a grin, "I don't know anything about being a minister. And, yes, the proposal still st—"

The last word was never spoken, for she went into his open arms, both pairs of lips seeking the other. This time the kiss bore no trace of gentleness, but rather was a wild, tempestuous expression of an exquisite passion.

As Ford and Mariah were reaching for each other, Laurel Simmons, once more ensconced in her own kitchen, was reaching for another cup of coffee. Her son, Jeff, was reaching for his courage.

"Of course I was thrilled that J.C.'s going to be all right, but I don't know, your grandmother seems to have gone senile."

Jeff Simmons had heard about the marriage ceremony. It was all his mother had talked about since getting home that morning.

"She's going to live with him—just like they were actually married! I tried to tell her that, no matter what Ford had said in that mock ceremony, they weren't husband and wife. Not legally. That no court of law would recognize the marriage."

Laurel sat down at the table, absently adding cream and sugar to the steaming brew.

"She told me that she didn't care what any court of law said, that, in the eyes of God, she was married and that she intended to live openly with J.C." A horrible thought crossed Laurel's prim mind. "Oh, my word, you don't think they've been . . . I mean, Mother did spend a lot of time over at J.C.'s . . . Surely, they weren't . . . No . . . no, Mother wouldn't . . ." *Would she?* hung in the air like a cloud in a rain-threatened sky.

Laurel sipped at her coffee thoughtfully.

"Well," she announced finally, sanctimoniously, "as always, we can lay this at the feet of Ford. If he hadn't taken it upon himself to perform this ludicrous ceremony—"

"I want to talk to you," Jeff said.

"—we wouldn't be watching Mother make a complete fool of herself."

"Mother, I want to talk to you."

Laurel Simmons, halting her cup in midair, glanced at her son. Something in the tone of his voice, his suddenly very mature-sounding voice, held her attention.

Jeff, dressed in jeans, T-shirt and sleep-ruffled hair, pushed his hips from the cabinet and sauntered barefoot toward the chair opposite his mother.

"I want to talk to you," he repeated. The way he said it, quick and nonsensical, suggested if he didn't do it now, he never would.

"What is it, Jeff?"

The mother-son exchanges that had transpired since Jeff's father's death had been few and far between. Neither mother nor son had seemed to know quite how to approach each other.

"You're wrong about Ford... Reverend Dunning."

"What do you mean?"

"He's not teaching promiscuity."

"Oh, you're talking about sex ed..."

"I'm talking about sex ed...and real life." Jeff squirmed. "I, uh...Megan and I, we, uh...we would have made a wrong choice about something if it hadn't been for Ford."

Laurel absorbed all that her son had just said...and all that he had not. "I see," she said.

Jeff forced his eyes to hers. "Ford, he, uh... he talked to us about responsibility...sexual responsibility."

"I see," Laurel repeated because it seemed all she was capable of.

Jeff swallowed. "If you were wrong about what he teaches in sex ed, maybe you're wrong about this other thing, too. I mean, about him and Miss Calloway. And what difference does it make if he did kiss her? Everybody kisses someone, don't they? I mean, God's not against kissing, is he? And you don't know what went on in that motel room. No matter what you think, Ford...Reverend Dunning...wouldn't preach one thing and do another. And even if something had gone on, he's only human. Besides," he added, his voice rising with each word, "I don't see what the big deal is about Gran. If God knows they're married, what difference does it matter whether the State of Louisiana does!"

Laurel Simmons sat, stunned into stillness. Jeff, too, was stunned. At his own audacity. He lowered his eyes. Fixing them on his hands, as if they had become the only pair of hands left in the universe. There was at least one other pair, however, for they reached out to cover his.

"When did you grow up, Jeff?" Laurel asked huskily.

Without looking up, he shrugged his muscle-bound shoulders. "I don't know," he mumbled.

"I'm sorry, Son," Laurel whispered. "I've been so busy grieving over your father, that I never noticed."

In apology, a mother squeezed her son's hand.

In forgiveness, her son squeezed back.

LATER THAT AFTERNOON, Ford and his father strolled through the latter's small backyard. Spring and its gentle ways had coaxed the daffodils into bloom, making the flower bed a profusion of sunshine yellow. Nearby, a sloe tree, its trunk gnarled with age, wore its tiny white blossoms like the finest of pearls.

"I've got good news and bad," Ford announced, his hands thrust into the pockets of his freshly creased khaki slacks.

Three hours before, he'd dropped Mariah back at her house, where they'd talked and planned and kissed until putting some distance between them seemed the better part of discretion. He'd returned to his trailer intent upon a shower and a shave and some sleep. He'd had to settle for the first two. He was so high on love he couldn't have slept if someone had put a gun to his head. Strangely, even after a sleepless night, he didn't feel tired. In fact he'd never felt more invigorated. At 3:15, he'd decided to visit his parents. There were certain things he wanted them to hear from him. God love his mother, she had sensed something was wrong and had insisted the two men share a look at the daffodils.

"Let's hear the bad first," John Dunning said, he, too, aware that his son needed to talk.

"I may be kicked out of the church."

"The music too loud or your sex ed teaching too raw?"

"The latest allegation is fornication."

John Dunning looked at his son, then back at the beautifully sculptured daffodil he was stooped before. The way his fingertips brushed the velvet, one would have thought he was confronting the richest of topaz. "So you're moving up to the big time, huh?"

Ford shook his head and laughed. "Somehow I wasn't expecting that to be your first comment."

"What were you expecting? Me to ask you if it's true?"

Ford considered. "Yeah, I guess."

The older man, in deference to age-weary joints, got slowly to his feet. "Well, I figure it either is true or it isn't. Either way, it's between you and God, not me and you." He indicated the lawn chair and both men sat down. "I assume the other party involved is this Mariah Calloway I've heard so much about, but never met?"

Ford grinned. "I haven't mentioned her that much. Have I?"

John chuckled. "No. It's just that the time or two you did, you lit up like a Christmas candle." The older man's smile faded. "Your mother and I haven't seen you smile over a woman in a long while. It made an impression."

Ford sobered, too, as he recalled the hellish years following Mei-Lee's death. "Yeah," he said simply, "I thought I'd forgotten how to smile."

"So Laurel Simmons—that is her name, isn't it?"

Ford nodded. Over the months he'd confided in his father about his staunchest opposition.

"So Laurel Simmons has found something else to broil you with?"

"Yeah. We took a group of kids to Florida. Laurel, Mariah and I chaperoned. She claims I spent the night with Mariah."

"It's gonna be hard to prove you didn't."

"It's gonna be damned hard since I did."

John looked his son straight in the eye. "You don't have to tell me anything, Ford."

"I know that. But I want to. I did spend the night with Mariah—she'd almost drowned earlier that evening, and she and I were pretty emotional about it. I stayed with her until almost 4:00 that morning—3:43 Laurel says. I did not, however, know her in a Biblical sense."

"Between you and me, it wouldn't have been the worst thing to ever happen if you had. Two people in love should answer only to God and themselves. I assume you do love this Mariah Calloway?"

"Yes," Ford said softly, adding, "very much."

Something strong and warm passed between the two men.

"Good. Damned good."

There was something more that Ford felt compelled to say. "Before you go getting the wrong idea, though, I want you to know it wasn't your son who was all that noble. If she'd pushed ..."

"Like I said, it wouldn't have been the worst thing to ever happen. There's a reason God picks his servants from among mere mortals. They understand the temptations of the flesh.''

Ford grinned. "It's plain to see where I get my liberal views from."

"Can't afford to be too rigid in this life," the elder minister said. "Besides, rigid ain't a whole heap of fun. And God intended us to have a little fun." Returning the conversation to the original subject, he asked, "So what're you gonna do if they kick you out?"

Ford's grin widened. "Find another church. And if I can't find a church willing to put up with my heretical lack of respect for convention, then I'll preach from the street." His voice mellowed. "You were right, Dad. I am a minister."

"I never doubted it. Just took me a while to convince you of it. Well, enough of this so-called bad news, which if you're wise, you'll let God sort through. What's the good?" He grinned, a wide, thoroughly contagious smile that matched his son's. "As if I didn't already know."

"We're getting married. Next month." Ford made the announcement as if he still couldn't quite believe it himself. "Oh, Dad, you're gonna love her. She's...she's... she's Mariah."

"If you love her, your mother and I'll love her. It's that simple." A frown dotted the older minister's face. "But be forewarned that marrying so soon after the charges of fornication will only convince some of your guilt."

"I know that. But I'm marrying her, anyway. In fact I'd marry her tomorrow. It's she who insists on waiting a month. She wants the wisteria to be in full bloom." Ford revealed Mariah's wish as if he thought it the stupidest reason he'd ever heard of to postpone a wedding—particularly when he didn't want to wait another minute.

His father laughed. "Welcome to the world of marriage. I swear before God a wife does nothing that makes sense and, though you'll never learn to truly understand her, I can assure you, you won't want to live without her."

"They never make sense?"

"Only on those rare occasions when they agree with you."

A cool March breeze blew across the yard, blowing the smile from Ford's face. It was replaced by the most earnest of looks. "Will you marry us?"

At the unexpected request, Ford's father's eyes glassed over. He had to clear his throat before answering. "With great pride and with great pleasure."

Saving the men from an awkwardly emotional moment, the back door fortuitously opened and Jessie Dunning shouted, "Phone call, Ford! It's a Laurel Simmons!"

Father looked at son, son at father.

"Oh, no, what have I done now?" Ford said between grim lips as he pushed himself from the chair.

CHAPTER FOURTEEN

EVERYTHING WAS SET.

The wedding had been scheduled for the first day of April, in the afternoon, in the backyard of the Calloway house, in front of the wisteria-covered arbor. Ever true to unconventionality, Mariah had asked all three sisters to be her maids of honor. No one, least of all Mariah, seemed concerned at the unequal number of attendants, Mariah's three to Ford's one. Ford has asked Jeff Simmons to stand up as his best man, an honor his young friend was taking most seriously. Ford had been deeply touched by Jeff's intercession on his behalf. Though he didn't know precisely what Jeff had told his mother, he suspected it was far more than the young man had ever intended, far more than the young man had really wanted, to share regarding his intimacy with Megan.

Whatever Jeff had said had altered Laurel's attitude, though to be certain, she was a woman who would always be narrow-minded. Ford figured that every rose had to have a thorn; in truth, it probably made the rose smell sweeter. Laurel had publicly announced that she might have been mistaken about Ford, that the church at least owed him the benefit of the doubt. Then, looking Mariah straight in the eye, she proclaimed that sometimes things weren't what they seemed. Since then, the two women hadn't been confectionately friendly—it was a word Mariah used to mean sticky-sweet—but Laurel had made certain overtures that Mariah had met more than half-way.

The only thing that concerned Ford was that certain others in the congregation, some of those who'd never been happy with his approach to preaching, had left the church, despite Laurel's plea, and joined another church in Bossier City. John Dunning had tried to make his son see that dissension was part and parcel of the ministry. People had a right to unite with those on their same spiritual wavelength, their same heart length. Equally, Ford not only had the right, but also the obligation, to preach the Gospel as he was inspired.

One other thing increasingly concerned Ford, as well. How was he going to get through the month, the long month, the long, long, *long* month, without taking Mariah to bed? He was still seriously asking the question the night before the wedding.

"Oh, Ford, it's beautiful," she whispered, reverently fingering the cameo broach he'd just presented to her as a wedding present. It was an antique he'd accidentally come across at a pawn shop in Shreveport. How anyone would have, could have, parted with anything of such rare beauty, he couldn't fathom. He only knew the instant he saw it, that it reminded him of Mariah—her own beauty, her one-of-a-kind uniqueness, the cool composure he saw developing, almost by the day, in her. She seemed more settled than he'd ever seen her, as if for the first time in her life she had a positive purpose, as if the time had been right for her to realize that she'd been so preoccupied with death, that she'd never allowed herself to experience life.

"Do you like it?"

"Oh, yes, I love it," Mariah said, smiling up at him from where she sat beside him on the trailer sofa. Both Tess and Jo had arrived home for the wedding, leaving the

Calloway house the last place to seek any privacy. When Mariah's lips fastened on his, however, he fervently wished he had her back at the house.

He allowed her to hungrily dine on him for all of about ten seconds. Growling, he yanked his mouth from hers. "A verbal thank-you will do very nicely."

"You're no fun at all," she teased, tracing her fingertip across his lips.

"And you're too much fun," he said, as he pulled her hand away. "Besides, you keep that up and you're going to get more than fun."

"Promises, promises," she taunted, her mouth one huge grin.

"I promise you tomorrow night I'm going to..." The rest he whispered in her ear.

"You can't say that! You're a minister."

"A horny minister," he said, nibbling at her fingertip despite himself.

"The very best kind," she purred, slipping her finger into his mouth.

He groaned and stood, dragging her and the velvet jewel case in her hand, up with him. "I'd better get you back before I ravish you. Or more to the point, before you ravish me."

Mariah laughed, the sound cascading like a wind-teased waterfall.

Suddenly Ford halted in mid-step. His face grew serious. "You did go to the doctor, didn't you?"

"Y-yes," she answered, hoping he didn't pursue the matter further.

Her hope went unheeded.

"You got a diaphragm?"

Knowing how frightened she was of childbirth, Ford had insisted they shelve the subject of children. He'd reiterated more than once that he was asking her to marry him, not have his child. If she never wanted to have a child, he could live, contentedly, with her decision. His attitude only made her love him more. But because she loved him, she wasn't blind to the fact that he would make a wonderful father and that, while he wasn't old, he wasn't getting any younger, either. Most men were fathers long before the age of thirty-eight.

"I took care of everything," she hedged, this time not giving him a chance to ask further questions. Batting her golden lashes provocatively, she said, "Want to try me out?"

With a groan, Ford shoved her out the door.

LATER THAT EVENING, as both moon and spirits rode high, the four sisters painted their nails in anticipation of the following day's festivities. Tess, Jo, and Mariah sprawled on the floor, while Eden sat on the sofa. At Mariah's side lay a telegram from Nick, wishing his best friend all the happiness in the world.

"I still can't believe it," Eden said, tears of happiness in her eyes every time the wedding was mentioned. And even when it wasn't.

Jo, her red hair loosely tied atop her head, moaned. "If you don't stop crying, Eden . . ."

"Well, I think it's wonderful," Eden protested, brushing the clear polish on her thumbnail. She had opted, as suited her personality, to wear a natural polish in lieu of color.

Tess, her divorce final since February, just smiled at Mariah. Mariah thought the smile the phoniest she'd ever seen and was determined to find a few minutes to speak to her sister privately. Then again, maybe she wouldn't speak to her at all. Maybe she'd just hold her hand.

"And I think religion's been set back three hundred years," Jo said.

Mariah took a wad of cotton left over from plugging her toes, so the carnal-red polish could dry undisturbed, and threw it at her sister. Both Jo and Mariah grinned.

"What are you painting your toes for?" Eden asked. "No one's going to see them."

"Of course someone is, idiot," Jo teased. "Ford is."

Eden blushed. "I . . . I . . . I meant . . ."

"You've never had your toes kissed, Eden?" Mariah teased.

"My toes what?"

"Kissed, as in—"

"We get the picture, Mariah," Tess said softly.

Eden shivered. "Sounds perverted."

"Kinky," Tess added.

"I don't know," Mariah said. "Sounds to me like it has possibilities."

"Four hundred years," Jo said dryly.

From there, conversation went from the ridiculous to the thoroughly ridiculous. Somewhere after midnight talk faded.

Breaking the silence, Eden said, "I wish Daddy could be here tomorrow."

"Today," Jo pointed out. "It's already tomorrow."

At the mention of her father, Mariah felt a thousand conflicting emotions. She lowered her eyes, lest they give something away. The three other women noticed her withdrawal. Looking at one another, Jo finally nodded. Eden stood and quietly exited the room. Minutes later, she returned and held out an envelope.

"What's this?" Mariah asked, her brow furrowed.

"We went through Daddy's things this afternoon," Eden answered. "We found this in the back of a drawer.

We were saving it to give to you on your wedding day. Sort of Daddy's gift to you. Since it's already your wedding day..."

Mariah's fingers clasped the age-yellowed envelope. Her eyes curiously lowered to the simple instructions scrawled across the paper. For Mariah, the words read. At the recognition of her father's handwriting, pain strummed through Mariah's heart, as though someone had hurtfully plucked a tender string on a guitar. How many times had she prayed that it would be his handwriting she saw on her birthday card and not "Daddy" written in Eden's or Martha's hand? How many times had she been disappointed?

The flap of the envelope had been tucked inside, enclosing within the papery walls a small, near weightless something that had slid into a corner.

"What is it?" Mariah repeated.

"Open it and see," Eden answered.

At Mariah's hesitation, Jo encouraged, "Go on."

Running a now-dry nail beneath the flap, Mariah flipped the envelope open. She poured the contents onto her palm. It was a ring. A simple, gold band with tiny entwining roses delicately engraved around the endless circle.

"It's Mamma's wedding ring," Eden said softly.

Disbelievingly, Mariah picked up the ring, looking inside at the inscription. It, too, was simple, simple like the man, simple like his all-encompassing love for a woman he'd met late in his life. Always, it read. Which was exactly the length of time that Ben Calloway had promised to love his Grace. It was a promise he'd kept.

All the strings of the guitar seemed plucked at once, making Mariah's heart seem too full of song. She felt her eyes watering. She glanced up at her sisters. "B-but why me?"

"Maybe because he felt he had to make something up to you," Jo said, pragmatically admitting what they all knew to be true—that, although the others had suffered because of their father's grief, it had been Mariah who'd suffered most.

"Maybe because you reminded him so much of Mother," Tess said.

"Maybe because it was his way of saying that he did love you," Eden said.

Mariah tightened her hand around the ring, feeling the pure gold burn into her flesh. Her lower lip trembled in prelude to the tears that began to silently stream down her cheeks.

Eden's eyes watered, too. Even Jo's eyes looked suspiciously moist, although everyone knew that Jo never cried. Tess simply reached for Mariah's free hand.

The four sisters sat thus for a long while.

Finally Mariah, wiping at her tears, said, "I always thought he blamed me for her death. I always thought he would rather I had died instead of her. I would have given anything, anything, if he'd looked at me—really looked at me—just one time."

"You weren't the only one who wanted his attention, Mariah," Tess confessed quietly.

The other three sisters looked at her with varying degrees of incredulity.

"How can you say that?" Mariah asked. "You were his favorite. I remember the two of you sitting out in the arbor for hours."

"But we never shared anything but the quiet."

"Still that was more than he ever shared with me," Mariah said, unable to keep the anger at bay.

"I know," Tess said, "but I forced him to share it." She smiled wanly. "The real Ben Calloway no one could get close to. And Lord knows I tried." The smile grew slightly. "You tried to be outrageous to gain his attention, and I tried to be perfect." At the word *perfect*, the smile vanished. "If I could just make one more A on my report card, if I could just make Honor Society, if I could just run faster and sing sweeter, maybe then Daddy would notice me. Or maybe Mamma never would have gone away..." Her eyes glistened with tears. "But, guess what? I wasn't perfect. Not by a long shot. I couldn't even keep my marriage together." Tess spoke in a tone of abject defeat and undeniable sarcasm.

"It takes two to make a divorce," Jo pointed out. "And none of us is perfect."

"It was Vance Langford who threw in the towel," Mariah said. "Not you."

Tess had been reticent about her divorce, saying only that her husband had decided he no longer wanted to be married. She still offered nothing more, leaving Mariah to wonder what had gone wrong with something that had seemed so right. She vowed never to let the same thing happen to her and Ford.

"It wasn't your fault, Tess," Eden said. "And nobody blamed you for Mother's death, Mariah. I don't even think Daddy did. I think he was just caught up in his own grief."

"No, that's not true," said Jo. "I mean, about no one blaming Mariah." Three pairs of eyes sought out the flame-haired woman. Jo's olive-green eyes looked deeply into Mariah's. "I did. I don't think I realized it until just now, though."

The admission hurt—Mariah could feel its sting—but, strangely, the admission didn't surprise her. It accounted for too much. Like how she and Jo always seemed to be at odds. Like how their sparring, on the surface a tease, always drew drops of blood before either would back away.

Like how Mariah always sensed that a wall stood between them.

"I remember the day Mamma went to the hospital," Jo said, her voice soft and wistful. "She was smiling. And I kept wondering why I felt so scared if Mamma was happy, but I did feel frightened. As if something was going to happen. I remember throwing myself at her—" atypically, Jo's voice choked; typically, she swallowed back the emotion "—as if I was trying to stop her from walking into whatever this bad thing was. She sat down on the sofa and drew me up beside her and explained how she was just going to the hospital to get the new baby, that there was nothing for me to be afraid of. She promised me that she'd be back. She promised," Jo added quietly.

Each sister, in her own way, felt the pain of the little girl Jo had been that day. When Jo's eyes once more found Mariah's, Mariah saw Jo's pain, as well. She also saw how easy it would be to blame the new baby.

"I was angry with Mamma for reneging on her promise," Jo admitted. "And I was angry with the baby who came home in her place." Tears fell onto Jo's porcelain-like cheeks. As adults, Mariah had never seen her older, her always so strong, sister cry. "I'm sorry, Riah."

The combination of an apology and tears left Mariah totally defenseless. Wordlessly she reached for Jo, and the two sisters, for the first time in their lives, communicated without snipping at each other first.

"It's okay, Jo-Jo," Mariah murmured. "It's okay."

It would have been hard to say which woman—Jo or Mariah—felt more uncomfortable with the tears. Or which wiped at them first when Jo later announced, "Good grief, are we getting maudlin, or what?"

"I think we're getting maudlin," Mariah agreed with a giggly grin. Both Tess and Eden were crying openly.

Jo groaned. "Will you two stop crying..."

"I think Eden ought to bare her soul," Mariah said. She still held her mother's ring. For a reason she couldn't explain, she wanted it near. No, she could explain it. It had everything to do with the warmest of warm feelings, the feeling that her father truly had cared about her. "She's the only one that hasn't."

"I agree," Jo said. "C'mon, Eden, share a deep dark secret."

Eden sniffed. "I don't have a deep dark secret."

"Sure you do," Mariah said. "Everyone does. Did you blame me, too?"

"Of course not. I was too busy taking care of you all to have time to blame anyone for anything."

"Well, there it is," Jo said. "Didn't you ever resent taking care of us?"

"Of course not."

"Oh, c'mon, Eden," Tess said, getting into the act, "how could you not have resented sacrificing your personal life? And if you weren't sacrificing it for us, you were for Daddy. You took care of him just like he was one of us kids."

"Yeah, look at you," Mariah said, "you're the only one of us who hung around the house."

"I love this house—"

"I know," Mariah interrupted, "but don't you ever want to break free and do something wild?"

Eden grinned. "I'm not sure I'd recognize wild if I saw it."

"You're hedging," Jo said.

"I'm n—"

"Yes, you are," Tess said.

"All right, all right!" Eden cried. "Yeah, I guess it would be nice to do something wild just once. And yes, it would be nice to have someone take care of me for a change. But..." She stopped.

"But what?" Mariah urged.

"But there won't be a Ford in my life," Eden said softly.

"You can't possibly know that," Mariah said. The mention of Ford's name melted her heart until it felt all gooey inside her chest.

Eden just smiled. "You be happy enough for me, too."

"Yeah, be happy," Jo added.

"Hang on real tightly to each other," Tess said, a note of sadness once more in her voice.

Tightly.

Later that night, as Mariah tried to fall asleep, she held tightly to her mother's wedding ring. It was strange, but the single event of her mother's death, like a rock tossed into a pond, had rippled throughout the lives of those she'd left behind. Her daughters had all reacted in different, but equally forceful ways. Jo had fought it with anger, Tess with a grief that matched her father's and led her to seek a perfection that couldn't be found. Eden had been forced into a maternal role that had stolen her youth, while Mariah herself had never been able to rise above guilt... and the feeling that no one, not even her father, loved her. She realized now that wasn't true. Ben Calloway had cared for her, as had her sisters. Always her sisters, for they were bound together through the love of their mother and father. Her sisters were friends. Her sisters were family. Her sisters were home.

But now, this day, she would have a new home, too.

She tightened her hold on the ring. Yes, she would do as Tess had said. She would hold on tightly to Ford. As tightly as family held to family, as tightly as lover held to lover, as tightly as Ben Calloway had held on to the memories of his beloved wife.

THE DAY WAS GORGEOUS. And Mariah no less, though it was hard to tell because she was so filled with a giddy happiness she could barely stand still. She resembled a whirlwind that jumped from here to there, then back to here again.

"Be still," Jo admonished, as she straightened the folds of the full-length white satin bridal gown, the bodice of which was decorated with swirls of fragile ivory bugle beads. The antique cameo rested in the vee of the mandarin collar, while tiny pearl studs—a single pair—peeked from her earlobes.

Eden was adjusting—or trying to as Mariah squirmed— the gauzy veil that Mariah refused to let be traditionally draped over her face. She insisted, instead, that from the beginning it be laid back against her silver-white hair, so that she could see the man she was marrying with no obstruction.

"Here," Tess said, handing her the fragrant bouquet that had arrived at the house that morning. The flowers had left all four women breathless; ivory roses nestled among creamy-white, purple-throated orchids and woven throughout were delicate clusters of lavender wisteria.

Similar wisteria, as though it well knew the specialness of the day, wound and curled in full-blossomed splendor among the latticework of the arbor. A small gallery of chairs, already filled to capacity, had been installed at the right side of the arbor, while to the left stood a white baby grand piano which had been rented especially for the occasion. The church organist was filling the air with sweet lover's music.

From her out-of-sight position at the side of the house, Mariah could see little, however. And nothing at all of Ford. It seemed like an eternity since she'd seen him, though it had only been the night before. Did it seem like an eternity to him, too? When they'd spoken by phone that morning—she to tell him of the gift of her mother's ring— she'd ached all over with the need just to be near him. Had he ached with a similar need? *And how much longer did she have to wait to become his wife?*

Suddenly, mercifully, the wedding march began.

"How do I look?" Mariah whispered.

"Beautiful," the sisters responded unanimously.

Mariah watched as first Eden, then Jo, followed by Tess, all dressed in the palest of lavender, began the trek down the ribbon-lined, petal-strewn path toward the arbor.

"You ready, little lady?" J. C. Hardcastle asked, offering Mariah his arm.

"Ready," she said, smiling up at the man who'd recovered so rapidly from his heart attack that his doctors were still amazed. J.C. said that, pure and simple, love had cured him. Mariah didn't doubt it. She knew its power. She had seen firsthand how it had transformed her.

As she walked at J.C.'s side, Mariah marginally noted the guests. All the senior citizens had turned out and were seated in the first rows. Behind them sat Ruth Doege, who wore her new spiritual marriage like a crown, and Megan Blake, who one day hoped to be the bride of the young man standing near Ford. Even Laurel Simmons seemed to be off duty in her patrol of the world's morality. She also seemed filled with more than pride for her son. Seated beside Laurel was Jessie Dunning, dressed in beige and good wishes for the son she loved and the soon-to-be daughter-in-law who each day captured just a little bit more of her affection. Various and sundry other faces made up the guests, none of which registered at all, marginally or otherwise, the moment Mariah's eyes found Ford. Dressed in a black tuxedo, he stood tall and sure against the beautiful blue afternoon. So very sure. It was one of the things she liked best about him. If he believed in her, how could she not?

When his eyes touched hers, she felt as if she'd been kissed by life ... and by all of its infinite and vast beauty. Within the crook of J.C.'s arm, she brought her finger to attention and wriggled it at Ford. At the same time, she grinned like a precocious imp.

Ford, not even attempting to hide it, matched her grin with one of his own. She was so beautiful ... and crazy! And this beautiful, crazy creature was his! All his, he thought, watching the silver-haired vixen as she stepped closer and closer into his life. But he'd have to be careful of his creature. He'd have to make certain she was bound to him only by the silken chains of love, for to shackle her with anything else would be to snuff out her spirit. And her unique spirit was too valuable a thing to deprive the world of.

With a smile of purest pleasure, J.C. released Mariah to the loving custody of her bridegroom. When Ford took her hand, he reassuringly tightened his fingers. Mariah squeezed back.

"We are gathered here this afternoon to unite this man and this woman in the state of holy matrimony ..." began a proud John Dunning.

Eden began to cry; Jo gave her a will-you-stop-that look.

Mariah simply couldn't take her eyes off the man beside her, the man safely holding her hand in his. She longed to trace the angular bones of his cheeks, his slightly dimpled chin, the thick brows, the column of his strong neck. A breeze, seemingly coming from nowhere, riffled through his brown-black hair, tumbling strands onto his forehead. His eyes, tawny and intense, dared her to brush them aside.

As always, Mariah couldn't resist a dare. Handing a startled Tess the bouquet she held in her left hand, she raked the fallen locks aside. Ford smiled. Mariah answered in kind.

"Do you, Ford, take Mariah Grace Calloway to be your lawfully wedded wife..."

The smile disappeared from Ford's lips as he listened to his father complete the question, with all its attendant pledges and vows. His eyes sealed with hers, personally, privately, making each pledge, each vow, and a thousand others besides. Promises that would last the days and nights of their lives.

"I do," he said at the appropriate place, the husky timbre of his commitment purling across Mariah's heart and soul.

"Do you, Mariah, take Ford Edward Dunning to be your lawfully wedded husband..."

The words, perhaps predictably, unbalanced Mariah's serene, contented mood. It wasn't a full tilting, but rather the delicate tipping of the scale. The reality of what she was about to do revealed itself to her carefully, fully. She was about to chain herself to this man, to this town, to this commitment. Was it really what she wanted? More to the point, was it something she could stick with? Had she sufficiently come to terms with why she'd spent her life running to be able to give it up for healthier endeavors?

Suddenly, she shivered with the faint stirrings of fear.

No! Don't be afraid! Ford's eyes begged. *Trust me. You've already made the commitment. And you have all it takes to see it through. We'll see it through together. We'll run together.*

Slowly at first, then more swiftly, the fear receded, disappearing far out, farther out than ever before, into the sea of her emotions. She was left with an odd feeling, simply because she'd never experienced it before. It was called lack of fear, the absence of guilt. Into this emptiness Ford silently poured the wine of peace and serenity, corking the vessel with the promise that he'd always be by her side.

"I do," she whispered.

Ford's hand tightened around hers.

"May I have the rings?"

Jeff Simmons, now on stage for his performance, produced the rings—both the ring Ford had selected for Mariah and Grace Calloway's wedding band. They were quietly, and very solemnly, passed to Ford's father.

Over the wide gold band that Ford and Mariah had picked out, John Dunning began, "The ring is an outward symbol of an inner commitment..."

In seconds, Ford eased the ring, inscribed with Always and Forever, onto Mariah's long slender finger, the nail of which shone a beautiful and brilliant red.

"With this ring, I thee wed," he repeated, not needing his father's coaching to complete the ceremonial vow that ended, "...I pledge thee my troth." His voice was low, resonant, the words swollen with feeling.

The promise echoed through Mariah's heart.

"This ring," said John Dunning as he held up the thin, rose-engraved band, "is a very special ring. It belonged to Mariah's mother. Mariah has chosen to wear it alongside her own wedding ring."

With this, John passed the ring to his son, who, supporting Mariah's hand with his left hand, slipped the ring on. It cozied next to the shiny wide band as though seeking a friend, a mate.

"I promise," he said, "to love you as devotedly as your father loved your mother and, should you precede me in death, I vow to hold your memory as close as he held hers, so that it might brighten the twilight years of my life."

Mariah's eyes watered. She and Ford had decided together that she would wear her mother's ring, but Ford alone had written the vow. Its simple message touched her deeply.

His words appeared to move everyone gathered there, for more than one handkerchief appeared and was sent to dab at moist eyes. Eden and Tess sniffed, and this time Jo didn't chastise them. She was too busy fighting her own tears.

Overhead, the sun seemed to momentarily shine more brightly, casting down its warmth on the wedding party, on the wedding couple, on the wedding rings that glowed in the solar brilliance. Mariah fancied the warmth as symbolizing her mother's and father's love. She knew it wasn't Ford's love, or the love she felt for him. Both far surpassed the passion of the sun.

Within a remarkably short time, Mariah had placed a gold band on Ford's finger, and his father was ending the ceremony.

"By the power vested in me, I now pronounce you husband and wife. What God hath joined together, let no man put asunder. You may kiss your bride."

No one moved. No one spoke. Even the breeze ceased to blow. It was as though a hush descended, a soft, fragile, crystallike hush. In the silence, the nearby creek trickled out a woodsy song.

Ford didn't hear the creek, however. He couldn't hear it for the joy singing in his heart. Mariah, too, was unaware of the silence, the creek, the way everyone watched the newly married couple with bated breath. She was aware only of the happiness humming through every cell of her being.

Slowly, reverently, Ford lowered his head. He brushed his lips across hers, whispering tenderly, "I love you."

"I love you," she whispered into the sweet heat of his mouth.

And then, he raised his head. And grinned. Hugely.

Mariah grinned back. Just as hugely.

Suddenly a breeze appeared, weaving its way through eager leaves and the fragrant clusters of wisteria. Suddenly birds began to chirp. Suddenly the crowd, the day, the world seemed magnificently alive—all in celebration of the union of two loving hearts.

CHAPTER FIFTEEN

"MARIAH'S DONE IT AGAIN!" Jo cried an hour later.

Behind her the guests milled about the backyard in quiet enjoyment. Jeff, still looking as proud as a peacock for having been asked to stand up for Ford, bent his head to speak with Megan, while his mother, Laurel, chatted with Jessie Dunning. Ruth Doege fussed over J.C., who protested, but loved every moment of her caring attention. John Dunning circulated among the other guests, agreeing with everyone that it was, indeed, a lovely ceremony, and the arbor a lovely place to hold a wedding.

"Done what?" Eden asked vaguely, studying the fast-emptying trays of food. She was clearly more concerned with whether she had enough finger sandwiches.

"She's disappeared! And at her own wedding reception!"

"She's upstairs changing into her going-away suit," Tess explained, collecting abandoned punch cups.

"Yeah, sure," Jo said. "It takes a half hour to change from a wedding gown to a suit."

Eden smiled. The softness of her expression, the romantic gleam in her eyes, transformed her into a beautiful woman. "It might if your new husband was helping you."

"Yeah," Tess added, "cut her some slack."

Despite herself, Jo grinned. "It was a gorgeous wedding, wasn't it?"

Both sisters agreed.

"And Mariah did look so pretty," Jo said.

Both sisters agreed again.

"And she and Ford make such a perfect couple," Jo added, qualifying her words with, "If you accept the premise that opposites attract. And yet," she added ponderingly, "Ford has a lot of the rebel in him, too. Yeah, maybe they're more alike than I thought. Anyway, with his dark looks and her blond, they look great together."

"Why, Jo Calloway," Eden teased, "don't tell me beneath that rough exterior beats a romantic heart."

"I think romance is wonderful," she said. "I just don't have time for it with my busy schedule. I'll leave it to you and T—" At the realization that Tess was looking a little forlorn at the subject of men and romance, Jo hesitated.

Eden, too, had noticed Tess's withdrawal. Placing her arm about her shoulders, she started from the backyard and up the steps to the kitchen. "C'mon. We need a few more sandwiches."

Jo, eager to make amends for her too-big mouth, fell into step beside them. "Watercress and avocado—they make wonderful sandwiches, Eden. You ought to try them."

UPSTAIRS, in Mariah's old bedroom, Ford and Mariah were engaged in their own discussion of food—soul food, or, more to the point, the nibbling, the biting of one mouth as it consumed another.

Ford, leaning with his back against the door, moaned as Mariah's tongue brazenly explored, for at least the dozenth wonderful time, the interior of his mouth. He sucked her sinuously curled tongue deep, then released it quickly. Sighing, he fought to maintain his control.

"I thought," he whispered, brushing her hair back from her face with a trembling hand, "that you brought me up here to help you get out of this dress." The net and lace and beflowered veil lay discarded across the foot of the bed. Ford, his fingers ever eager for the touch of her hair, had taken it off her the moment they'd entered the bedroom. Which had seemed like only minutes before, but which was bordering on thirty.

"Actually I brought you up here to seduce you," Mariah said, her face radiant with love.

"Well, let me assure you you're doing a whale of a good job," he breathed, his body aching in places he didn't know a body could ache—and he thought he knew every one. Thoroughly.

"How good a job?" Mariah teased, deliberately running her hand down the front of his tuxedo pants—the enlarged front of his pants.

He grabbed her wrist just as her hand reached his fly. "So good," he said thickly, "that if you do that one more time, we're likely to have the honeymoon right here."

"You want to?" she taunted, looking for all the world like the green-eyed enchantress she was.

"Here? Now? With the guests downstairs?"

"Yeah," she whispered, her nose nuzzling his. "They probably think we are, anyway."

The idea, having been exposed to his heated body, caught fire and flamed as brilliant a red as the fingernails raking lightly across his cheek. "You want to?" he asked hoarsely.

"Do you?"

"Do you?"

She giggled at their silly indecision, then gave his question some serious thought. Did she want to consummate their marriage here and now in the white-hot heat of quick passion? Slowly, the smile vanished, washed aside by a tide of seriousness. "Do you?" she whispered again, her hand now soft against his cheek.

He thought. Then groaned. "No, dammit! I've waited too long to rush now." As he spoke, he nibbled, as though in consolation, at her lips.

Mariah nibbled back. "I can't believe we can—at last—and aren't."

"I have visions of celebrating our fiftieth anniversary and we still haven't consummated this marriage."

Mariah smiled she-devilishly. "I assure you, if that's the case, we will excuse ourselves from the festivities and . . ." She said something wildly sexy.

Ford groaned, thinking that his vocabulary was fast being reduced to nothing more than moans and groans, with an occasional whimper tossed in.

"If we're not going to make love," she said, "what if I just drive you a little crazy?"

"You mean you haven't been?"

"I haven't told you my little secret."

"Am I strong enough to hear this?"

"You're certainly hard enough," she teased, pushing her thighs into his.

He grinned on a quick intake of air. "I swear you're going to pay for this, Mariah Call—Mariah Dunning. Mariah D-u-n-n-i-n-g."

Relishing her new name and his provocative threat, she purred, "What would you say if I told you that beneath this very prim and proper wedding dress, I'm wearing a red garter belt and red panties?"

Ford wouldn't say anything. He tried to, but couldn't. That is, if he wanted to continue breathing. He couldn't even moan or groan. Both stuck midway of his tightened throat. All he could do was look at her with a have-mercy-upon-my-soul expression.

It was the same look he gave her ten minutes later as he glanced up from the foot of the outside kitchen stairs and saw her standing at its head. He had stayed in the bedroom just long enough to unfasten the endless row of buttons that ran down the sweet curve of her back, then had made a fast exit. To have remained another moment with the knowledge that he wasn't going to touch her would have put him in the category of sainthood, a state, however, he would have been cast out of later when he did all the wickedly wonderful things he planned to do to her.

Now, his eyes on hers, he silently asked if she was wearing the scarlet garter belt and panties beneath the pencil-slim skirt of her white suit. The vixenish quirking of her lip, the sparkle in her eye, the sultry sway of her hips as she started down the stairs in her mile-high heels all said, "Why don't you find out for yourself?"

He grinned and she understood clearly that he swore he would. But right now he had to watch the customary tossing of the bridal bouquet, for which the guests had gathered.

"C'mon," Eden said, hustling all the available women forward, several of whom were in their seventies and giggling louder than the younger women. She and Jo and Tess, each for her own reason, hung, clung, to the outer semicircle.

Mariah looked around, studying the intent faces of the female guests and the unintent faces of her sisters. Eden was still trying to persuade someone to take another finger sandwich, while Tess was smiling at something J.C. had said. Jo was filling someone's ear, probably about some cause-oriented something or other. Mariah smiled, deciding she'd cheat just a bit.

"Ready?"

A chorus of "Ready" sang around her.

With perfect aim, she arced the bouquet high, sailing it right into the hands of a startled Jo. The older woman's initial reaction was that she'd caught a sweet-smelling alien. She jerked her head upward. Mariah just grinned, while everyone around them applauded. Slowly Jo smiled. The bonds of sisterhood had been soldered just a little more strongly.

Jo's smile, however, soon metamorphosed into a teasing, "Not on your life will I marry next."

Mariah's perkily said, "You never can tell."

Then, promising herself that she'd send flowers to both Tess and Eden the following day to symbolize that she hoped marriage was in their near future, too, Mariah turned her attention to her new husband. The crowd parted for her as she moved down the steps to join him. Slinging his tux jacket over his shoulder, Ford possessively slid his arm about her waist and ushered her toward the waiting car. Good wishes rained down upon them. There was one last hug each from the sisters and one manly handshake from Jeff, and then they were off to the Shreveport hotel that was to be the site of their two-day honeymoon. Mariah herself had suggested waiting to take a longer honeymoon, because, as she'd pointed out, she had to be available the following Tuesday to escort the senior citizens to the race track in Hot Springs, Arkansas. Wisely Ford had asked no questions.

Few words were spoken on the drive. But then, few words were necessary. The silent language of love—a look, a touch, a melding of single-thoughted minds—said it all and a thousand things more. Mariah was deliberately provocative. She gnawed her lip invitingly as she blatantly sent him a hot stare. She played with the hair on the nape of his neck, hair that curled slightly over the collar of the staunchly starched white pleated shirt. She sat at a Jezebel

angle that displayed her ivory-stockinged thigh, pur-
posely leaving Ford to wonder if it was the red garter belt
holding up the lovely silk hosiery.

Are you wearing it? his eyes asked.

Am I? hers teased back.

With a possessive defiance that made her heart tumble
over itself, Ford sought the answer. Dividing his time between the road and her, he ran his hand under her skirt
and, not roughly, but then not tenderly either, shoved the
fabric upward. His heart raced into double time at the sight
of red lace and a strip of red elastic, the silver clasp of
which bit gently into the ivory stocking—just the way he'd
like to gently bite the creamy skin exposed beneath it. He
settled for edging his hand under the elastic binding. The
warm flesh of his palm mated with the warmed flesh of her
thigh, while his fingers rested daringly near the seat of an
even greater heat.

Her eyes hazed at the intimacy.

His breath hissed.

Ford told himself to move his hand away before both he
and she ignited into flames, but he couldn't. So he just
prayed that he wasn't stopped for speeding or swerving or
copiously salivating on a public highway.

Still wordlessly, still with his hand at her thigh, he pulled
into the hotel parking lot. Awkwardly cutting the motor
off with his left hand, he moved his body toward hers and
leaned forward. Cupping the back of her head, he drew her
mouth down on his—harshly, fiercely, without preamble.
At the same moment, his hand squeezed her thigh, tightening his fingers until she could feel a fine quivering of restraint.

She whimpered and parted her lips, giving herself up to
the deep hunger inside of her.

Hard and furiously, he kissed her, his tongue filling her with the urgency of his need. At last, he lifted his head.

"I'm through waiting," Ford said.

The fire in his tawny-colored eyes underscored the truth of his words. That, and the way he threw open the car door.

BUT WAIT HE WAS destined to do—at least for a little while longer.

The moment they were shown into the bridal suite, an elegant room decorated in teal-blue and rose, Mariah excused herself and disappeared into the bathroom. It, too, with its gold and crystal fixtures and its Jacuzzi, bespoke luxury. When Mariah closed the door, Ford, like many bridegrooms before him, was left to wait with only his impatience to keep him company.

Standing before the window, he peered down at the Saturday sunset that was just beginning to streak the sky in apricot and pink. He was but barely aware of the scurrying of weekend traffic, barely aware of the speeding sunset, barely aware that a cool April breeze fluttered the leaves of a nearby oak tree. He was wholly aware of the almost unbearable ache that consumed him. The ache had begun the first time he'd seen Mariah at the Midnight Hour and, with any luck, would never completely end.

Restlessly, he glanced behind him at the closed bathroom door. He grinned at his own anxiousness and reminded himself that no one had ever died of sexual frustration. If one did, he would have been dead a long time ago. Popping open the black bow tie and leaving it to dangle, he began to unbutton his shirt—first the difficult top button, followed by the remainder, which he unfastened only after dragging his shirt tail from his pants. He had just released the confining cuffs when he heard the faint sound of the bathroom door.

He turned. At the sight of Mariah, his wife, his breath slowly ebbed away.

As always, her hair was a mass of planned disarray, frizzing and waving and curling onto her shoulders like a silver-blond mantle. Her cheeks glowed with an anticipatory pink not unlike a faint blush, while her eyes sparkled a verdant green. Her lips were the color of newly picked cherries . . . and as shiny as though a spring rain had sprinkled its fresh moistness upon them.

She wore a gown of crimson silk—transparent crimson silk that left not a single doubt as to every generous curve of her feminine body. Thin straps, no more than one-sixteenth of an inch in width or, measured another way, the exact width of the control Ford had left, draped across her bare shoulders. Embroidered into the bodice of the gown, in an elaborate flowered motif, were darker scarlet threads. Within the swirls, the rosy tips of her breasts created the centers of the floral design. From there, the gown billowed to her ankles, displaying within its sheer folds the shadow-silver hair at the apex of her legs. Her bare feet, the toenails painted the color of her lips, dug into the rose carpet. It was the way they dug into the carpet that spoke so eloquently . . . that, and the suddenly unsure expression on her face. The vamp, the vixen, the consummate tease, was suddenly shy.

The shyness strongly appealed to Ford's masculine protectiveness—he wanted to fit her within his arms and never let her go. It also, inexplicably, made him want her more. The one-sixteenth of an inch of control dissipated to a fragile one-thirty-second. The first emotion, that of protection, rode watch, however, over his desire.

"Come here," he ordered, carrying out his own command by starting for her.

Mariah stepped toward him, wanting, needing, the strength in his arms. She was suddenly so...unsure. Not about the marriage. That she couldn't have been more positive about. What she was unsure about was being not his wife, but his lover. Had she promised more than she could deliver? What if she couldn't please him? What if she didn't know how to please him? What if—

The warmth of his knuckles grazing her cheek stopped her foolish, rambling questions. She felt his strength, his certainty, flowing through her.

"Do you know how much I love you?" he asked huskily.

"Yes," she whispered, inclining her head until her mouth found his wrist. It tasted salty, yet sweet and was altogether too small a morsel of him. She wanted to taste all of him...little by little by lot. And she wanted him to taste all of her, every desire-laden inch.

"I'm going to tell you, anyway," he said, her lips at his wrist sending undulating waves of pleasure coursing through Ford. He fought to speak. "I love you more than I thought it was possible to love. I love you so much that my heart hurts. Sometimes it feels so full I think it'll burst wide open."

His knuckles had moved to her lips, her oh, so sweetly curved lips, where they brushed back and forth against the red lushness of her mouth.

"I promise you you'll never be sorry you married me," he swore.

"I know," she breathed.

"I'll slay your dragons, I'll fight the demons that haunt you and, if I can't destroy them, I'll run with you."

"I just want to run to you," she answered, adding, "I'll never make you sorry you married me." This she promised as she drew her left hand to his cheek.

"I never would be," he said, taking her hand in his and drawing it to his lips. He kissed the two rings encircling her finger.

"I'll be a good wife."

He kissed her palm.

"And I'll learn to be a minister's wife."

"Just be yourself. That's all you ever have to be. That's all I ever want you to be."

Laying her hand within the folds of his shirt, he flattened it against his bare chest, at the same time pulling her into his arms. He buried his face in the crook of her shoulder, in the fullness of her fragrant-smelling hair.

She brought her right hand to join her left. She luxuriated in the feel of the softly curled hair matting his chest before wrapping her arms, still beneath the shirt, across his muscle-hard back. Ford edged his hands onto the swell of her hips and urged her into the hard, hurting heat of him.

Mariah's breath caught, and she involuntarily shifted her weight, seeking more of him with slowly writhing movements that were both graceful and primitively sensual.

Ford moaned, using his hands to shape the firm curve of her sinuously dancing hips. With his nose, he nuzzled aside her hair, kissing the first bit of neck he found before bestowing slight, nibbling bites along her shoulder, discovering nerves she didn't know she had, making her shiver as desire raced in the wake of his mouth. Retracing his route, Ford kissed the shell of her ear, tracing its delicately sculptured outline with his tongue. When the tip of his tongue played across the lobe, he likewise drew it across the tiny pearl studding her ear. He pulled both lobe and earring into his mouth and suckled gently.

Mariah sighed and turned her head, instinctively searching for whatever it was giving such exquisite and tormenting pleasure. But he denied her what she sought. Instead, he teased with kisses to her jaw, to her chin, to her neck, which she prettily arched to receive the bounty he so generously graced her with. Even so, her mouth restlessly trembled for his.

"Ford," she whimpered, desperately, unknowingly, adding, "Ache...oh, how you make me ache...!"

"Welcome to the club," Ford responded. Now as needy as she, he hurried his mouth to hers. Though he took her lips hastily, trying to appease the hunger gnawing at both of them, he nonetheless forced himself to kiss her slowly, savoringly, as though she were a sumptuous dessert that could only be eaten slowly. Mariah, however, wanted more and more and more still, evinced by the digging of her fingers into his back, the ravenous hunger of her lips, the soft mewling in the back of her throat.

Ford tunneled his fingers through the hair on each side of her temple, anchoring her head and attempting to temper the kiss. When her mouth opened wider, instinctively begging for more intimacy, Ford forgot temperance and scooped her into his arms. Crossing to the bed, he placed her upon it. Her hair splashed wildly about her, while passion glazed her eyes. Her breath escaped in an uneven, serrated rhythm.

Suddenly, seductively, she grinned as only Mariah could. "Ah, Rev, you make me have the most decadent thoughts."

Ford grinned. "Yeah? Tell me one."

She slid her hands through the slit of his shirt, drawing the starched material away from his chest. Her eyes and her hands roved in the dark forest of hair whorling in thick abundance. Her fingers traced the white-edged scar, the only blemish on the perfectly tanned skin.

"I wonder," she whispered, "what this would feel like next to my bare skin...next to my bare breasts." She lifted her eyes to his. The last vestiges of the smile had disappeared, replaced by something akin to desperation. "I want to feel you everywhere at once."

Her honest need of him was humbling and the greatest of all aphrodisiacs. When he spoke, his voice was as gritty as sand. "I don't think that's possible, Lady Bear. You're gonna have to decide. Do you want me here—" he kissed her lips "—or here—" he brushed his lips against her shoulder "—or here?" His mouth closed over the clothed peak of her breast. Beneath the sheer fabric, amid the intricate embroidery, the nipple knotted, looking for all the world as though it were part of the embroiderer's beautiful design.

Mariah made a simpering little sound and arched into his pleasure-giving mouth. He laved, washed, tongued the rosy bead of her breast before shifting his attention to the other. This time Mariah cried out. Ford's mouth closed over hers, drinking in the priceless clamor of passion. As his lips worked a slow magic on hers, he dragged the shirt from his shoulders and carelessly threw it to the floor. Using only his hands and his instinct to guide him, he felt for and found the straps of her gown. Pulling them down, he thrust the filmy material to her waist. He then slowly, completely, stretched his body over hers, mating his chest with her breasts.

A long, low moan escaped them both. Mariah clasped her arms about his back, reveling in the warm muscularity. Ford rubbed his chest on hers in an act filled with languid, liquid motion. He traced along her rib cage, the heels of his hands grazing the softness of her breasts that naturally plumped to the sides. He then squirmed again, sending the pearled tips to stab into him like fleshy little daggers.

"Well," he rasped, "how does it feel?"

How did it feel? How did the most tender of softness, already sensitized to the point of screaming, feel abraded against the most masculine of skin? How did it feel to want to cry out as the plush crinkly hair toyed teasingly with both her nipples and her senses? How did it feel to be light-headed and hope to God the dizziness got worse before it got better? How did it feel to try to tell your lover this, but couldn't because the words couldn't get past the heavy breathing in your throat?

"Ford..." she tried, her hands growing restless.

Almost naively restless, Ford thought on some subliminal level as he corralled her hands in his and pulled them high above their heads. At the same time, he rolled to his back, taking her with him. She now lay atop him, stretched within the cradle of his legs. Using his arms and body to draw her up his chest, he dipped his head and took the swollen tip of her breast deeply into his mouth. He rhythmically tugged on her, tenderly, even roughly, coaxing a response from her. Her composure shattered into a thousand little cries, and she shivered from her hungering need.

"Easy, easy," Ford whispered, tumbling them once more until he lay above her. His hips fit between her naturally spread thighs. Taking his hand, he brushed back the hair from her passion-rouged face.

"I...I want to please you," she whispered, "but I don't know if I know how."

If Ford had been thinking with anything above his waist, he might have realized how strange a comment it was. But he wasn't...and he didn't. "You please me by just breathing.'' He pushed himself, his aroused self, against her. "See how you please me? Hell, if you pleased me any more, I'd be totally senseless!"

Sense. Mariah tried to hang on to a thread of sanity, but she was beyond thinking. She could only feel. What she felt was an ache, a need—a wonderfully terrible ache, a terribly wonderful need. Unknowingly, instinctively, she pushed his hand between her legs, to the seat of that heavy, throbbing need. Even through the fabric, the heat and moistness reached out to him.

Heat. Moistness. Both branded themselves across Ford's consciousness. In that moment, he realized he'd never truly known what either meant before now. Heat, that threatened to blaze into an uncontrollable fire. Moistness, that threatened to drown him in its sensuality. Unable to stop himself, he molded his palm to the feminine mound. Fire burst into being within Mariah's body, rippling outward in rhythmic rings of fevered feeling, compelling her to twist slowly beneath his caress.

He stifled a groan and tried to shelve his own need. How he wanted her! Wanted to bury himself so deeply within her that they'd never be two again, but he'd promised himself that he would make love to her properly. And that meant waiting just a minute longer.

"Not yet," he said. "In a minute, but not yet."

Abandoning the sweet cradle of her femininity—she cried out at the loss—he took her leg in his hands and raised it from the bed. Surprise danced across her face even as the gown slithered downward, piling between her legs in a modest heap that curiously looked a thousand times sexier than had she been exposed. Ford tried to concentrate on what he was doing. He grinned. "I've waited a long time to prove my point."

"About what?" she managed to say.

"About toes being an erogenous zone," he answered, darting his head and starting to deliver kisses to the calf of her leg—slow, candy-sweet kisses that made her moan from the moment mouth met flesh. He kissed the heel of her foot, then slowly bit the back of her ankle before lazily streaking his tongue across the smooth ivory skin. On a muffled cry, Mariah writhed, sending the gown scurrying upward.

Ford felt his body tighten, felt his heart sprint forward. He told himself to close his eyes, but he couldn't. The gloriously feminine sight before him was altogether too beautiful. So he stoically bore his own torture as he kissed the ball of her foot and then its arch. When his lips reached her toe, a whimper filled the room.

Mariah heard the softly bleated sound and realized that it was she who was making it. She vaguely wondered if it sounded as filled with sensual abandon as she thought... then ceased to think or care about anything except the endless sensations swarming along the nerve endings of her body. That and the ache. The hollow ache. The heavy ache. The ache that seemed to go on and on and on... She closed her eyes and prayed that it would cease... and, conversely, that it wouldn't.

Suddenly her foot was released, suddenly the gown was tugged from her hips, suddenly Ford's naked body loomed before her. She had only seconds to realize how masculinely perfect he was before his body covered hers. Wordlessly, his face grim with passion, he maneuvered himself between her legs, positioning himself for entry. Unable to wait longer, he pushed forward, sheathing himself in the moist sweetness of her body. At the sudden resistance he met, at the unmistakable, almost unpassable, tightness, he stopped. Dead cold. And fixed his eyes on hers.

"M... Mariah?" he asked disbelievingly.

She tried to grin. "Now's a real bad time to tell me you don't like virgins," she whispered.

Virgin. The sultry, teasing vamp was a virgin! His wife was a virgin. No man had ever touched her intimately. He wasn't sure what he had thought—the truth was, he hadn't allowed himself to think much about the subject—but he hadn't expected her to be a virgin. The discovery rocked him to his very soul; he felt a curious moistness sting his eyes. He started to withdraw.

"No!" she cried.

"I can make it easier," he breathed, desperately trying to forget his own need.

"No," she said, cupping his buttocks in her hands and pulling him downward as she pushed her hips upward to meet him. She cried out as he tore through the tender membrane.

"Oh, sweetheart," he whispered, kissing the neck she'd instinctively arched in her moment of pain. His breath was warm and consoling, his lips gentle as they moved from her neck to her mouth. He kissed her deeply, thoroughly, running a hand along her thigh in an attempt to force tightened muscles to relax. He made himself remain motionless, giving her body time to adjust to his supreme invasion.

At last, and restlessly, she began to stir beneath him.

He stilled her. "No, let me."

As his lips teased hers, his hips began to shift, his body started to slide into hers. Slightly at first, then with a building force, but always slowly, tenderly. She whimpered, then despite him, because nature ordained it, she, too, began to move. This time he let her. Over and over, he entered her. Over and over, she took him into her.

"Ford..." she whispered pleadingly as the spiraling emotions built within her. They were more powerful than

anything she'd ever experienced and screamed for sur-
cease. Her hands, her legs, dug into him, just as her hips,
writhing against his, begged him to complete the act.

His hand eased between their bodies, seeking out in the
swollen sweet flesh the bud of her desire. He stroked it but
twice before a wild release claimed her. She raggedly cried
his name at that ultimate moment of satisfaction.

As the tiny convulsions sucked at his body, his senses,
he felt his own climax rushing at him. It started before hers
had ended and there seemed no way now to tell hers from
his, his from hers. Which was perhaps just as it should be,
he thought, filling her with heated life, because just as their
bodies had mingled, just as their cries had merged, so had
their lives. Two had become an inseparable, and forever,
one.

"ARE YOU A GOOD LOVER?" Mariah asked the question a
long while later, after passion had cooled, after the Jacuzzi had ministered to their love-tired bodies, after dinner had been served in their room.

Ford was growing accustomed to her off-the-wall questions, yet she still sometimes managed to take him by surprise.

"I don't know. What do you think?" he said, the finger lazily tracing her spine hesitating only briefly before
resuming its delicious journey.

"Oh, I think you are. It's just that I have nothing, no
one, to compare you with. I was wondering where you
thought you stood—comparatively speaking."

He could feel her grin burrowing into his belly. He could
also feel her breasts bare and loose against his chest. Just
as he could feel the current subject doing arousing things
to his libido. She had to feel those arousing things, too,
since she was lying across his thigh.

"World-class," he said in answer to her question.

She inclined her head, looking upward. He looked downward. Both were grinning. "Somehow I just knew you would be."

Before she could turn away, he asked the question that had been on his lips a thousand times since they'd made love. He'd always had the feeling she'd wanted to avoid its being asked. "Why didn't you tell me you were a virgin?"

"I forgot," she responded flippantly.

"Why, Mariah?" he insisted, refusing to let her off the hook.

She glanced away from him and back to his chest, where the dark hair endlessly fascinated her. Shrugging, she said, "I don't know."

He could tell her answer was honest. "Why do you think?"

"I didn't want you concentrating on it, making a big deal out of it."

"And?" He'd heard a silent *and*.

"And I was afraid you'd ask me why I was a virgin."

"Why were you? Not that there's anything wrong with that."

She glanced back at him. "I really don't know, Ford. I guess I just didn't want to get that close to a man. I've dated a lot of men, but I never met anyone I wanted to be that close with. Maybe I was afraid he'd disappoint me." In a second, she added, "The way my father did."

"Or that you'd disappoint him the way you thought you had your father?"

She shrugged again. "Maybe."

He suspected *maybe* was a definite yes. "You didn't disappoint me, Mariah," he said quietly, tenderly dropping his lips to hers.

Oh, she tasted sweet!

Oh, he tasted warm!

"You never could disappoint me. In fact, on a scale of one to ten, you pleased me about a two billion."

"I'll learn," she said so earnestly that he fell in love with her all over again. "I mean, you're a sex ed teacher. You can teach me, right? I'll learn all the different ways to carry piggies to market."

Ford laughed. "You do a great job of transportation as it is."

"I'm serious, Ford. I'll study *The Joy of Sex*. I'll read the *Kama Sutra*. I'll—"

"Do whatever comes naturally."

"You mean like this?" she teased, kissing the hollow of his throat.

"Exactly."

"And this," she added, nibbling at his nipple.

"Exactly."

"And this," she whispered, her hand skimming beneath the sheet to feather against an area that was growing incredibly alert.

Ford moaned.

"Tell me something, Rev. Sizewise . . . I mean, comparatively speaking—"

"World-class," he interrupted.

She giggled, and he rolled her to her back, pinning her beneath him.

His smile fled as he looked down into the face of his wife. "I love you."

She grazed his cheek with her knuckles. "I love you."

"I'm glad you were a virgin," he said, his voice suddenly thick with emotion. "It wouldn't have mattered if you hadn't been, but . . . I'm glad. I love knowing I'm the only one."

Mariah brushed back a wisp of hair that had fallen across his forehead. "I love the cameo."

It seemed a strange segue, even for Mariah, but Ford went with it. "I'm glad you like it."

"You didn't think it strange I didn't give you a wedding gift?"

He shrugged the broad shoulders that cast a loving shadow over her bare body. "Not really," he said honestly.

"I was saving mine for tonight."

Ford rubbed his nose across hers in love play. "It was the best of all gifts."

"Not my virginity."

He raised his head. His expression said he was a little perplexed, but not gravely so. "Does that mean I have to give it back?"

She smiled. "No, you can keep that, too."

"So what was my gift? Your sexy bod?" He teased a nipple, nudging it with his nose, then wetting it with his tongue.

"I didn't get a diaphragm."

He stopped the sensual game at her breast. His eyes found hers. They were now clearly perplexed. "What did you get?"

"Nothing." The word hovered in the room.

"I don't understand—"

"I want to have your baby." When he gave no reply, Mariah, finding his silence a little awkward, added, "Actually, I guess I'll have to wait to give you your gift. At least nine months. Maybe longer if I miscalculated my ovulation chart. I guess I should have gotten Jeff to figure it for me," she added with an attempt at levity.

Ford still didn't speak. He didn't even smile. Finally he said, after a long, deep swallow of emotion, "Mariah you don't have—"

"I know I don't have to."

"We decided to wait to discuss this."

"I decided not to wait." She smiled, touching his cheek with her fingertips. "I won't be afraid if you're beside me. You will be beside me?"

He was still visibly moved; his voice reflected it. "I'll be beside you, no matter what, for the rest of our lives, but—"

"Good. Then it's settled."

"Mariah, I can't let you do this. Not now."

"You have no choice. It's a gift." The tone of her voice brooked no argument. And neither did her body as it arched and stretched and otherwise caused havoc with his senses. "In fact," she added, shifting her hips just so the tip of his manhood poised at a most strategic point, "now that we've started, I think we ought to keep right on working on it. Besides," she purred, her crimson lips pouted in the epitome of seduction, "I feel truly inspired to learn another of your lessons."

Before Ford could respond, he felt the breeze of her breath against his lips, felt her skin move across his like a warm summer zephyr, felt her woman's body sheathe him like the forceful passion of a wild tempest. On a low satisfied growl, he acquiesced—lost, hopelessly, irrevocably, in the awesomely wonderful storm of love.

"Oh, Ford..." she whispered.

"Mariah...Mariah...Mariah..."

Ford heard her name spilling throughout the room and had no idea where it came from. Perhaps he had spoken it, perhaps his heart had beat it or perhaps it was simply the wind singing the sweet song of its sister.